"I will wed Fiona.
She* will *step forward."

Aliss and Fiona glared at Tarr, neither making a move.

Tarr folded his arms over his chest and circled the twins slowly. He lowered his arms and walked up to stand only inches from Fiona.

She noticed that the warm color of his sundrenched skin made the scar cutting through one eyebrow and another on his jawbone below his right cheek more prominent. His dark brows arched over eyes she had first thought black, but were a deep brown, with faint gold specks that were visible only when the fire's light caught them and turned them brilliant.

He was, she decided, a handsomely compelling man.

"Now that you have assessed me, what say we wed, Fiona?"

She laughed in order that her shock at him guessing her identity would not show. She moved next to her sister so that they appeared mirror images of each other. "I cannot assess you in one glance. It takes time to know the manner of a man. And you cannot be sure who I am or what manner of woman I am."

Other **AVON ROMANCES**

ALAS, MY LOVE *by Edith Layton*
BEYOND TEMPTATION: THE TEMPLAR KNIGHTS *by Mary Reed McCall*
MORE THAN A SCANDAL *by Sari Robins*
THE RUNAWAY HEIRESS *by Brenda Hiatt*
SOMETHING LIKE LOVE *by Beverly Jenkins*
WHEN DASHING MET DANGER *by Shana Galen*
A WOMAN'S INNOCENCE *by Gayle Callen*

Coming Soon

COURTING CLAUDIA *by Robyn DeHart*
DARING THE DUKE *by Anne Mallory*

And Don't Miss These
ROMANTIC TREASURES
from Avon Books

THE MARRIAGE BED *by Laura Lee Guhrke*
MARRY THE MAN TODAY *by Linda Needham*
TILL NEXT WE MEET *by Karen Ranney*

DONNA FLETCHER

THE DARING TWIN

AVON BOOKS
An Imprint of HarperCollins*Publishers*

This is a work of fiction. Names, characters, places, and incidents are products of the author's imagination or are used fictitiously and are not to be construed as real. Any resemblance to actual events, locales, organizations, or persons, living or dead, is entirely coincidental.

AVON BOOKS
An Imprint of HarperCollins*Publishers*
10 East 53rd Street
New York, New York 10022-5299

ISBN: 0-06-075782-5
www.avonromance.com

First Avon Books paperback printing: July 2005

Avon Trademark Reg. U.S. Pat. Off. and in Other Countries, Marca Registrada, Hecho en U.S.A.
HarperCollins® is a registered trademark of HarperCollins Publishers Inc.

Printed in the U.S.A.

10 9 8 7 6 5 4 3 2 1

For Bruno,
a very special man in my life,
for teaching me that
you can't run away from love
no matter how hard you try!

Chapter 1

North Scotland, 1558

"I would rather rot in hell than wed him," Fiona said, her tone as sharp as her brilliant green eyes. "I have a right to wed whomever I wish or to wed not at all, if I so choose. Leith *may* be chieftain of the MacElder clan . . ."

She lapsed into silence knowing full well her protests would serve little purpose.

"Our cousin Leith will have his way." Her twin sister Aliss acknowledged what Fiona had already realized.

Fiona drew up her legs to her chest and wrapped her arms around them, stared at the stream a few inches from her booted feet. She had not expected this turn of events. There had been talk that a powerful chieftain searched for a wife, but it meant nothing to her. She had all intention of finding her own husband, but that had changed fast enough.

"Leith believes this union will prove beneficial to our clan and many agree," Fiona said. "There is talk that Tarr of Hellewyk will stop at nothing to gain more land and power. With his father's recent passing he is now, at twenty and nine years, chieftain, and with his land bordering MacElder land—" Fiona shrugged.

"Our clan fears he will attack us so it is better to keep him friend rather than foe," Aliss finished.

The twins sat in silent companionship on the edge of the bank. Autumn had barely arrived and summer's warmth continued, allowing the flowers' last blooms.

Fiona could not make sense of the last few months. Word that Tarr of Hellewyk searched for a wife spread throughout the clans, and many women were interested in the mighty warrior. So why did he choose one who has no interest in him?

Leith had informed her little more than a week ago that he, as chieftain of the MacElders, had entered into an agreement for her to wed Tarr of Hellewyk. She had laughed at him. His face reddened and he yelled that she would do her duty to her clan.

She had named several women in the clan who would gladly agree to the arrangement. But Leith was adamant; she was the chosen one. And now she would wed a stranger. The idea of never achieving her dream of finding love rankled her and had kicked her stubborn nature into action. She had made it known that she would not wed Tarr of Hellewyk under any circumstance. The clan had claimed her selfish, many refusing to speak with her while others outrightly belittled her.

Aliss interrupted her musings. "I never gave thought to us separating."

Fiona fisted her hands at her knees. "We will not be separated."

"Tarr of Hellewyk wants no burden of a sister-in-law."

"He will get no wife in me and therefore no sister-in-law, and it is a selfish one he is to think to separate twins." She would fight the devil himself to keep Aliss and her together.

"They plan your wedding at this moment and what follows," Aliss reminded.

"They think we have no say in the matter." Fiona picked up a twig off the ground and with two fingers snapped it in two. The thought that the skinny twig could be Tarr's neck relieved some of her tension.

Aliss drew closer to her sister's side. "You have an idea?"

Fiona tossed the piece of twig aside, her round face brimming over in a smile. "A plan of sorts that just might work. It will not be easy, but it will certainly delay the wedding and may ultimately prevent the union from ever taking place."

"Tell me."

"Leith made it clear that Tarr looked for a strong woman to give him sturdy sons to carry on his clan's name. Even when I insisted that Tarr had his pick of solid women who fit his requirements, Leith had countered that none matched my courage. And none irritated him as much as I do, though he dared not admit it.

My wedding Tarr would serve two purposes. Leith would be rid of me and gain a strong ally."

"He had intended this all along," Aliss said with surprise.

"And kept it from me until he felt there was nothing I could do but surrender to his decree."

Aliss laughed. "Leith always underestimates you."

"Us," Fiona corrected. "For my plan involves the two of us."

"Go on."

"What if one twin could not be distinguished from the other? After all, we share identical features, bright red hair, green eyes and good birthing hips. Those in the clan even have trouble telling us apart. It is our opposite natures that make us distinct."

Aliss nodded slowly.

"I am strong-willed and outspoken and I like riding, hunting and weaponry, whereas—"

"I am soft-spoken and softhearted, my interests that of herbs and healing," Aliss finished.

"We are both independent," Fiona said, "though many believe you dependent on me and that is only because of your gentleness. They do not know of your courageous nature and it is that strength you must rely on if we are to carry out this charade. We will need to combine our opposite natures so that there will be no distinguishing one from the other. You will need to speak up more, be a bit more bold—"

"And you will need to speak more softly, temper your quick wit."

"The best part is," Fiona said, and lowered her voice

to a whisper, "that no one will realize that we are both skilled enough in each other's interests to make the ruse believable."

"With us both displaying similar skills no one will know who is who."

"Leith will certainly make his disapproval known." Fiona looked about to laugh. "It will give me great pleasure to see him squirm and demand that we obey him. You realize he will threaten us, but what can he do to us? Separate us? He cannot tell us apart. His hands will be tied."

"There is Tarr of Hellewyk to consider," Aliss reminded.

Fiona laughed this time. "He will not be getting his way."

"Which will anger him."

"It is his own fault. He deserves to be made the fool. He demands I wed him and produce babes for him without even meeting me."

"We must be cautious. He is known for getting his way at all costs," Aliss said.

"Something he and I have in common."

"Tales have it that he knows only victory."

Fiona shrugged. "Then it is time he tastes defeat."

"Let us hope he tires of our game and decides to leave us in peace."

"We will be relentless, and he will see it is futile to press the matter."

"I hope you are right," Aliss said, and quickly blessed herself for added measure. "For if not we will certainly feel the repercussions of his anger. I heard that many quake in the mighty warrior's presence. I can only imagine the response to his anger."

"What man does not show anger? They bluster and shout, demand and expect and generally make a horse's ass out of themselves."

Aliss giggled. "With your high opinion of men, it is no wonder at twenty and one years you remain unwed."

"Need I remind you that you also lack a husband?"

Aliss hid her laughter behind her hand.

"Do not even hint that it is my fault you have not wed," Fiona challenged.

Aliss's words rolled out with her laughter. "You chase all prospective husbands away."

"I am your older sister," asserted Fiona.

"Ten minutes older."

"Older nonetheless, and therefore I am responsible for you and thus far no man has proven worthy of you," Fiona said, adamant in protecting her sister. "And do not tell me that there have been any who have interested you. If any man had caught your attention, I would not have interfered."

"I must admit I am content with life. I enjoy working with herbs and learning all I can about healing. I do not know if I would have time for a husband."

"Of late I have given a husband thought," Fiona confessed. "Remembering the easy and caring love that mother and father shared has made me realize that I wish the same for myself. I do not recall any harsh words ever being spoken between them, though we knew when they were upset with each other. It did not take long before one would reach out to the other and it would be settled, and they would be smiling once again."

"And the stories of how father loved mother from afar, not having enough courage to approach her until one day—"

"He accidentally knocked her on her bottom and mother gave him a tongue-lashing." Fiona laughed.

"His cheeks turned scarlet and he lost the ability to speak."

"Mother felt sorry for him and comforted him."

"He apologized and offered her his hand," Aliss said with poetic flair.

"And they never parted from that day on . . . until father passed on."

Aliss sniffed to keep tears from falling. "I miss them."

"I do too. And I remember how mother insisted we never separate. That we were to remain together and protect each other until—"

"We each found love," Aliss finished.

Fiona rested her elbow on her knee and her chin on her hand. "I wish to find love, or perhaps for love to find me, to have cupid's arrow strike me when I am not at all expecting it, to have my heart race when I see him and to see love reflected in his eyes every time he looks at me. And that is not possible if I am forced to wed a stranger."

Aliss stood and offered a hand to her sister. "Then let us go, for Leith is sure to be already upset with us since we have not hurried when summoned."

Fiona reached for her sister's hand, though she knew she was reaching for much more. They were forming a pact, an agreement that might place them in harm's way, but together they both were willing to accept that possibility and do whatever was needed to succeed.

With a quick lurch Fiona was on her feet, an eager smile on her face. "Do you realize that it will not be necessary to pretend to be each other? All we need to do is switch our natures on occasion and no one will be the wiser."

"It sounds easy, but it will take vigilance on our parts to make sure we confuse people."

"We should be extra cautious around Tarr," Fiona suggested. "His warrior skills will keep him alert to our every action and response. He will grow annoyed when he realizes there is little he can do in determining our true identities."

"Hopefully he will tire of the charade and leave us in peace."

"What if he does not?" Fiona asked, knowing it was best when going into battle to have covered all possibilities. "What if he simply grabs one of us and demands a marriage, thinking the more courageous twin will step forward to save her sister?"

The dire thought faded Aliss's smile.

Fiona however brimmed with confidence. "If that should prove true then we both will turn into weaklings who cry and protest and beg for his mercy. He would certainly grow disgusted and think twice before chancing a marriage to such a childish woman."

"A good solution," Aliss said.

"Part of the battle plan," Fiona warned, "however, we will enter a far different battle than the imposing warrior is accustomed to. We will enter a battle of wits."

Chapter 2

"We look a fright," Aliss said, trying to shake her brown wool skirt free of dirt and hay while attempting to keep pace with her sister.

Fiona did not bother to pluck the bits of hay stuck to her white linen blouse or protruding from her red hair. "It is better we appear unkempt, another reason for Tarr of Hellewyk to find fault with us."

"Better that he would have watched us rolling around in the hay, then he would have thought us mad and want nothing to do with us."

"When we are through with him he *will want* nothing to do with us. Besides, Leith's second summons left no room for us to freshen our appearance," Fiona said. "His message was clear—get to the common house now."

"Then let us not keep him waiting." Aliss grinned

and hurried her steps, Fiona now having to keep pace with her sister.

As they entered the common house, they saw that the clan was gathered, waiting word on the final arrangements that would secure the MacElders's safety by joining forces with the clan Hellewyk. Eyes rounded with curiosity, mouths dropped open in shock, heads shook in bewilderment, and whispers ran rampant when clan members caught sight of the disheveled sisters.

Whispers turned to wagging tongues as grins appeared on many a face and bets were soon being made as to the outcome of the meeting between Tarr of Hellewyk and Fiona of the clan MacElder.

The sisters stood for a moment surveying the room where important matters were discussed between the elders and the chieftain, disputes settled, and celebrations enjoyed. The common house was a good-size, wattle-and-daub walls, a timber frame, a thatched roof and it could hold nearly all the clan members. Trestle tables and benches occupied most of the room and a large stone fireplace consumed a good portion of one wall. Today it was brimming over with men, the tables providing seating along with the benches. Not all of the men wore the MacElder colors, yellow, green and red, yet the others wore the Hellewyk colors of green and black.

Their cousin Leith stood at the far end, tankard in hand. He was tall and broad and thick in the waist, with long brown hair and a crooked nose, and at twenty and five years with the death of his father Tavish, was now clan chieftain. He looked to be in good spirits, laughing and often raising his tankard to drink. The tankard stilled at his lips when he saw the twins, and then a towering shadow above him began to move. Slowly at first, then it appeared to drift away from Leith, taking shape and form until, from the dark into the light, a man emerged beside Leith.

He appeared to stand a good two to three inches past six feet, and for once Fiona was glad for her five feet seven inches. She would not feel thwarted by the size of this man Tarr of Hellewyk, for he could be no other.

His stance was one of pride and confidence. He was bulky and broad, though his mass was muscle not fat. His face was round and his features sharp, his shiny auburn hair fell past his shoulder while slim braids hung along both sides of his face.

His green and black plaid was wrapped tightly around and crossed over his broad shoulder and full chest. He wore a pale yellow linen shirt beneath and brown leather boots. A dirk was tucked at his waist and his claymore was strapped to his back, the silver handle visible behind his head. His features were more compelling than handsome, and the look in his dark eyes—one of warning. He was not a man to cross.

Fiona sensed her sister's fear and reached out to clasp their hands together, giving the impression she was the weaker twin.

Aliss gave a grateful squeeze and, holding tight, took the first step forward.

Fiona joined her determined pace until they stopped in front of Leith and Tarr.

Their cousin looked from one to the other, his brown

eyes looming large as though in shock. His cheeks glowed red and his nostrils flared, he appeared ready to erupt.

"Your appearance insults."

Aliss stuck her chin out and struck with a sharp tongue. "You demand our immediate appearance and now offend us?"

Leith's face reddened even more. "You knew wedding arrangements were being made, Fiona."

"Against my wishes," Fiona snapped.

Leith's head jerked left to stare at the twin he had assumed was Aliss. "What game is this you play?" He looked from one to the other then slammed his tankard on the corner of a table, the ale sloshing over the sides. "Fiona, step forward."

The twins dropped hands, folded their arms across their chests, and took a step forward.

Leith shook his head, stared at the two women, then reached out and grabbed Aliss. "You cannot fool me, Fiona. You will wed Tarr of Hellewyk this day."

Aliss began to beg pitifully. "Nay, please do not force me to wed."

Leith instantly released her and grinned with satisfaction, which vanished as soon as Fiona joined with her sister in begging for mercy, their pitch growing to a piercing shriek.

"*Enough!*"

The thundering shout had men jumping in fright, walls trembling, and immediate silence reigning.

Tarr stepped forward, his stern glance shifting from twin to twin, then to Leith. "You told me all was settled."

"Along with Fiona's strength comes a mind of her own."

"What of obedience to her chieftain and duty to her clan?" Tarr focused on the sisters, his dark eyes intimidating in their scrutiny. "I will wed Fiona. She *will* step forward."

Aliss and Fiona glared at him, neither making a move.

Tarr folded his arms over his chest and circled the twins slowly. "They appear no different, and if the weaker can appear stronger then she has the courage I seek. I will wed either one."

"But does she have the strength you seek?" Aliss asked.

Fiona grinned, her sister's remark so caustic that she thought she herself had spoken.

Tarr lowered his arms and walked up to stand only inches from Fiona. He remained silent, as did she. She noticed that the warm color of his sun-drenched skin made a short, narrow scar that cut through one eyebrow, and another on his jawbone below his right cheek, more prominent. Except for these two scars, his face bore no other marks or blemishes. His dark eyebrows were not thick, though they were full and arched over his eyes as if applied with perfect strokes. His eyes, she had first thought black, were a deep brown with faint gold specks that were visible only when the fire's light caught them and turned them brilliant.

He was, Fiona decided, a handsomely compelling man.

"Now that you have assessed me what say we wed, Fiona?"

She laughed so that her shock at him guessing her identity would not show. "I cannot assess you in one glance. It takes time to know the manner of a man, and you cannot be sure who I am or what manner of woman I am."

"Strength, honor, courage, I would say you possess all three."

Aliss stepped forward, her eyes roaming over him slowly. "Arrogant, demanding, impatient, I think you possess all three."

Gasps could be heard but were interrupted by Tarr's thunderous laugh.

"Your tongue is quick and sharp," Tarr said, his laughter subsided.

"*She* must be Fiona," Leith insisted, walking to stand beside Tarr.

"Are you sure about that?" Fiona asked. As the two men stared at Aliss, she moved next to her sister so that they appeared mirror images of each other. "Tell me you are certain I am not Fiona."

Leith moved his mouth, yet no words emerged.

Tarr did not react; he simply glanced from one twin to the other.

"I demand Fiona step forward," Leith said sharply.

The women looked at each other, then to Leith and laughed.

Fiona caught the corner of Tarr's mouth twitch as if to laugh before his expression turned stern and uncompromising. He finding them humorous made him less intimidating to her.

"I have a few days before I must return home. I can be patient," he said, looking to Aliss.

"Time will not help you," she said. "We do not wish to wed."

"It matters not what either of you wish. A marriage contract has been arranged and will be honored."

"We will see," Fiona said with a challenge.

Tarr walked up to her until their faces almost touched. "It is done. There will be a wedding before I leave here."

"But who will be your bride?"

"Fiona will be, I am certain of it." Tarr stepped back and, without looking at Leith, he ordered, "Food and drink, it is time to celebrate."

Fiona and Aliss moved quickly aside, out of the path of rushing women who hurried in with overflowing platters and bowls of food. It did not take long before the tables were crowded with feasting men and women and the celebration began.

Fiona was starving and about to dig into the richly scented lamb on the platter when she realized that her appetite far surpassed her sister's. If she ate as she usually did there would be no doubt to her identity. The problem was that she doubted Aliss could eat the amount of food that was her custom. She would have no choice but to eat as sparingly as her sister, then fill herself later when they returned to their cottage.

Fiona caught Aliss's glance. She had realized the situation and waited. Fiona reached for a small piece of lamb and nibbled at it.

Aliss reached for a similar piece and did the same, her relief obvious only to her sister.

Seated on Tarr's right, Fiona envied the hardy way he ate and silently cursed him. She had to admit, though, he was not disgusting in his manners as most warriors were. And he was cleaner than most. When he had stood next to her he had smelled of fresh earth and pine, and his long hair shined as though it had recently been washed. But then he had thought it to be his wedding day. At least he had been considerate enough to bathe for his bride.

Annoyed that her thoughts centered on Tarr of Hellewyk, she grabbed for another piece of lamb and ripped off a piece she could certainly eat without a problem, though Aliss could never finish such a thick slab.

She smiled, then reluctantly handed it to Tarr.

"Aliss," Leith accused wagging an accusing and greasy finger at Fiona as he leaned past the real Aliss. "Only Aliss would be so thoughtful. Fiona would never share her food."

Tarr took the meat from her slowly, his finger lingering on hers before he slipped it out of her hand. "But would Fiona be unselfish and eat less so that her sister would not have to eat more and their ruse could continue?"

Fiona admired Tarr's intelligence. It was no wonder he was a victorious chieftain, feared and awed by friends and enemies alike. He would be a worthy opponent in this battle of wills.

He tilted his head toward her. "I will have my way."

"So will I," she whispered.

Tarr nodded slowly as he turned away from Fiona and turned his attention to Aliss, seated on his left. "I admire you and your sister's actions."

"I thought you would. You are after all a warrior and a true warrior respects his opponents."

"This battle will end in your opponent becoming your husband."

Aliss laughed beneath her breath and shook her head, sending a bit of hay raining down on her shoulders. "Only if *I* so choose."

Tarr plucked a piece from her blouse. "The choice will be mine."

"We shall see," she said, and yanked the hay from his fingers.

Fiona had been watching Leith while Tarr conversed with Aliss. He huddled at the end of the table with a group of men. She suspected they planned something, but what? How would he think to uncover their charade?

It did not take long for Leith to hatch his plan. Soon one of the men at the end of the table got up and joined a group of clansmen at another table near the door. It took only minutes for the man to suddenly begin moaning and complaining about his stomach until he soon collapsed to the ground, rolling and yelling in pain.

Fiona hurried to his side and with a far gentler manner than she cared to use, she proceeded to tend the supposedly ailing man. He complained viciously about awful pains in his gut. He was certain he was dying, and Fiona was all too ready and willing to send him to hell where he would know real pain.

She glanced to Aliss who attempted to conceal her concern for the ill man. Fiona's healing skills were limited, but they were sufficient enough to handle the writhing man at her feet. Her sister would just have to trust her on this one.

Fiona noticed the way Leith had made his way to Tarr's side and was whispering in his ear. She knew his words, though could not hear them. Leith filled his head with Aliss's healing skills and how she would certainly know if the man was truly sick; Fiona however, would not and therefore this little farce would uncover the true twin.

The man did an excellent job at suffering and Fiona intended to do an excellent job in seeing that he healed himself.

She told him that she would cure him in no time. She grabbed a tankard of ale off the table, plucked leaves off a platter, tearing them into pieces and added them to the ale. She kneeled beside the man and helped ease him up to sit.

He moaned and groaned and held his gut.

Fiona leaned down, her lips near his ear. "I have a brew here for you. Now the problem is that if I am Aliss the brew will certainly heal you. If I am Fiona, then the brew will surely kill you. So I leave the choice to you. Drink or not to drink."

She held the tankard to his lips.

His decision was quick. He pushed the tankard away and stood of his own volition. "I feel fine," he said and hurried out the door.

Fiona was pleased to see Leith's face turn red with fury, and she would not have been surprised if smoke spewed from his nostrils. Tarr on the other hand appeared impressed.

He looked ready to approach Fiona when the door

opened suddenly. A stranger entered, looked over the room and, when his eyes connected with Tarr, he hurried toward him.

Tarr met him halfway, a concerned look on the warrior's face.

"Raynor has attacked the keep."

Tarr's men were on their feet reaching for their weapons.

Tarr turned to Leith. "I leave shortly. Have the twins ready for the journey. They go with me. When I find out which sister is Fiona, I will wed her and return Aliss to your clan."

Chapter 3

Fiona and Aliss were on horseback before they were given a chance to refuse. Their meager belongings had been hurriedly packed with the help of a few clanswomen, and Fiona had grabbed Aliss's healing basket as she was rushed out the door of their cottage.

They had been placed protectively in the middle of the Hellewyk procession of warriors, riding beside each other.

"Victory is ours in the first skirmish," Fiona said, her words for her sister's ears alone.

"True enough, but Tarr retaliated by spiriting us away. He is not giving up; he is waging war, and he intends to win."

"As do we. If we keep him confused he will grow frustrated and finally surrender and send us home."

Aliss disagreed. "I do not think so. He is a warrior intent on victory."

"Then we must remain vigilant at all times."

"And *patient*," Aliss reminded. "It will take *patience* to outwit Tarr."

"I have a lot of patience," Fiona snapped. "It is an idiot I have no patience with."

Aliss cringed. "I can see that lack of food has made you grumpy."

Tarr's sudden presence interrupted any further complaints from Fiona.

His gorgeous black stallion pranced and snorted on approach and nestled close to Fiona's gray mare.

"I have been told that Fiona is an excellent hunter, skilled in various weaponry, and that Aliss is a superb healer."

"You think to determine our identity that way?" Fiona asked, though she sounded more as if she accused.

Tarr was just as blunt. "Your identity will be made known sooner or later. Our clans will unite through marriage and there is nothing you can do to stop it."

"You think so?" Aliss snapped.

"I have no time to debate this matter." He glanced from one to the other. "If your skills are needed use them."

"Who is this Raynor?" Fiona asked, prepared to fight if necessary.

"Raynor of Blackshaw is a Viking Scottish chieftain who claims that a section of my land belongs to him. It has been an ongoing battle for years."

"Obviously with you continuing to be the victor," Fiona said.

"What is mine remains mine." Tarr reined the horse away from Fiona. "Remember that and keep alert. Raynor is unpredictable." He rode off with a shout to one of his men.

"He is a handsome and fit man," Aliss said.

Fiona turned her head with a jerk. "If you think so favorably of him, you wed him."

"I am not interested in marriage. I just took more notice of him while he spoke with us. His features are not hard to gaze upon and though the size of him can intimidate, it offers protection. His clansmen must certainly feel safe with him as their chieftain."

"I can see how his people would feel safe," Fiona grudgingly agreed. "But his features mean nothing if he is not a man a woman can trust and depend on. And as for you not being interested in marriage? Love can change all that."

"I do not want it to," Aliss said with a firmness that had her sister raising a brow. "I do not want my work replaced by love. I would like love to compliment my work and I do not believe there are many men who would find patience with my propensity for healing the ill."

"Find an ailing man and you both will be happy." Fiona laughed; Aliss did not.

They camped just before nightfall and the atmosphere was one of caution. Guards were posted around the camp, and several men disappeared into the shadows of the night presumably for added protection.

Fiona was disappointed when no food was offered, and she wondered if she would last until morning without a morsel to fill her protesting stomach. She almost hugged her sister when she passed her a hunk of bread and cheese as they lay huddled next to each other by the fire.

"I knew you would need nourishment," Aliss whispered.

"Bless you," Fiona murmured, and feasted with joy.

The morning brought a rush to break camp and be on the way. Aliss informed Fiona that she had heard the men talking and that they would reach Hellewyk land by midday, and that many of the men expected an attack before they reached the keep.

"This Raynor anticipated Tarr's return, or forced it," Fiona said as she and her sister mounted their horses. "Keep alert and your weapon close."

"I am not as skilled with a weapon as you," Aliss said nervously.

"You are skilled enough. Just find cover where you can. I will not let anything happen to you."

Aliss nodded and soon they were once again on the trail.

The day was beautiful, not a cloud in the sky. The smell of heather was heavy in the air, summer having appeared to refuse autumn's total reign. They traveled along a path made worn by many travelers, the earth packed hard and solid. A smatter of trees lined one side and a vast meadow could be seen beyond, framed by low-rising hills. The other side was dense with foliage with a few croppings of large rocks here and there.

"I wish there was time to search the woods for herbs," Aliss said eagerly.

"A good place for Raynor's men to be hiding," Fiona reminded. "And Tarr knows that. I have watched the way he directs his men and how he himself is aware to all that goes on around him. He is a wise warrior."

"You admire him."

"His warrior skills impress and he strikes an imposing figure on his horse. He sits straight, his shoulders wide, his eyes intent, and his weapons close. He is prepared for anything. He will not be caught off guard."

Aliss jerked her head from side to side. "You think we are watched now?"

Fiona shook her head. "You think it wise to make it appear as if you nervously look about for lurking warriors?"

Aliss dropped her head, gave it a shake, then stuck her chin up. "I am devoid of warrior abilities."

Fiona laughed. "I do not know about that. You wield a mean bone needle."

Aliss smiled. "I surely do."

"We have discussed this before, Aliss," Fiona said seriously. "Seek cover as quickly as possible and keep safe. Your skills and strength will be needed after the battle ends."

"I worry about you."

"And I worry that if you do not keep safe, who then will tend me if necessary? We each have our talents and it is best we use them wisely."

"I am so glad we remain together—"

"So am I," Fiona chimed in. "And we will stay together. *No one,* absolutely *no one* will separate us."

A screech like that of a wounded animal pierced the air a mere moment before a horde of warriors descended on the Hellewyk troop.

"The rocks," Fiona said to her sister as she reached for her sword in its scabbard on the side of her mare.

Aliss grabbed the knife from her boot, slipped off her horse knowing her mare was trained to seek safety during battle, and ran for the cropping of small boulders a few feet away.

Fiona entered the battle first making certain she cleared a path for her sister to get to safety. Once Aliss was behind the rocks she charged full hilt into the thick of clashing swords.

Fiona swung her sword with skill and strength, toppling warriors from their horses as if she swatted them off like pesky insects. She delivered several severe kicks, blooding faces when attempts were made to tear her off her horse, and she felled one man with the butt of her sword handle to his hard head.

She had trained her mare well for battle, and the horse remained calmly aware of her master's every move and command. Fiona saved one or two of Tarr's men from the point of a sword. Her strength grew with each kick, thrust and swing, the heat of battle racing her blood.

The skirmish over, Tarr sat looking over the battlefield. A few of his men were hurt while three of Raynor's men lay bloody and moaning on the ground. He was relieved no graves would be dug this day for his men, and more relieved that one would not be for his future wife.

At first he thought to protect the twin he saw in the thick of battle, but it was soon obvious that she was an accomplished swordswoman. When she assisted him in dispelling his opponents, he knew she possessed the courage he was searching for in a wife. She fought like a true warrior. The other twin however hid behind a rock. Had he found Fiona?

He thought he had the answer when he saw the other twin emerge from her hiding spot supporting one of his warriors whose injured leg was carefully bandaged. She sat him gently on the ground and then rushed to help the wounded.

Bloody lacerations and agonizing moans did not deter her as she was soon stitching torn limbs, head gashes and bandaging less severe abrasions, the hem of her brown skirt being torn again and again for bandages.

"You will find us both courageous," Fiona said, halting her mare beside him.

"You both fight but in different ways," Tarr remarked with admiration. "Perhaps I was right about it not mattering which twin I wed."

Fiona grinned. "Does it not? You requested a specific twin. Will you settle for less than what you bargained for?"

She rode off with a laugh and it brought a smile to his face. She was quick-witted and perceptive. Damned if she had not understood his pride in having the woman he had agreed upon.

"Raynor's been captured!"

The yell drew everyone's attention, and Tarr swiftly directed his stallion to converge upon the bloody man sprawled on the ground. He watched one of his warriors shove the twin away as she attempted to help Raynor. She shoved back, causing him to stumble, and dropped down on her knees beside Raynor.

As soon as the warrior had steadied his footing, Fiona had her sword at his throat. "Touch my sister again and it will be you who will need tending."

"Sheath your sword," Tarr said sternly as he swifty dismounted, grabbing Aliss's arm and yanking her to her feet. "You will waste no time on Raynor."

She jerked her arm free with such force that she stumbled, though hastily righted her footing. "He is severely injured; he needs immediate attention or he may die."

"I care not," Tarr spat. "He attacked my clan and suffers his own consequences."

"I cannot just let him die when I have the skill to help him."

"You would heal him so that I could hang him?"

"I would heal him and hope that you would have mercy and bring a senseless feud to an end."

"Feud? I fight to protect what is mine," Tarr said angrily.

"And he?" Aliss snapped. "Does he not do the same?"

"He is my enemy."

"He is not *my* enemy," she said firmly, and dropped to the ground to tend the unconscious man.

"We leave as soon as I see to my men. If Raynor cannot travel he remains behind to rot." Tarr marched off, his warriors following.

Aliss's attention remained on Raynor while she addressed her sister. "You know what to do."

"I will see to it," Fiona said, and with speed and skill born of experience she fashioned a hauler out of tree branches, grass, and moss and hooked it to her saddle with thick vines.

Aliss continued working on Raynor who remained unconscious.

"How bad is he?" Fiona asked.

"I am not certain. He suffered a wound to the head, which I have stitched, though much too swiftly. The rest of the blood on him is not his. I have cleansed what I could with what little water I have. I do not know if a fever will claim him before he wakes or if he will ever wake again."

"You did what you could."

"I will do more once we arrive at Tarr's keep."

"If he allows you," Fiona reminded.

Aliss's head shot up, her green eyes defiant. "I will see to his care regardless of Tarr of Hellewyk."

"I doubt any one of Tarr's men will lift a finger to help their enemy."

"It matters not. You and I have moved a larger man."

Fiona did not argue or object for in fact the man they had moved had been their ill father. With a blanket and much sweat and tears, they had gotten their father onto a bed they had fashioned on the floor in front of the hearth, and Aliss had made her first attempt at healing.

Raynor nearly matched Tarr's height and though

slimmer, his body was dense with muscle. His features were hard to distinguish from the blood that covered his face from his head wound. Aliss had cleaned him off as much as she could but much blood remained and was beginning to crust around his eyes, nose, and mouth. It would take a patient cleansing before he would be able to open his eyes, but that was the least of his worry.

Few survived a severe head injury, and the bumpy journey and a damp, dark cell would not help his recovery.

Aliss covered Raynor with her own blanket and had him ready to go before Tarr was prepared to depart.

"Tarr does not look happy," Fiona warned as she watched him approach.

Aliss had just finished securing her healing pouch to her mare and turned to Tarr glaring down at her from his saddle. She glared back.

He looked from one twin to the other. "Hear me well, for my word is law. Raynor sealed his fate when he attacked my land. You attempt to heal a dead man."

Tarr rode off with a loud snort from his horse punctuating his departure.

Aliss mounted her mare. "He has no heart and soul. It is good you will not wed him."

"He is a stubborn one," Fiona said as they slowly joined the procession of warriors, though this time they were left to follow.

Aliss groaned. "Do not tell me that now you find him appealing?"

"I find him interesting."

"Nay, you find him a challenge."

"A man should be a challenge," Fiona insisted. "I

could not abide a spineless man, one who would find my strength intimidating."

"Tarr is more than a challenge."

Fiona grinned like a child with a naughty secret. "I know."

Chapter 4

Tarr arrived home to discover no damage to his keep and no clansmen hurt. He immediately questioned the validity of the message that had been delivered to him. If Raynor had attacked his land why was there no evidence of it? He intended to have answers, though first he had prisoners to see to, three including Raynor. The other two prisoners had suffered leg injuries and had not been able to flee. They would heal and more than likely, he would allow them to return home. Raynor was a different matter.

A celebratory atmosphere filled the air as clansmen and women greeted the returning victorious warriors. Wives welcomed husbands with open arms, children hurried to their fathers' sides, and smiles of pride were settled upon their brave chieftain, Tarr of Hellewyk.

Tarr acknowledged the smiles with nods and waves, and noticed the curious glances given to the twins. His clan knew he had left to bring home a wife, and here he was with two identical women. Gossip would spread like wildfire. Soon all would be involved in attempting to solve their identities.

Tarr watched the sisters dismount, their only concern for Raynor as one kneeled beside him and the other stood nearby. He had hoped to find differences in them, but, thus far, they had succeeded in doing an excellent job at appearing identical in all manner. Both had raging, brilliant red hair that curled past their shoulders near to the middle of their backs. The green of their eyes reminded him of fresh meadow grass and their lips held the color of ripened apples. Their cream-colored skin was smooth, their round chins held high when they challenged, and their smiles broad. They were stunning women.

He ordered two of his men to follow him as he directed his stallion over to the twins.

"A cell awaits Raynor in the belly of my keep along with his men," he said from his saddle.

Aliss did not look up at Tarr when she responded. "Then I remain there with him."

"And I remain with my sister," Fiona chimed in.

Tarr corrected both of them. "You both will stay where I put you."

Aliss bolted to her feet and nearly shoved Fiona out of her way to walk over to Tarr. "Have you no heart that you would condemn a dying man to a prison cell?"

"He is my enemy and he condemned himself when he invaded my land."

Aliss pointed at Raynor. "Can he hurt you now? Do you fear him so much that you imprison him when unconscious?"

Tarr felt her insult like a slap in the face. "I fear no man."

"Then spare him more suffering with the short time left to him. Place him in guarded chambers if you must, but allow him to die in some comfort."

This twin cared too much, Tarr thought. She had to be a healer, which meant she was Aliss.

"Please," Fiona implored, her voice quavering.

Fiona's plea shattered his opinion of both sisters and confused him even more. He had thought her the one who bravely fought beside him, or was she now playing her part well?

"A bargain, then," he said, a sudden thought giving him a taste of impending victory. "Let Fiona step forward and I will keep Raynor from my dungeon."

Aliss spoke up. "You must think us fools to bargain over a man who death will soon claim."

Fiona moved to her sister's side to show solidarity.

A groan from Raynor caught all their attentions.

Aliss rushed to his side.

"You accuse falsely," Fiona said. "It appears your keep was not attacked. What brought Raynor here? Do you not care to know the truth?"

Her thoughts mirrored his own. He was curious over the very same questions, which had come to mind when he arrived home. If by chance Raynor survived, he would learn the truth, so perhaps letting the twin see to his care would prove beneficial.

"Take Raynor to the bedchambers across from mine

and place two guards outside the door," Tarr ordered his men.

"A wise choice," Fiona said.

"We shall see," Tarr said curtly. "My concern now is to end this game you and your sister play. You will both join me in the great hall for the evening meal. It is time we three got to know each other."

Raynor continued to groan as four hefty warriors transported him on the hauler to the second floor of the keep. He quieted when he was placed on the bed, but only for a moment, then he continued to moan softly and steadily.

"Help me rid him of his boots," Aliss said to her sister. "Then we will see to his shirt. I want to make certain I missed no wounds."

Fiona went to work on one leather boot as Aliss saw to the other.

"Tarr demands our presence at supper," Fiona said, dropping the boot to the floor.

"I have work to do here. I have no time to eat." Aliss collected both boots and set them aside. "His shirt."

Aliss eased the wrapped plaid from his shoulder.

Fiona made quick work of his blood and grime-soaked shirt with her knife, slicing it down the middle, and with a few more quick swipes of her blade the shirt was off.

Fiona grabbed hold of her sister's arm to get her attention. "If we both do not appear at supper, Tarr will grow suspicious. I imagine he already thinks that the healer of the twins will remain with Raynor. We must attend supper together." Fiona released her sister.

"I cannot leave him for long." Aliss bent over Raynor to examine the bruising.

Fiona paced beside the bed. "What if we debate between us which one of us will return to help him? It would confuse Tarr—"

"And give you an opportunity to eat more with me not there."

Fiona sighed with delight. "That sounds wonderful for I am starving."

"And I am not," Aliss said, and pushed the wooden chest in front of the bed around to the side.

Fiona hurried to help her sister until they had it next to the top of the bed.

Aliss placed her healing pouch on top. "I am going to need more candles, a bucket of water, and clean cloth—and that fire needs stoking. I do not want this room to grow cold."

Fiona saw to the fire, adding several logs from the stack next to the hearth and stoking the burning ashes. "I will find candles and get you water, but remember you must be ready for supper and you must show no concern about rushing back to Raynor."

"Do you think this ruse is for naught? Tarr has made it clear that he intends to marry one of us, and he is a man who is accustomed to having his way."

"You think we are incapable of defeating him?" Fiona sounded cautious.

"We are stubborn, you and I." Aliss's smile faded with her words. "But so is Tarr. He is attentive and listens well, hearing even what is not spoken."

"I realized the same myself," Fiona admitted. "He

hears beyond what people say and understands well their actions."

"Which is why you pleaded for Raynor?"

"You left me little choice, sister. You demonstrate extreme courage when it comes to defending the weak and ill. I could see in Tarr's dark eyes what he thought."

"That I was Fiona, his future bride."

"We have done well together thus far in keeping him confused. Now our chore becomes more difficult."

"I thought the same," Aliss said. "Tonight when you return from time spent alone with Tarr, you will need to tell me all that you and he discussed. We will need to apprise each other of all discussions we separately have with him."

"This way he will never be certain which twin he speaks with."

A pitiful moan had Aliss turning to Raynor. "I need water to tend him."

"I will get it for you, but make certain you leave time to freshen yourself for I cannot abide the grime that sticks to me and I intend to scrub myself clean."

"Do not worry. I will do the same."

Fiona stopped before reaching the door. "We will win this, Aliss."

"If so, will our victory be as sweet as we anticipated?"

The twins entered the hall. They had washed off the dirt and blood of battle and donned fresh clothes, dark green skirts and pale yellow blouses. Their skin shone and their cheeks glowed pink. Their long red hair was tied back, though one twin's stubborn strands fell loose while none were out of place on the other. They approached the table together.

"No victory celebration?" Fiona asked, stopping in front of Tarr and glancing around the empty hall. "I expected to find you at the dais flanked by your men raising tankards in triumph, yet you sit at a common table with a lone man."

"She certainly speaks her mind," the man said with a deep laugh.

"And you are?" Aliss asked with overt sweetness.

"Kirk," he answered, standing as if he had been gently called to task.

Tarr made the introductions. "Kirk is a good friend and a new father."

"How delightful," Fiona said with a single, loud handclap. "A son or daughter?"

Kirk grinned, his thick chest growing wider and his full face bursting with pride. "A son."

"Much good health and happiness to him," Aliss offered sincerely.

"And who do I thank?" Kirk asked teasingly.

"The choice is yours, Fiona or Aliss," Aliss said.

"Then, I thank both and look forward to getting to know both." Kirk grabbed an apple from a bowl on the table. "I must be on my way. Enjoy supper and good night to you all."

His absence left Tarr alone with the twins. He had even instructed the servants not to disturb him, having had the table stocked with platters and bowls of food and pitchers of ale and wine. He wanted his attention fixed on the twins and nothing else. He had first thought to wait to speak with them, thinking the twins fatigued from the skirmish. Weariness, however, had its advantage and he hoped one of them would falter and he would be victorious twice this day.

Fiona and Aliss sat on the bench opposite him.

He watched them pile their plates high as he filled their goblets with wine.

"Leith told me that you came to live with the clan MacElder ten years ago, when you were both eleven years." Tarr said.

"Leith's father Tavish was our father's brother. Uncle Tavish attended our father's burial and our mother informed him of her own illness. He promised her he would return for us and raise us as his own," Fiona said.

"Uncle Tavish came for us five months later," Aliss added, and turned the attention on him. "We were sorry to hear of your father's recent passing."

"I will miss him. He taught me much."

"And your mother?" Aliss asked. "What of her?"

"She has past one year now. She was loved by all and her presence is sorely missed."

"Do you have siblings?" Aliss asked, nibbling on a piece of venison.

"Nay, I am a lone child."

"Is that why you want sons?" Fiona asked bluntly.

"My blood, my clan name, shall continue with my sons and their sons."

"What if you have only daughters?" Fiona was quick to ask.

"I am confident I can produce many sons."

"What if your wife thinks otherwise?" Fiona smirked.

"A good wife will do as her husband asks."

"Good thing you did not say obedient wife," Fiona said, stabbing a chunk of cheese with her knife.

"You should go see to Raynor," Aliss instructed, carefully slicing an apple.

Fiona shook her head. "Your turn."

"I have already spent my time with him."

Tarr raised his hand. "Stop. One of you go. I care not who and know not who, but I need no more of your play-acting this day."

"I will go," Aliss said with annoyance, and took a bite of the apple and hurried off with a wave.

"Would you be a good wife?" Tarr asked, returning to their conversation.

"To a husband I loved."

"A woman's fancy—love." Tarr leaned in, resting his arms on the table, prepared to defend. "Bards write poetic nonsense about love, minstrels sing endlessly about it, and women foolishly wait for a gallant knight to claim them. I prefer a woman of substance, courage, and honor. One who will stand beside me, in battle if necessary, and one with the strength to birth me fine sons so that what we build together will forever continue."

"And love?"

"Love is the courage to face all of life with each other."

Fiona dusted her hands. "You are poetic?"

"Do not insult me," he half laughed.

"I speak the truth as do you. You let it be known what *you* searched for in a wife."

Tarr noticed how her green eyes turned brilliant, then

softened along with her emotions. Her quick responses hinted she was not afraid of a challenge, and her natural red lips tempted him to kiss her.

"And what benefits such a union could bring," he said.

"You must have had many offers."

"You wonder if you were my first choice?" he teased, and watched her green eyes spark.

"Fiona would be your best choice," she said curtly.

He laughed. "Actually you are correct. Out of all the clans who submitted proposals to me, Fiona was the only choice I seriously considered. Her reputation was well known."

"What reputation?"

"I heard she is a skillful horsewoman as well as a talented hunter. She can handle most weapons as well or better than a man and she protects her sister like a mountain lion would her cub. I knew then that Fiona would protect her children with her life and that was the type of woman I wanted as the mother of my children."

"These could be tales and not truths."

"Nay, I heard enough to know them as truths." He smiled slowly. "I particularly enjoyed the story of a young lad named Edward who challenged Fiona to an archery competition. He claimed he would win and in so doing gain Aliss's hand in marriage."

"He was stupid."

"And embarrassed from what I was told. It seems Fiona beat him badly, and he foolishly accused her of cheating."

"Which is why Fiona had to thrash him senseless."

"Your clan tells the tale with much spirit and pride, the men demonstrating how fists flew, and Edward found himself sprawled in the dirt with a bloody nose, then Aliss came to his aid."

"A healer does that, which is what started the whole mess in the first place. After Aliss tended a minor abrasion for Edward, he fancied himself in love with her, though Aliss made it clear to him she did not feel the same way. Fiona made Edward understand the error of his presumption."

"You are a beautiful woman."

Fiona seemed taken back by his words and shook her head while her eyes turned wide.

"Aye, you are beautiful. The tales speak of the twins' beauty, many claiming that the raging red hair provides Fiona with her fierce passion to defend and Aliss with her fierce passion to heal. I wonder what other passion Fiona possesses."

Fiona froze as Tarr leaned over the table, cupped her chin, and brought his lips to hers.

Chapter 5

Fiona's senses returned like a splash of cold water to her face, and she jerked free of Tarr. "You presume too much."

"A kiss from my future wife is not too much to ask," he shrugged.

"Do not play foolish games with me, for you will surely know defeat," she snapped, and grabbed for an apple to slice since she momentarily toyed with the notion of using the knife on him. "If a kiss is the type of tactic you plan to use in determining our identities, you are doomed to fail." She more shredded than peeled the fruit.

"What makes you think it was the kiss I assumed would help me?"

She stilled the knife and stared at him, her irritation growing in leaps and bounds.

"Reaction reveals much about a person."

Fiona continued her peeling at an alarming speed, furious with herself for not being more alert to his intentions.

He rested his arms on the table. "Your actions now tell me you are annoyed, a response more associated with Fiona than Aliss."

Fiona bit her tongue to prevent from lashing out at him and sliced at the apple hard, thinking it his head. Pain seared her finger and she looked down to see her blood spilling over the apple.

Tarr immediately reached out to grab her hand.

She pulled it away from him. "I can see to my own care."

Tarr shook his head and snatched the clean cloth wrapped around a pot. "You are a stubborn one," he said as he handed it to her.

"My reaction disappoints you?" She took the offered cloth and wrapped her finger, then stood. "Be careful of what you wish for in a wife, Tarr. You may just get her—then what will you do?"

Fiona marched out of the hall, her annoyance obvious in every step she took, and she did not care one bit. She took quick steps in a rush to see her sister. She ignored the two dozing guards at the bedchamber door and entered the room.

Aliss looked up from where she sat in a chair near the hearth grinding herbs in her pestle. Raynor remained unconscious in the bed.

Fiona held up her wrapped hand. Her sister rushed to her side.

"What happened?" Aliss asked anxiously, directing Fiona toward the light of the hearth.

"Do you know what he did?"

"Tarr did this to you?" Aliss asked incredulously, carefully unwrapping the cloth.

"Nay, I did it to myself, but it was *his* fault."

"He must have made you awfully angry for you to cut yourself. You are too skilled with a knife for such a foolish blunder."

"I was damn foolish." Fiona plopped down in the chair.

Aliss pulled the small wooden stool in front of her sister and went to work on tending her wound. "Tell me what happened."

"He tried to kiss me."

"Oh dear!"

"It was not the kiss that upset me, but rather his intention that infuriated me."

"His intention?" Aliss shook her head.

Fiona eyes sparkled like fiery emeralds. "He wished to see my reaction."

Aliss looked up. "So the kiss was but a ruse."

"He did not *want* to kiss me."

"Did you want him to?"

"Nay," Fiona answered hastily, and turned away to stare at the flames in the hearth.

"Fiona," Aliss said gently.

Fiona slowly shook her head at her own idiocy. "I grew excited at the thought of his kiss. I was foolish."

"No you were not," Aliss insisted.

"I was," Fiona said stubbornly. "I thought he

wanted to kiss me and that I would taste my first kiss. How silly of me. I let down my defenses and suffered for it, but never again. I am more wise to his tactics now."

"You have a right—"

"I have no right to be stupid."

"But you have a right to find love," Aliss argued.

"It was a kiss, nothing more," Fiona said defensively. "You have been kissed."

Aliss laughed gently. "A few pecks by young inexperienced lads do not qualify as kisses."

"But they were enough to let you know someone cared, had feelings to take a chance and steal a kiss, if only a quick peck. I have known no such demonstrations of feelings."

"You wanted Tarr to *want* to kiss you?"

"No—yes." She tossed her hands up. "I told you I was foolish. Why would I even consider kissing him? I have no wish to wed the likes of him."

"He is a handsome man and a fine warrior. Why not share a kiss and see if you like it?"

"And what if I did like his kiss?" Fiona asked. "What then?"

"That would be up to you."

After Fiona retired to the bedchamber they were to share, Aliss remained vigilant at Raynor's bedside. She had made a soothing potion that would help remove the crusted blood on and around his eyes more easily, though it remained a tedious task.

She had to repeatedly and gently bathe his eyes, especially his long dark lashes. When he woke she wanted him to be able to open his eyes without difficulty, for fear he would think himself blind.

His features held an air of familiarity: a strong defined chin that most certainly meant he was a stubborn one, and creases between his eyes, which attested to a man with heavy thoughts. His face was round, his flawless skin sun-drenched, and his hair auburn.

It would be interesting to see the color of his eyes.

She jumped as her wrist was suddenly grasped.

"I cannot open my eyes. Where am I and who tends me?"

His grip promised punishment if he did not care for the answers. Aliss realized that he was much too alert to have awakened from a deep sleep, and he must have roused earlier from unconsciousness, listened to his surroundings to ascertain his whereabouts. His only recourse was to hold her prisoner to gain knowledge of his capture.

She remained calm and spoke soothingly. "You are in Tarr of Hellewyk's keep. I am Aliss, a healer, and you shall have your sight back if you allow me to continue bathing the crusted blood from your eyes."

He did not release her, though his grip loosened. "My eyes were injured?"

"Nay, it was a blow to your head that produced so much blood. I stitched it and it will heal with rest."

She felt his hesitation in letting go of her, but finally his hand dropped away.

"I am not in the belly of Hellewyk's keep. It is a soft bed that cradles me."

Aliss returned to gently bathing his eyes. "Tarr's choice."

Raynor grinned. "I think not, fair lass." He winced as the cloth caught on a chunk of crust that refused to budge.

Aliss felt his twinge and quickly apologized. "I am sorry. I meant you no pain. My tiredness makes me clumsy."

"I will bear any pain if it returns my sight. I beg that you continue."

She understood he felt vulnerable not being able to see, and her heart went out to him. "I will work until I can keep my eyes open no longer."

"You are surely an angel."

"A simple healer is who I am."

"Nay, your touch is beyond gentle, your voice heavenly, and your skin smooth to the touch. You must be an angel sent from the heavens to rescue me, and I look forward to seeing your lovely face."

"You may scream in fright," Aliss teased.

"I will gaze in amazement on true beauty."

"Do you charm all women as you attempt to do with me?"

"Intelligence and beauty, I am impressed." He yawned.

"You should rest. Your head wound needs it," she said with concern.

"I do not want to return to the deep sleep I fought so hard to escape."

"No one knows you have awakened. You are safe for now."

"I am safe with you by my side." His speech slowed as sleep crept over him.

"Then worry not and rest."

Before his eyes closed, he whispered, "Do not leave me, Aliss."

She worked until she began to nod off to sleep. A few times Raynor had stirred, reached out and touched her arm, then settled once again in slumber. She thought he would not wake again until morning, a mere few hours away, so she stretched her back ready to stand.

His hand instantly found her wrist. "Do not go."

Before she could reassure him, he drifted back to sleep, though his hand remained around her wrist. Try as she might, she could not break free of his grip unless he woke, and she did not want anyone to know he had regained consciousness. Her eyes grew heavy from the exhaustion she had kept too long at bay. She had little choice. She rested her head on Raynor's chest and fell fast asleep.

Chapter 6

"Let go of my sister or I promise you will feel my knife spear your worthless heart."

Aliss woke to Fiona's threat and to a pair of arms hesitant to release her, though they drifted slowly off her.

"When did he wake?" Fiona asked, helping her sister to stand.

Aliss stretched her sore back and arms. "Sometime last night and he did not threaten me."

"A wise choice, and one he would do well to remember unless he wishes me to make good on my promise."

"An angel who has the devil as a sister," Raynor said fearlessly.

Fiona leaned over him. "The devil will also be tending you, and I dare say her touch is not near as gentle as the angel."

Raynor's laughter was mixed with a groan. "I fear you not. The angel will not let you harm me."

Fiona rolled her eyes at her sister.

"Your silence tells me I speak the truth and have nothing to fear."

"How do you get people to trust you so quickly?" Fiona asked, stepping away from the bed in fear of throttling the injured man.

Raynor answered her. "Her heart is honest and pure. There is anger, though courage, in your heart. You both are easily distinguishable."

"It is a good thing he is not Tarr," Aliss said.

"Sounds as if you do not favor Tarr," Raynor said, sounding pleased.

"That is none of your concern." Fiona pressed a finger to her lips, warning her sister to be careful of what she says. "We must go, Aliss."

"You cannot leave me, Aliss," Raynor protested.

"She most certainly can," Fiona informed him.

"You are presently my eyes. Do not leave me to suffer in darkness."

Aliss sat on the bed beside him.

"Touch her and I keep my promise," Fiona warned, and received a scathing look from her sister. She shrugged it off and kept her hand on the hilt of her sheathed knife at her belt.

"I will not be long. I will return with food, and once you have eaten I will again tend to your eyes," Aliss assured him.

"How long before I see again?"

"Hopefully by the end of this day," she said. "I will

leave a soaked cloth over your eyes in my absence, perhaps it will help." She examined the stitches on his head. "Your head wound heals nicely. There are no signs of impurities and only minor swelling; with rest you should heal better than I anticipated."

"You thought I would not survive?"

"You were unconscious. I could tell nothing."

"Yet you refused to give up on me."

"It is the healer in me," Aliss said.

"It is your pure heart," Raynor corrected.

"Enough," Fiona snapped. "We need to go."

Aliss placed the water-soaked cloth over his eyes. "I will not be long."

Fiona hurried her out the door and down the hall. "Tarr waits on us for the morning meal."

Aliss stopped her sister before they descended the stairs. "I do not know if it is wise to tell Tarr that Raynor is awake."

"Tarr has a right to know his enemy is alert. He could, with his eyesight restored, prove dangerous. I know you fear Raynor's fate, but Tarr is right when he says Raynor sealed his fate when he chose to attack us."

"I will inform Tarr that he stirs and may wake soon."

"Once his vision is clear you tell Tarr or I will."

"Agreed," Aliss said, satisfied. "Now, let us hurry; I am starving."

"Heavenly words to my ears and my rumbling stomach." And with a dash Fiona challenged her sister to a race, both laughing as they entered the great hall at the same time.

Tarr acknowledged them with a nod before returning

to his conversation with Kirk. The twins were left to enjoy their meal and talk by themselves, which suited them perfectly.

Aliss ate more than usual, doubting she would have enough time to eat again before the evening meal. She had to tend to Raynor, and while he rested she hoped to see how the other wounded warriors were fairing.

"Calm yourself." Fiona whispered a warning. "You look ready to take flight."

"I have much to do."

"Tarr probably has plans of his own for us. He has made it clear enough he will see this ruse of ours finished soon, which means we must, under all circumstances, remain alert not only to his watchful eye but to our actions."

"You do better with Tarr than I do, and since he cannot tell us apart, he has no idea which twin he spends time with. He can spend all the time with you and not even know he has held company with the same sister repeatedly. All you need do is act differently at times and he will never know."

"Why do I get stuck with him all the time?"

Aliss lowered her voice to a bare whisper. "Because you would kiss him if given the chance, where I would not. And I think you should find out if perhaps Tarr would make a fine husband."

"I look for love, he does not," Fiona reminded her sister.

"Love can strike even the most uncooperative man."

"Ladies," Tarr called out, startling both women. He stood and walked toward them. His smile started slow and languished as if uncertain, then suddenly it burst free and spread across his handsome face along with a devilish glint that sparked his eyes.

Fiona responded instantly, a smile bursting out before she could stop it.

"It is a fine morning for a walk. Who will accompany me?" He did not give either one a chance to respond; he reached out for Aliss.

Fiona could detect the panic in her sister, though she contained it well enough. Tarr did not notice that her smile was forced and that her eyes pleaded with Fiona for help.

Fiona struck with a curt remark. "Good, I had enough of your company last night."

"You both play this game well. I admire challenging opponents," Tarr said, and tugged at Aliss's hand so that she would stand, and as she did he brought his face close to hers. "Perhaps we shall share another kiss today."

"I warned you last night that you go too far if you think I will willingly kiss you," Aliss said.

Tarr released her and frowned at Fiona.

She fought the smile that lurked beneath the surface. It did her heart good to see him unsure of his own choice. "I have an ill prisoner to tend."

"I think not," Tarr said. "You shall be the one to accompany me on a walk."

"Are you certain?" Fiona asked. "You appear indecisive today."

"You think to befuddle me, but it does not work. I know whom I ask to walk with me," he said firmly.

"Who is that?" Fiona challenged.

He reached out and grabbed hold of her hand. "A twin who will rue the day she has challenged me."

Fiona was almost out the door when she turned her head and grinned mischievously at her sister.

"Where do we go?" Fiona asked as they left the keep.

"To show you the strength and wealth of my clan, and have you understand why I need to wed a woman of equal strength."

"I would be honored to view your holdings," she said sweetly, and his brow knitted. "Perhaps I can offer you advice on how to run your holdings more efficiently."

"You think yourself capable of leading a clan?"

"I *know* myself capable of leading a clan," she smiled, and sauntered on ahead of him.

The day was overcast though warm for autumn. Soon enough the weather would change and daylight would grow shorter. The clansmen and women were busy gathering the last of the harvest and seeing to repairs to their cottages before winter set in.

Fiona waited for Tarr to catch up with her, then she walked beside him in silence. She needed no one to tell her of the strength and pride of the Hellewyk clan. It was there in everything she saw from the well-maintained cottages and fields to the excellent weave of the cloth the clan's people wore, to the healthy animals grazing in the pens and the delicious smells wafting out of cottage windows. Hellewyk was obviously a prosperous clan.

Tarr needed no advice. He was an exemplary leader and certainly a man any woman would be proud to have as a husband, any woman but her.

She was greeted with smiles, waves, and a shout of welcome now and again. They did not stop to speak with a single soul, this walk was not to introduce her to anyone since how could he; he knew not who she was. This walk was for her to be introduced to a home, a home that could be hers if she so chose.

It had its appeal, she had to admit, as did the man walking beside her. The gleam in his eyes spoke of pride for his people, his confident gait announced him a strong leader, and the width of him left no doubt he could defend his clan with honor.

"I have much to offer a wife."

He was right. He had much to offer a wife, all that most women would want, but she was not like other women. She wanted to look with love upon the man she wed and feel it deep within her heart. She wanted to ache to touch her husband and feel content when she cuddled in his arms. She wanted her babes conceived from love for she did not know if she could submit to a man out of mere duty.

"Your thoughts are deep."

He attempted to step closer to her, but she placed a distance between them with the sudden thought that if she foolishly began to feel for this man and he did not return her affection, she would suffer for it.

"My thoughts are private."

"I will share them with no other."

"True enough, for I will not speak of them." She walked on ahead of him and intended not to glance back to see if he followed. Then she realized that he might return to the keep, visit with Aliss and learn of her deception regarding Raynor.

She turned in a hurry and collided with Tarr. His arms wrapped around her to steady them both, and his dark eyes caught her in a grip that sent gooseflesh rushing over her. She tugged to free herself, but he held strong.

"Free me," she demanded in a harsh whisper.

"You are not my prisoner."

His face was much too close to hers, his breath whispering like a warm breeze against her cheek. It sent another rush of gooseflesh running over her.

He stepped away from her suddenly and she stumbled back. This time he did not offer her help and she steadied herself.

Kirk approached them on a run, stopping at Tarr's side. "Raynor's men lurk in the woods to the north."

"I did not think they would desert him."

"They could be waiting for a reinforcement of warriors," Kirk suggested.

Fiona offered her opinion. "Or waiting for the injured to heal and see what they can find out about their leader."

"His dead body will be returned to them," Tarr clarified.

"If he should survive his wounds, what then?" Kirk asked.

Tarr shrugged. "It matters not, for his fate remains the same."

"Will you not question him first? Learn what you can? Learn why he attacked you?" Fiona sounded as though she disputed his decision.

"Raynor will answer many questions before he meets his fate, though his answers will not change his destiny," Tarr answered confidently. "His capture will, however, end the senseless dispute that has raged between our clans."

Fiona thought of the man Aliss now healed only to die. Her sister would not be happy with the decision and might very well put herself in danger to help Raynor. She fought hard to save the ill and wounded, and saw only senselessness in executions and torture. Fiona did not always agree with her sister's opinion, since there were those she felt deserved the hangman's noose.

"Do what you must," Fiona said, appearing unconcerned. "I will leave you to discuss the matter." She did not rush off, though she wished to dash to the keep and alert Aliss to the pending problem. She strolled as if enjoying the day and the sights of an active, thriving village. With measured steps she entered the keep and, once inside, made a dash for the stairs.

"It is difficult to judge her character," Kirk said, turning to Tarr as the twin entered the keep. "She appears headstrong and demanding one moment and then sweet and pleasant the next."

"They wish to keep me puzzled."

"I think they are succeeding." Kirk coughed away a laugh. "The mighty Tarr has been duped."

"You know me not if you think that, my friend."

Kirk wisely let it be and returned to the previous matter at hand. "You will question Raynor if possible, will you not?"

"Aye, I want to know if I had been his intended target or was I merely in his way? I hope to have the chance to ask him."

"Then his fate has yet to be settled? Yet you told the twin—"

"What I wish her to know. His answers will seal his fate, so let us hope he wakes and answers to my satisfaction."

Chapter 7

Fiona sat on the steps of the keep bored to death. In the last two days, she had done nothing but trade places with her sister to keep company with Tarr. Not that Aliss wanted to trade places, she was too busy tending the ill and making certain no one discovered that Raynor had woken.

Aliss had been especially worried after Fiona had warned her that Tarr expressed no pity for his prisoner. True to her nature, Aliss wished to heal and protect, which meant she found excuse after excuse to see that Fiona spent more time with Tarr than she did.

A large shadow fell over her, blotting out the bright sun.

"You look lost," Tarr said.

She caught her tongue before she could claim boredom. The twins appeared busy enough with all the healing Aliss had done. Letting him know she was bored would alert him to her identity.

"I am relaxing in the early morning sun."

He stepped to her side so that the sun could once again drench her.

She smiled at his considerate action and got the sudden urge to spend time with this man who so intrigued her. But she did not wish to stroll his land, or sit and talk. She wanted to be involved with his daily routine and discover his true nature.

"What are you doing?" she asked, standing.

"I am going hunting."

She almost jumped for joy. She had not hunted in weeks and ached to feel her bow in her hands, but again that would alert him to her identity.

"Would you like to go with me?"

He laid a trap for her, knowing full well Fiona would jump at the chance to hunt. Besides, his dark eyes glistened with a hint of mischief and a smile lurked at the corners of his mouth. He obviously enjoyed this little trick, thinking he was about to snare his prey.

Fiona set a trap of her own. "I would like to see how good of a hunter you are."

He appeared ready to laugh. "You doubt my skills?"

"Not all warriors make good hunters."

He pounded his chest. "I am good at everything I do."

Fiona let loose with laughter.

"You doubt me?"

She stifled the last bit of laughter, amazed with his sense of humor. She had believed him a staunch warrior who thought of nothing but battle and gaining wealth, but there was more to this mighty warrior.

He was respected and loved by his people and he provided well for his clan, *and* he had a good sense of humor.

"I need proof," she challenged.

He held his hand out to her and she eagerly took it.

"You shall have fresh meat for supper this evening."

They walked into the woods, Fiona wishing she had her bow. Unfortunately, she would be a spectator only for this hunting expedition.

She caught the sight of tracks early on but said nothing to Tarr. Her father had taught her to hunt well, and she had sharpened her skills through the years. She would not chance ever going hungry.

"I would teach you how to track," Tarr whispered. "But silence is best when hunting."

She nodded and paid careful attention to his steps and actions. It did not take long to realize his trap remained set and that he waited to snare her. Fiona drifted away from him to purposely cross the animal's tracks that she had seen and had thought Tarr ignored.

He grabbed her arm and shook his head. "Follow in my footsteps. You trample tracks."

Fiona looked with eager eyes at the ground around her. "Where?"

With an exasperated huff, he tugged her behind him.

She pursed her lips to keep her giggle silent. She could only imagine how confused he must feel, and a part of her sympathized with him—but only a tiny part. After all, he had brought this on himself and would suffer his own consequences just as he had proclaimed for Raynor.

They moved along, Fiona turning her footsteps light so they could barely be heard. When finally a rabbit was spotted, they both stilled. Tarr took aim and missed.

She could have told him his aim was off just by the way he held his bow, but she remained quiet and alert. She wanted to grab the bow from his hands when he missed the second animal, but wisely remained quiet.

She was glad she had, for when he missed the third she knew then that his haphazard aim was off on purpose. He truly was a skilled warrior, especially adept at subterfuge.

"I think you need some practice," she whispered in his ear.

He turned. "Let us see if you are any better."

She could not refuse his offer since he shoved the bow into her hands. The smooth wood was warm from his grasp, but without the sweat found on the bows of warrior's lacking confidence.

Tarr had no such problem. He had a faith in himself that Fiona admired. At first, she had believed him arrogant and dictatorial, but lately, after getting to know him, she had revised her opinion. He was a man of honor and distinguished pride, and of course a proficient strategist, even at a moment's notice.

He grew more appealing the more he intrigued her.

She fumbled with the bow and arrow, though it was unfair to Aliss. Fiona had taught her sister the fundamentals of bow hunting in case the need should ever arise, and she had hit her target often enough.

For now at least, Tarr expected a difference between the twins, and she did not intend to disappointment him.

Fiona laughed as she clumsily attempted to connect bow and arrow. Tarr stood watching her until, finally, shaking his head, he took the weapon from her. He moved close beside her, his body leaning into hers, and she let him.

She waited to see his intention, and in that moment of awkward silence, she thought she heard the steady beat of his heart. It was a strong, rhythmic thumping, not too fast or too slow but sturdy and dependable.

The solid strength of him had impressed her, but this self-assurance made her realize just how worthy an opponent he was.

"Why are you so opposed to this union?"

His question startled her. "You ask such a question while hunting?"

"We hunt not only for food but the truth, and you are well aware of that."

"The truth is Fiona never wanted this marriage, and with many willing MacElder woman to choose from this all could have been settled by now. If you search for the truth, then I suggest you begin with yourself. Why did you pick Fiona?"

She shook her head before Tarr responded. "Do not bother with the same explanation. Tell me something different."

He answered fast enough. "I wished a woman of multiple talents, not merely the basics."

"Why?"

"So that we would have interests to share and I would not grow bored with her."

"Are you sure it is not love you look for?" she asked.

"Why are you so insistent on loving?"

"Love bonds."

"Commitment bonds. Love has nothing to do with it."

Fiona scowled. "You are cynical when it comes to love."

"And you are childish to believe such fairy tales of everlasting love."

All but ready to lash out at him she kept a tight rein on her mouth. Instead, she asked, "Why are you afraid to love?"

He stared at her as if she had just pierced his heart with an arrow. "I fear nothing."

She shrugged. "Deny it if you wish, but it is obvious."

"And what do you fear," he retaliated.

"Not being loved," she shot back.

A sudden sound had both their heads turning. A large buck stood still in the distance as if just catching their scent.

Tarr raised his bow and with arrow ready, he took aim, held, and released as the buck took off. The arrow whizzed past the animal's head.

"Damn," he muttered.

"You aimed too high." She bit her tongue too late.

He shoved the bow at her in a challenge.

She shook her head. "I hunt the truth today."

He took a quick step toward her, dropping his bow.

"Then tell me how this makes you feel." He reached out, took her in his arms, and kissed her.

He stunned her, and for a moment she did not respond. Then, when she felt the full force of his solid lips pressed to hers, she lost herself in the taste of him. She allowed herself to surrender completely to the magic. She did not think or grow anxious or question; she simply enjoyed the kiss.

She allowed time to stand still, for sounds to vanish, and for there to be only the two of them locked in a loving embrace and devoured by a kiss.

He brushed his lips over hers several times when he finished and rested his forehead to hers. "You owe me an answer."

She took a moment to catch her breath before smiling. "It makes me feel alive, like the sky is more blue, the air more crisp, the sun brighter."

"Be careful, you may be falling in love."

She pulled away from him, annoyed at his teasing tone. "You may know how to kiss, but you do not know how to shoot."

"This hunt is over."

"For today."

Tarr bent to retrieve his bow.

A sudden sound had Fiona turning to a deer running into view. She quickly drew an arrow from the pouch strapped on Tarr's back, grabbed the bow from his hand, and with light steps hurried forward readying her weapon.

She halted and stilled all movement, her weapon ready to shoot. With strength born of determination, she drew the bow back and fired. The arrow felled the deer.

Fiona handed the bow to a stunned Tarr. "I return to the keep. While you gut the animal, you can wonder who I am—healer or hunter?"

Chapter 8

"Stop! Stop and leave it for Aliss to do," Raynor complained, pushing her hand away from his face.

"Aliss is busy with Tarr. You are stuck with me, and I am just as gentle," Fiona insisted.

"As gentle as a stomping bull. You and your sister are as different as your voices."

His remark stunned Fiona silent, though only for a moment. "There is no one who can tell our voices apart."

"I can, and with ease."

The door flew open suddenly and Aliss stood in the doorway appearing flustered.

Fiona knew immediately that something troubled her sister, and Tarr had to have been the culprit.

"I think I have made a dreadful mistake." Aliss's chest heaved as though she had run miles.

"I assume things did not go well?" Fiona asked, standing and dropping the washcloth in the bowl of warm water on the chest beside the bed.

"Tarr did not hurt you, did he?" Raynor asked, his effort to rise proving futile.

With a firm hand to his chest, Aliss pushed him back on his pillow. "Nay, he did not."

"This should not be discussed in front of the prisoner," Fiona said sharply.

"My concern is for Aliss," he snapped. "She has been kind to me and I will not see her hurt. Tarr is not dimwitted, and in no time he will distinguish the difference between you two, since it is obvious you play a game with him."

"Tarr knows nothing," Fiona said, bending over Raynor. "*You* would do well to keep any knowledge of our identities to yourself."

"You threaten me?" Raynor made to move again.

Aliss held him down and nudged her sister away with her shoulder. "Stop, the both of you. Threats will settle nothing."

"Nor speaking in front of the prisoner, as I have advised time and again," Fiona said, frustrated. "We need to speak in private."

"My eyes, Aliss, you promised."

"There are more important matters than your eyes," Fiona said.

"You will open your eyes this night, I will make certain of it," Aliss assured him. She squeezed the warm cloth in the bucket and placed it over his eyes. "Leave this on and rest until I return. I will not be long."

They walked outside, Fiona insisting a reprieve from the keep would do them both good. They smiled, presenting a perfect picture of twin sisters taking a leisurely stroll, and all the while Aliss detailed how Tarr attempted to kiss her and how she had gotten flustered, they tripped, he landed on top of her, and she had frantically pushed him off.

Fiona realized that her sister thought she would be mad, but she smiled. "I would have loved to have seen that."

"You are not upset?"

"Why would I be?" Fiona asked as they left the group of cottages to walk in the open meadow.

"For one, I feared I exposed my identity; and second, I think you begin to care for this man and I worry I may have hurt your chances with him."

"I admit he stirs an interest in me. I am amazed at his patience in dealing with us. I thought by now he would have been frustrated and returned us home." She shook her head. "Instead, with patience, he shows us all he has to offer a wife"

"Do you wish to alter our plan?"

"Not unless I see a reason to change it."

"What if Tarr actually toys with us?" Aliss asked. "What if already he can tell us apart?"

"Not likely," Fiona said with confidence. "He has demonstrated that he is a man on a mission. He is as determined to have a strong wife who will defend his land and bare him mighty sons as I am to wed for love."

Aliss stopped and turned a soft glance on her sister. "You and Tarr are much alike."

Fiona crunched her face, about to shake her head.

"You cannot deny it. You are both skilled hunters, strong-willed, independent," Aliss said. "You match each other perfectly."

"Where is love in all this?"

"Perhaps it would grow if you wed and gave it a chance."

"And if it does not? I am stuck."

"The problem is that time is running out, and quickly," Aliss said, addressing the obvious. "This ruse cannot go on for long, one of us is bound to make a mistake or Tarr, sharp-witted as he is, will figure out that he is actually spending more time with Fiona than Aliss. Then there is Raynor. I have not healed him only to see him die."

"Is it that you favor Raynor? He is a handsome man and well-endowed." Fiona smirked.

"He is an ill man in need of tending, nothing more. I told you many times that I, unlike you, am not interested in finding love. I wish to continue studying the healing arts, which means I have no room for a husband in my life."

"You may regret it one day."

"Then it will be mine to regret, but now I wish to pursue my interests."

"You know I will always support whatever choice you make," Fiona assured her. "I think it would be wise of us to place a time limit on this charade."

"You mean a time limit to see if you could possibly fall in love with Tarr."

"Whatever way you wish to see it as." Fiona shrugged. "One month's time, then we leave or stay unless an earlier departure proves necessary."

"Tarr will not let us leave," Aliss said.

"I know someone who would probably welcome us and protect us."

Aliss looked perplexed.

"Think about it, Aliss. Where is the perfect place to hide?"

Aliss smiled. "Raynor."

"He would not deny us protection. He feels indebted to you."

"He would need our help."

"If we need his help, then so be it," Fiona said. "How long before he is well enough to attempt an escape?"

"Two, perhaps three weeks."

"See if you can stretch it into a month. If we time this right, all can fall into place easily."

By the time they were done, it was agreed that nothing would be said to Raynor until it was deemed necessary. As for Tarr? He was for Fiona to deal with; Aliss wanted nothing more to do with him.

Aliss returned to Raynor and Fiona went to the pen where her mare was stabled.

She grabbed a blanket and reins and prepared her horse for riding. Within minutes, she was flying across the meadow, a cool wind in her face, her raging red hair flying wildly about her head and the pure joy of freedom beating wildly in her heart.

Fiona was not familiar with the land but that made no difference. She feared little, her knife sheathed at her waist and her sword strapped securely to her horse.

Most men feared a woman with a sword, not knowing whether she was skilled or if it was simply a ruse. Once she unsheathed it, though, men quickly learned she knew exactly what to do with it.

She rode with sheer abandonment until, spying a stream through sparse woods, she slowed her mare, guiding her to the water.

Resting on the edge of the stream while the horse drank, she tossed a stone or two into the running water. "I know you follow me; show yourself."

A moment passed and no one emerged from behind the trees or bushes.

"Have it your way, but I know you are there. For a fierce warrior, one would think you would be a good tracker, or is this another ruse like our hunting expedition?"

The taunting did it; Tarr stepped out from behind the trees. His stallion headed straight for the stream.

"How?" was all he asked.

"I caught you from the corner of my eye when my sister and I parted. You followed me, and not as unobtrusively as you should have."

"You let me follow you?" Tarr asked.

"I wanted to see what you were about, then I realized." Fiona turned and threw another stone; it skipped clear across the stream. "You wanted to see how skilled I was with a horse to determine if I am Fiona or Aliss. I confuse you, and that annoys you. Or are you annoyed because you find you favor kissing me?"

Tarr walked over to her, grabbed her arm, swung her around, and planted his lips on hers with a challenge to her to deny him.

She did not give it a thought. She wanted to taste him as much as he wanted to taste her. The kiss was more a battle than a tender embrace. Their tongues darted, their lips demanded, and their bodies pressed into each other. Did one intend to emerge a victor?

Fiona made no protest when his hand grabbed her firm around the neck and his mouth grinded against hers with a passion that sent her toes to tingling.

Damn if he did not taste good like a flavor of the finest wine or the freshest fruit that tempted the soul and made you hunger for more. His strong fingers dug into the muscles at the back of her neck while he kissed her, and Damn, Damn if it did not feel as good as the kiss.

She leaned into him and grabbed hold of his powerful arms, hugging them as if she needed their support. The kiss seemed to go on forever, and that was fine with Fiona until they both came to their senses and let the battle wane, their foreheads dropping to rest against one another.

"I do not even know who I kiss," Tarr said on a deep breath.

"The question should be why do you kiss me?"

"You tempt my soul, woman," he said, and bit gently at her bottom lip.

She grinned and licked the taste of him off her lip.

Tarr shivered. "We could do well together."

"I could give you strong sons," Fiona said, and stepped away from him.

"We would enjoy creating them." He sounded pleased.

She stared blankly at him.

He stepped forward. "I would be good to you."

"Would you love me?" she demanded.

"In my own way."

Fiona's blank stare remained as she grabbed her mare's reins and mounted her horse without assistance from him. She rode off and did not look back.

She felt her emotions well up inside her. She enjoyed their kisses more than she cared to admit. She enjoyed the strength of his massive arms around her, the feel of his strong fingers kneading her neck and the heated intensity of his kiss and how it stirred her passion beyond reason.

Tarr was more than she bargained for, and the idea that she could be attracted to him troubled her. It could interfere with her choices if she was not careful. She could very well be tempted to justify a joining with him for no good reason, and live to regret it.

Her mother had filled her and Aliss's heads with tales of chivalrous men who wooed and won maiden hearts, and how in the end love conquered all, a tiresome tale to some, a poetic beauty to others.

To Fiona love was beauty in its purest form. She had watched the beauty of the way her mother and father laughed and loved together every day of their lives. When they argued, which had been rare, they both would be apologizing and hugging and laughing in no time. When her father had taken ill, her mother had tended him with loving care, never complaining, never crying in self-pity but sharing as much time and joy with him as she could right up until the very end.

They had shared the joys and sorrows with the same enthusiasm and had been content in each other's arms.

Fiona wanted a bond like her parents, a lasting bond that would travel beyond these earthly planes to the heavens above. She liked to think that her mother and father were happy, safe, and finally sharing an eternal love.

She choked back a tear, crying just did not suit her character and she rarely shed tears, the last being when her mother died.

Was she foolish to think that she could find such an everlasting love? She had no answer; she only knew that if she did not try she would always regret it. She found Tarr of Hellewyk attractive, and she knew there was more to the man than he let most see.

She wanted to know what lurked beneath the surface of the fierce chieftain that stirred fear and respect in the hearts of his enemies. And she had one month to do it.

Fiona smiled as she approached the keep. This was one challenge she looked forward to.

"A bit more and it will be done," Aliss assured Raynor.

"It takes too long," he said annoyed,

"The blood you lost from your head wound pooled in your eyes and since there was no time to clean them it crusted over your eyelashes good and hard. It takes time to remove it. There is not much left. You will see soon enough."

"Just rip my eyes open."

"No," Aliss said firmly. "The pain would be like you have never felt before."

"I do not care; I want this done."

"Why? So you can escape? You are not well enough

to go anywhere. Your head wound is healing but you require more rest."

"I will be the judge of that."

"You will not."

"You think to dictate to me?" he asked firmly.

"Nay, I simply speak the truth and advise you wisely. If you think to make haste and escape, you will collapse in no time along the trail and make your condition worse. But then I suppose few warriors have the good sense to be sensible."

"You are direct."

"I am honest."

"I look forward to setting my eyes on you," he said gently.

"You will have your wish shortly."

"How long?" he asked anxiously.

"An hour or so."

"Too long," he whispered harshly and shoved her hands away, ripping his eyelids apart before Aliss could stop him.

Aliss watched the pain wash over him and his eyes blink several times. He fought to keep them open. Finally, he settled a stare on her face.

"Oh my God," he said before he passed out.

Chapter 9

Tarr stood by the window in his bedchamber looking out at the starless night. All was not going as he had expected. He thought to have the twins' charade settled within a few days. A week and a half, and he was more perplexed than when this all began.

His desire was simple, a strong wife to bear strong sons. Instead he got twins who he could not possibly tell apart. Just when he thought he had it figured out, he realized he had not, and he would once again be back where he started.

He had even yet to determine if he spent time with the same woman or if they took turns. Their features were identical, and while their beauty appealed to him, what attracted him more was the bold nature displayed by one of the twins. Which one he was not certain, but it had to be Fiona. She was the sister with the bold personality. The one who would stand up to a man and, without fear, challenge him.

When presented with this ruse, he had given brief thought to wedding either twin. But he recalled the difference between them, and while he respected the skill of the twin who was the healer, he favored a wife whose confidence and bravery he respected.

He had not considered love; it was a useless emotion serving no good purpose. It caused intelligent men to make foolish mistakes. He had no time for such foolishness and definitely not for mistakes. He had a clan to consider and protect; he could not, nor would not allow, anything to stand in the way of his chieftain duties.

He rubbed his square chin then crossed his arms over his chest. The twins' face drifted in front of his eyes. It had to be Fiona who always spent time with him and the one who stirred his blood when they kissed.

Her passion matched his own, and there was no doubt they had desired each other. A good start for an arranged union; it bode well for their future together.

Fiona.

He had to have kissed Fiona.

He rubbed his chin harder, kneading his flesh with his fingers while staring off into the dark night, wondering who the devil he had enjoyed kissing.

A scream suddenly jolted the silence and had him running out of his bedchamber, across the hall, and into the room that held Raynor. The two guards who had been posted outside the door had already entered the room and were presently being held at bay by a twin who looked ready to do harm if anyone dared to touch the unconscious man in the bed.

"What goes on here?' Tarr demanded.

Before she could respond the other twin entered the room with a flourish and settled herself beside her sister. Their identical features startled the senses. There was no physical trait that could distinguish them. It was as if they were mirror images.

Raynor groaned, coming out of his faint.

Tarr stepped forward and Fiona braced her hands on her hips as if daring him to try and pass her.

"I will speak with him," Tarr commanded.

"Not now," Aliss said, and leaned over Raynor to whisper in his ear.

"Now!" Tarr was angry. How dare she dictate to him.

"He will make no sense," Aliss snapped. "Give him until morning. His head will clear and you will get answers from him then."

"Leave now, both of you."

"Go," Raynor ordered. "I will talk with Tarr."

Fiona took her sister's arm and nearly dragged her out of the room, but not before sending Tarr a scathing look.

He returned it in kind as the door slammed.

Tarr and Raynor were alone, the two guards having disappeared when they recognized the warning tremor in their chieftain's voice.

Raynor pulled himself up to a slumping position.

Tarr kept his eyes on his enemy's every move. He remained at the side edge of the bed, and though he lacked a weapon he did not fear. He knew Raynor was in no condition to fight him, and besides, he was confident in his ability to defeat him.

"You will answer my questions."

"You will tell me how many of my men you hold."

"I will tell *you* nothing," Tarr said through gritted teeth.

"I say nothing until I know of my men."

"My dungeon would better suit you."

"If you have any of my men there, I will join them."

"What brought you to my land?" Tarr asked, ignoring his demand.

"To claim what is rightfully mine."

"We have been through this, Raynor. The Isle of Non belongs to me."

"It connects to Blackshaw land—"

"And Hellewyk land. It is mine and there is nothing you can do about it."

Raynor smiled. "Aye, there is."

Tarr's laugh challenged. "You ride on my land with a small troop of warriors, attack me, get captured, and think you will claim my land? The blow to your head has made you delusional."

"We shall see."

Tarr did not care for the confidence in Raynor's voice. Something was wrong, and the only reason he did not overly concern himself with it was because he held Raynor prisoner. He held the upper hand.

"Why did you not attack my keep?"

"My plans did not call for attacking your keep."

So he had had plans, and from his calm response it appeared he was not concerned with the failure of those plans.

The door suddenly burst open and one twin followed close on the heels of the other twin.

"You have had your time," Aliss said. "He needs to rest."

Tarr did not argue this time. He would bide his time with Raynor and learn precisely what he was up to, in whatever way was necessary.

"We will speak again," Tarr said.

"Of that I am sure," Raynor replied in a challenging tone.

Tarr nodded, accepting his dare, turned and left the room. He did not go directly to his room; instead he went down to the next floor and waited by the twins' bedchamber door.

Fiona turned on Raynor. "You heeded my warning?"

"I spoke not of you or Aliss," he assured her. "Your secret is safe with me."

"Why should we believe you?" Fiona asked skeptically.

"Why should we not?" Aliss said, assisting him and carefully sliding him down to rest his head against the soft pillow.

"You trust too easily," Fiona said to her sister. "He is the enemy."

"Like Tarr?" Aliss asked. "Do you trust him?"

"It seems to me that you both find it difficult to trust," Raynor said, looking from one to the other twin. "Did your parents not teach you of trust?"

"Our parents were loving and wonderful people," Aliss said as Fiona shook her head. "What have I said wrong now?"

Raynor answered. "Your sister thinks you share too much information with the enemy. She does not realize

I am simply grateful for having had such a skilled healer save my life."

"Remember that well and hold your tongue where my sister and I are concerned."

"You do not need to keep warning me. I have told you your secret is safe with me and I mean it. I will not tell Tarr the ease in which he can tell you apart."

"You are so sure of that?" Fiona asked.

"Aye, that I am," he said and yawned.

"Enough," Aliss said. "You must rest and I wish to bathe your eyes again to make certain they are fully cleansed."

Fiona ignored her sister's decree. "What did Tarr and you discuss?"

"My capture and my men he holds prisoner."

"Conrad and Ivan have healed nicely and are doing well," Aliss said proudly.

Fiona groaned. "Keep giving him information."

"He is as much a prisoner as his men. Does he not always have two men outside this door?"

Fiona threw her hands up in the air. "I give up. Tell him everything. This way he can plan his escape." She turned and stormed out of the room.

"I could take you and your sister with me," Raynor said.

He sounded more like he urged Aliss to join him. "You need a few weeks yet to recover. Make your plans but tell me nothing; when it is time I will let you know if we will go with you."

Fiona stomped down the stairs, turned the corner, and caught a shadow from the corner of her eye. Her hand went to the knife at her waist. Before she could draw it Tarr stepped forward, the shadows clinging to his wide shoulders as though they refused to release him. One more stride and he was free; his features suddenly stronger, his strength more potent, his scent more alluring—and a faint passion lurking in his eyes.

"How long has Raynor been awake?"

Fiona kept her wits about her. She had no intention of lying to him, and she had no intention of succumbing to this sudden flush of desire that flooded her. "Several days."

"And you said nothing to me?" he asked moving toward her.

Normally she would have stayed her ground, but the sheer breadth of him so overwhelmed her that she backed away. She did not know if the shadows rushed after him and made him appear an enormous winged bat in flight, or if it was the strong scent of earth, pine, and male that beset her senses. She only knew she needed to distance herself from him.

He seemed to feel the opposite for he moved closer to her.

"He was in no condition to talk."

"I decide that not you."

"He was no threat," Fiona countered.

"Again my decision not yours."

"Then do what you will with him."

"You defend him no more?" Tarr asked unbelievingly.

"A healer heals; he heals well and soon will be fully recovered. I did what I had to do; now he is yours."

"So opposite," Tarr said, staring at her and moving his body so that he nearly imprisoned her against the stone wall. "One twin heals, the other wields a weapon with precision and intent."

"Think what you will; it matters not to me."

"Obviously since you kept the truth from me."

"You asked me nothing of Raynor's condition," she said.

"And you told me nothing."

"If you had asked—"

"Stop! I will not tolerate duplicity."

"Tolerate?" she said her voice harsh. "I am to tolerate being taken from my home, threatened with being separated from my sister, forced to wed a stranger who wants me to bare him sons, and you expect me to care what you think of my actions?"

"You would be wise to," he warned.

She stepped forward with such might that it forced him to retreat. "I have been threatened enough. I care not what you think of me or my actions and remember well, Fiona would not be a compliant wife, so take heed or you will find yourself saddled with a most undesirable woman."

She pushed past him and entered her bedchambers. He followed behind her, entering before she could close the door.

"You are not welcome here."

"This is my home."

"And this is my room while I am forced to seek shelter here," she said, her green eyes blazing like shimmering emeralds.

"Nothing here is yours."

She walked up to him and poked him in the chest, her

finger meeting solid muscle. "Nor would I want it to be."

"What you want matters not."

"Think again, Tarr of Hellewyk," she said with another jab of her finger. "What *I want* will decide *your fate*."

"No one decides my fate."

"And no one decides mine," she said with a final jab, and walked several feet past him then turned around. "Get out of my bedchamber."

Tarr faced her from where he stood, a grin slowly surfacing. "You are Fiona, for only she would have the courage to poke at me and challenge my word."

Fiona placed her hands on her hips and approached him. "If you are so sure, then get the cleric now and wed me."

A moment of doubt flashed in his eyes and his grinned faded.

"You asked for this battle, Tarr, though I do not think you were prepared for such worthy opponents."

"Stubborn opponents," he said tersely.

"Thank you," she said with a nod and a smile. "Stubborn opponents usually prove victorious."

"And what of foolhardy ones?"

"You should not be so harsh on yourself."

He was too fast; she did not even see him move. His hand grabbed her face and he gently squeezed her lips to pucker.

"Have your fun, but know now that this will be your home; you will be my wife, and I will do my damnedest to protect and provide for such an ornery woman."

He released her and walked out of the room, leaving the door open. She walked over and peered past the door, watching him. She admired the thick muscles in his legs—and then there was his backside, not too large but perfectly rounded and firm. She liked that, drooping backsides or flat ones did nothing for her. The width of his shoulders always impressed her, and she favored his auburn hair for he kept it clean and combed.

She sighed when he turned the corner and closed her door, resting her back against it. She liked that he returned her challenge. Men either cowered when she challenged or thought her foolish and simply ignored her, or at least tried to.

Tarr did not back down. He actually respected her as an opponent, and that sparked excitement in her. She wanted to experience more with him, after all he just might prove worthy of being a husband.

Provide and protect would he?

She laughed. "Only if I let you."

Chapter 10

Tarr watched the sisters from the front door of the keep. They walked among his clansmen as though they belonged, many calling out greetings to them. It did not seem to matter which twin was which. In two weeks time they both had earned the respect of his people, and they both answered to either name.

Would it really matter which twin he wed? His answer had been confirmed in a short time. He had found he enjoyed the sharp-tongued twin and the way she sparred with him. When the soft-natured twin surfaced, he lost interest. So he had a dilemma on his hands. He wanted to be sure he wed Fiona.

He grinned when a puppy came running to attack one twin's skirt. She scooped him up, hugged him to her cheek, and kissed his brown furry face before placing him on the ground and giving his fat little rump a pat and a shove toward a group of children.

They continued walking side by side chatting the whole time, though taking time to acknowledge those who called out to them. The twins were close and that very closeness was the reason he had insisted they be parted. He wanted no competition for his wife's attention to her duties.

He, her husband and their children, would be her priority. He needed no interference, and having watched Fiona and Aliss it was obvious they were inseparable. How he would finally separate them he was not sure, though he could see about wedding Aliss to someone, preferably a distance away.

He would mention nothing of it until all was settled, since he knew Fiona would not be the only one to protest. His clansmen had begun to seek Aliss's healing skills, and pleased they were with the results. He would worry about it later. First he needed to determine which one was Fiona.

Kirk joined him. "They look as one."

"I know. I can find no difference between them; they play their roles well."

"They should; they are twins." Kirk laughed.

"I need no reminding; they tempt my sanity."

"Everyone seems fine with them," Kirk said.

"Because they do not care which twin is which!"

"They simply accept them."

"What are you implying, Kirk?" Tarr asked.

"I know not who helped my Erin, but it matters not to me for she was tended for several days with a generous and loving heart, and my wife has improved much."

"What you say is that it matters not which twin I wed."

"Your stubbornness has you resisting. You picked Fiona so you want Fiona. Pick one and wed her and be done with it."

"They are different," Tarr insisted.

"How?" Kirk asked, and looked to the twins. "Their walk is identical, their laughter is identical, and their speech is identical."

"They are different," Tarr repeated. "I know it and I will prove it."

"To whom; it matters to no one."

"It matters to me." Tarr marched off, leaving Kirk shaking his head.

Tarr approached the twins and before he could say a word one spoke.

"I'll go see to Raynor; you tend to Tarr." One twin hurried off and disappeared into the keep.

"You remain apart more then together when around me. Do you fear me discovering the difference between you?" he asked, and watched for the familiar sparkle that shined in her green eyes when he confronted her.

There it was, like the sun reflecting off a shimmering emerald; he smiled.

"Do I entertain you?"

He held his tongue and took control of his smile.

She leaned into him, her shoulder nudging his. "I know what you think, but I wonder if you can satisfy my lusty thirst."

His eyes rounded.

"Do not look at me with an accusatory glare. I have known no man intimately, but I am not ignorant of sex.

I do not fear it and—" she lowered her voice—"I pray the man I love has much stamina, for sex is something I intend to master."

Damn, if she did not set his loins to fire.

"Be careful or you will have lessons before you are wed."

She grinned. "The lessons will be my choice."

He stared at her swaying backside as she sauntered off.

"I am healed," Raynor said after Aliss examined his head wound.

"That does not sound like a question."

"I know I have healed. I walk the room without growing dizzy."

Aliss watched him puff his chest in pride, an impressive chest fraught with muscles. He was a fine-looking man. Women probably would find his mixed Scottish and Viking features handsome, and his strange accent lyrical. She, however, thought of him only as an ill man needing tending.

He tugged at her hand. "I wait for confirmation."

"There is no dizziness at all?" she asked. "And be honest. It will do you no good if you are not honest with me."

"Damn, you have a way of making me feel guilty if I attempt to lie."

"I guess I have my answer." She walked away from him.

He swung his legs off the bed and braced his hands on either side of him as if preparing to stand. "I barely realize the dizziness."

"But it is there."

"How long before it is gone completely?" He stood slowly.

Aliss shrugged and sat at the table to work with her herbs. "That is difficult to know. It could be a day or two or a week or two. You will know when you feel your full strength return."

He began to walk around the room.

Aliss noticed how his steps faltered now and again, though not as badly as when he had first attempted to walk. He had had to lean on her, take short steps, day after day until he could finally stand on his own.

She had thought he would protest being dependent on her, but he seemed comfortable with her assistance.

He talked as he walked. "Tell me about yourself, Aliss."

"There is not much to tell."

"Tell me anyway," he urged. "Your voice has a way of soothing the soul, which I have no doubt aids in healing."

Aliss was never comfortable with compliments. Healing to her was a privilege and she respected her learned skill, and did all she could to learn more. She derived a sense of satisfaction and self-worth from her healing work and intended to continue with it for as long as she could.

"Where were you born?"

"Northwest of here, where the mountains rise so high you would think they reach to the heavens."

"Your parents still live there?"

"My parents passed on ten years ago, and what of you?"

"We talk of you not me."

She smiled. "Why do you and Tarr battle?"

Raynor broke into a huge grin. "Tarr is foolish to think that one twin is stronger than the other."

"My sister is much stronger than I."

"I see a balance of strength between the two of you," he said. "And I do not understand how Tarr cannot see the obvious differences between you."

"He does not look closely enough."

"I heard the differences," he said proudly.

"What did you hear?" she asked curiously.

Raynor paced slowly beside the table. "I heard a gentle caring in your voice." He laughed. "I actually thought I had died and an angel spoke to me, then I heard your sister." He laughed again. "For a moment I thought perhaps heaven and hell fought over me."

Aliss could not prevent herself from laughing, though she was quick to defend her sister. "Fiona has a good heart."

"I have learned that, but at the time the sharp tone of her voice warned me that she was not to be taken lightly. Where your hands healed, hers could do damage. You also have patience—"

"Fiona has—"

"Patience when it suits her," Raynor finished. "Your strength comes in your tender, caring nature. Fiona's strength comes in her quick mind and actions. She would defend you with her life."

"As I would her."

"A bond like yours is rare and I dare say cannot be broken."

"We will not let it be," Aliss said adamantly.

He walked over to her. "You and your sister can live in peace on my land. My people would welcome your healing skills, and they would welcome a warrior such as your sister."

"You tempt me with your generous offer, but the choice must be Fiona's. If she finds Tarr to her liking, then she will convince Tarr that we are not to be separated. Wherever we go, we go together."

"There are no conditions to my offer."

"I appreciate your generosity," she said, comfortable that he spoke the truth to her. He was a warrior in strength, demeanor and word, which made him an honorable man and why she was curious as to his battle with Tarr.

"I have little time here."

She held up her hand. "Tell me no more, for I will speak the truth when questioned."

"When the time is right, I will tell you everything, and you must trust me."

She was surprised by his adamancy. "I would trust that any decisions would be left to me."

"You are wise beyond your years, and I believe you would make a wise choice."

His answer disturbed her for it sounded more like a warning. She watched him make his way back to the bed, fighting to regain his strength in each step he took. Soon he would be fully recovered. She felt he probably was already planning his escape. Did he expect Fiona and her to go with him? And if they did not, what then?

She would speak with Fiona about this conversation

and see what she thought. It seemed that they needed to be aware of everyone around them. But then they had faced such a situation once before together.

She remembered when they had first arrived at the clan MacElders. Uncle Tavish had told them it would be their home and they need never worry again. The clan was their family and would always be their family.

While they had been accepted and treated well by the clan, they themselves always felt different. They remained close, doing everything together. They were sisters and best friends, and they allowed nothing to come between.

Fiona had sensed there would be trouble when Uncle Tavish passed on. He was a man who gave thought to his actions and consideration to his clan. His son Leith did not think on things; his actions were not always wise or beneficial to all, and he often considered himself before anyone else.

Aliss had known trouble was brewing, for Uncle Tavish and Fiona had talked often, he respecting her intelligence and forthright manner. It was obvious Leith had been jealous, and Aliss wondered, if it had been possible, would Uncle Tavish have left the leadership of the clan to Fiona?

Uncle Tavish had not been dead more than three days when Leith's rule could be felt and she and Fiona knew that it would take little time and effort on his part to bring the clan to ruin. If it were not for the match between Fiona and Tarr, the MacElder clan would know much unrest and suffering.

While neither she nor Fiona would wish such a plight

on their clan, it was not right that Fiona bare the sole burden of Leith's ignorance.

Aliss turned and glanced at Raynor stretched out and sound asleep on the bed. Had fate brought him into their lives? If this matter did not go the way Fiona wished, would this stranger be their escape to a more peaceful life?

She wasn't sure. She was just grateful that they would have a choice.

Chapter 11

"Which one rides with me today?"

The twins stopped talking to glance up at him from where they sat at a table near the huge stone fireplace in the great hall. Tarr had learned that they had arrived in the hall before dawn. The cook had advised him that they had seen to preparing their own breakfast, which they had taken to the table where they have been talking ever since the sun rose a couple of hours ago.

They looked at one another as though deciding, then one stood.

"I would like to ride."

"I will have the horses made ready." He glanced at the other twin. "How does Raynor fair?"

The twin that stood spoke, "Why not ask him yourself?"

"In time."

"You let him wonder over his fate."

Tarr turned to the twin who sat. "A warrior knows his fate; it is the consequence of battle."

"We decide our own fate," the other twin said.

"It is not always left for us to decide," Tarr said. "Fate sometimes has the right answer, we are just too stubborn to see it."

The other sister stood. "Then fate has a busy day today." She smiled and walked off.

He was not surprised to see her leave the keep. Each morning one of the twins would stroll the village and look in on those who were ill. He was not certain which twin repeated the daily routine or if they took turns. It was impossible to tell them apart. Their dress was always the same, either a green skirt or brown one, their blouses white or yellow and their red hair fashioned the same, swept up, tied back, or free to spill over their shoulders; today it was worn free.

Tarr extended his hand for Fiona to take the lead. "Let us meet our fate."

The weather was perfect, a warm day for autumn, not a chill in the air.

Tarr watched Fiona mount her mare, without any help from him. She grabbed the reins, swung herself onto her horse, and waited. He took a moment to talk with the young lad who tended his horses, and from the corner of his eye caught an impatient Fiona lead her horse away from the village.

Her mare was just as impatient, snorting and stumping the ground, her eyes fixed on the open meadow. The animal was itching to break free and run, as badly as he imagined Fiona wanted to run, and he doubted she would hold her back much longer.

Tarr purposely took his time to see what she would do. Would she wait for him or take off at a blazing pace?

His answer came only moments after he mounted his stallion. Fiona freed her mare to run and Tarr grinned as he urged his horse to catch her.

He could see how much she enjoyed her ride by the way she enthusiastically held her face up to greet the wind. Then there was the ease in which she rode her mare; theirs was a harmonious pairing.

Watching her now he realized that she had a natural ability with horses, actually animals in general. He recalled how the puppy was attracted to the one twin, and he had noticed that most animals around the keep responded to her, or was it both twins?

He shrugged away his confusion and decided today he would let fate deal with his dilemma. He intended to enjoy his time with Fiona, at least he hoped the twin was Fiona.

Tarr took off after her, his stallion having no difficulty catching up with her. When he rode alongside her; she challenged him with a smile and he accepted, pulling past her. Not for long, though. She caught up with him, and they rode neck and neck for a good distance before they both slowed their pace.

Tarr pointed to a stream not far off. They led the horses there to drink and rest while they did the same.

They sat not far from the water's edge, Fiona stretching her legs out in front of her and tilting her face to the sun.

"I am glad autumn allowed a touch of summer to visit for the day."

"Enjoy it now, for winter will soon approach and there will be few days spent outside." The prospect of being inside this winter appealed to him. He would have a bride to keep him warm and busy, and the thought stirred his senses.

"You think I will spend the winter here?" She sounded as though she laughed.

"I know you will." He sounded pleased.

"I am curious," she said, her tone now one of interest. "You think to make a wife of me or my sister, and shortly, as you have often reminded me. Yet you have done nothing but spend a few hours each day with us. What will be the deciding factor for who you wed?"

He favored her direct manner. Their would be no pretense between them; she would have her say whether he liked it or not, and that pleased him. He had no time for a woman who would whine and complain and never say what she meant.

"I am not sure," he said. "You both seem identical, but then I could be speaking with the same twin over and over. I sometimes think to grab one of you, wed, and have done with it."

"Yet you do not. Why?"

"My stubborn pride?"

Fiona laughed. "That can get in the way."

Her eyes sparkled along with her laughter before a lopsided smile settled on her face. He had never noticed it before, and he realized the funny grin made her all the more beautiful.

He had appreciated her beauty at first glance but of

late, he had begun to notice other things about her that appealed to him. She tilted her head when she laughed, her eyes rounded when she grew upset, she licked her lips slowly when deep in thought, and now this funny grin.

"So then you have no plan where my sister and I are concerned?"

"You should use tact when questioning your adversary."

"You are not my foe?" she asked.

Had he upset her? Her eyes rounded slightly.

"If not foe what am I to you?"

She leaned forward as if she would spit the words from her mouth, then grew still. She shook her head so briefly. "I do not know."

The wind rustled a cool breeze across the stream, whipping Fiona's hair in her face. Before she could brush it aside, Tarr reached out and gently ran his fingers into the strands, raking them back until his hand cupped the back of her head.

"Let us see if we can find out," he said, and leaned over her, his broad chest pressing her to the ground as his lips claimed hers in a hungry kiss.

She did not shy away or deny him. She eagerly joined him, sharing in the kiss and demanding as much as she gave, which fueled his already ignited passion. Her taste was not sweet; it was tart and pungent and intoxicating.

He loved her odd flavor and could not get enough of it. Her lips were firm and succulent, not soft mush like most of the women he had known.

Damn, but he favored the taste of her and the feel of her. She arched her body against his, her breasts pressing firm to his chest, and she wrapped one leg around his, hugging it tightly. She had locked onto him as if she had no intentions of letting go and the thought sent him reeling.

She wanted him.

He eased his lips from hers to trace down along her cheek to her neck, then nuzzled kisses along her silky flesh. She tilted her chin up, providing him easier access, and her strong moans let him know how very much she was enjoying his attention.

Her breathing grew rapid and her body moved beneath him as if she had an itch that needed immediate scratching. Her hands hugged his arms with a strength that surprised him, but when his lips drifted to her breast she suddenly ceased all movement.

He looked up to see a heated glare fixed on him.

"Touch nowhere that rightfully belongs to my future husband."

He grinned.

"My husband will be of my choice."

Now she could read his mind. He was about to remind her that she would wed him, and damned if he did not want the wedding to take place today. This vibrant, eager woman beneath him had to be Fiona.

He pushed himself off her and walked over to the water's edge. He leaned down and splashed water in his face several times. He was crazy for allowing this farce to continue, and yet somehow he did not want to stop it. He felt he was unraveling Fiona, discovering who she was bit by bit and enjoying it. By the time he turned around, Fiona was standing near her horse.

"You run away?"

She laughed and mounted with an agility and speed that startled him. "If I did, you would never catch me." She took off, her laughter trickling in her wake.

He mumbled several oaths as he mounted his stallion and went after her, a smile surfacing as he gave thought to the wedding night they would soon share.

Clouds arrived at the keep along with Fiona. She walked her mare to the pen, her thoughts on her response to Tarr's unexpected question.

If not foe, what am I to you?

She had believed him her foe. Why had she answered differently? And what was he to her? She raved and ranted about her situation and yet she found herself enjoying his company.

She looked forward to their discussions. He respected her opinions and never dismissed them as trivial.

Fiona released her mare into the pen and turned, intending to find her sister and talk. But Tarr walked toward her, his horse left to the care of a young lad who took the reins. A ripple of anticipation spread throughout her body tingling her senses. She had just left him, how could he seem more appealing to her in such a short time?

He wore no smile, his eyes were intent upon her, and his walk determined.

He wanted her.

She could sense it in every step he took, in the way his eyes refused to let go of her, in his strides that announced, I am coming to get you.

She had warned him that he would never catch her, and yet he did not give up. He came after her. The thought thrilled her. If he wanted her that much, could he possibly care for her?

He reached her, took her arm, and lead her behind the keep, away from curious glances and into the afternoon shadows that danced against the stone wall. There, he wrapped her so tightly in his arms that she could feel the rapid rhythm of his heart. His was a strong and steady thump-thump that soon had her own heart following suit.

She stared into his eyes and saw her own passion reflected in his heated desire. They mingled and mixed until fused together, and that is when he claimed her lips.

The taste of him never failed to excite her and within minutes, she was fully aroused, and wanting more, much more from him.

She refused to let the kiss end, nibbling at his lips urging his return, until he gently shoved her away from him.

"Think of what I am to you, for before I take you to my bed I want to know."

Fiona stared at his back as he walked away from her, and she wondered over his question and worried over her aching heart.

Chapter 12

The horn sounded late that night when the village had been just about tucked in for a good night's sleep. It roused everyone in minutes, the men running to their posts, the women rushing the children to the safety of the keep while other women prepared to defend against fires.

"Raiders from the north," Kirk shouted as Tarr burst out of the keep, claymore in hand.

Fiona and Aliss were close behind him.

"Remain in the keep," he ordered as he ran to issue orders to his men.

Aliss turned a knowing glance on her sister. "Do what you must. I will be ready to tend the wounded, though make certain you are not one of them."

Fiona with sword in hand hurried to help defend Tarr's land.

She knew at first glance that the raiders were more barbarians than skilled warriors, but then they could prove a far worse adversary since they cared little for life. They lived to war. Tarr's men handled them well, but the sheer volume of warriors made fighting difficult. You would just finish with one and two more would appear. That was how the barbarians won their battles, by flooding their enemy with a plethora of warriors.

Fiona kept her eye on Tarr's back while she fought with a skill uncanny for a woman. Some thought it a natural ability while others thought her in league with the devil, for no woman possessed such remarkable talent with weapons.

Her heart jumped with fear when she saw blood splattered across Tarr's naked chest, but he remained firm on his feet, which meant the blood belonged to his enemy.

She returned her attention to the battle, soon fighting off two large men, her temper growing with each thrust of her sword. They were large and strong and gave a good fight, but Fiona outmaneuvered them at each turn.

She caught one's arm with her blade and turned to finish the other when a third suddenly appeared out of nowhere. Before she could swing her weapon, his sword descended on her.

Steel clashed against steel and a powerful fist crashed into the warrior's jaw, dropping him to the ground. Before she could take the other warrior down, Tarr's sword swung, felling him in one swift blow.

She was about to thank him when a warrior raced up behind Tarr, her wide eyes warning him just in time, and another warrior fell.

The thick muscles tensed in his sweaty and blood-covered chest as he reached out and grabbed her wrist. "Get yourself to a safe place."

"I am in a safe place, beside you," she said, and pressed her cheek to his before returning to battle.

The night wore on with torches one right after the other igniting thatched rooftops, and the clash of steel echoing in the darkness. Fiona's skin turned to goose-flesh when she saw her sister along with other women creep onto the battlefield and drag the wounded to safety.

Victory was close, the last of the barbarians running off knowing defeat was imminent, when suddenly a large warrior wearing a wolf's headdress that near covered his entire face emerged from the darkness on a mare as white as freshly fallen snow and, with arrow in hand, plunged it into Tarr.

Fiona was too far away to help or to see how badly he was wounded, but she let loose with a bloodcurdling scream and advanced on the retreating warrior. Neither she nor Tarr's men could catch the half wolf, half man, and he was swallowed by the darkness that had spit him out.

Fiona was rushing to his side while her eyes frantically searched for her sister; Aliss was approaching. Fiona made it there first and pushed the men gathered around their chieftain out of her way.

Fiona dropped to the ground beside him. The arrow had gone straight through his arm several inches above his elbow. It would take tremendous strength to deliver such a powerful blow with a single hand.

His men already argued about who would pull the arrow out while Tarr shouted orders to secure the boundaries of the village.

Fiona silenced all when she shouted, "Quiet." Then she methodically issued clear orders on what the men were to do. They quickly obeyed once their chieftain nodded his approval.

Aliss kneeled beside Tarr.

"It cannot be removed yet," Fiona said calmly.

Aliss agreed with a nod after a quick assessment. "We must examine the possible damage before anything is done."

Fiona looked to Kirk who had returned after seeing that the men had begun carrying out her orders. "Get him to his bedchamber."

"I can walk," Tarr insisted, then directed his question to Kirk. "How many lost and wounded?"

"Surprisingly we suffered no losses, but we did suffer many injures. Thanks to—" Kirk looked from one twin to the other—"thanks to one of them, the wounded were removed quickly from the battlefield and their injures attended to. Many are doing well with very few having suffered severely."

Tarr looked from one twin to the other. "Will I lose any of my men?"

"I think not," one answered.

"And me?" Tarr asked.

Fiona answered. "I will not let you die." With that she and Aliss helped him to sit up, then assisted him to stand. The twins supported him with their shoulders, and slowly they walked him to the keep as he attempted to speak with Kirk, who followed along.

"Quiet," Fiona yelled. "You must save your strength."

Erin, Kirk's wife, ran out of the keep as they were about to enter. She rambled on about one of the men who had begun to bleed badly. Aliss slipped out from under Tarr and Kirk took her place.

Once in the room, Tarr refused to seek his bed; he insisted on a chair. He grabbed Kirk's arm. "Bring Raynor to me now."

Fiona examined his wound. "There is little blood," she said with worry.

He stared at her; her vibrant green eyes anxious, her touch uncertain, and fear straining her lovely face. She cared what happened to him and that thought struck his heart like a mighty blow. It made him want to reach out and comfort her, assuage her concern and kiss her until each melted into the other's arms.

He mentally shook the nonsense from his head. What was the matter with him? His clan had just suffered a fierce attack and he thought of kissing and making love with this woman.

He was not supposed to feel or want her. She was simply to be his wife and the mother of his children. But did he want more? His duty was to his clan and he could not allow love to interfere with that duty.

"Work your magic," he said gruffly. "The clan speaks of your healing talent; use it." He purposely challenged her. Why? So that he would know who cared for him?

He was denied an answer when Aliss rushed into the room and hurried to her sister's side. Suddenly he could not tell one from the other as they shifted positions and worked almost as one.

The sisters consulted in whispers and he grew annoyed.

"What do you discuss?" he snapped.

"The best way to remove the arrow so there would be little or no damage to your arm," Aliss said.

He was surprised by her candid answer and pleased. "I trust your decision."

"A wise choice, she is an excellent healer," Raynor said, entering the room.

"I can see that," Tarr said. "You have healed well."

"And sealed my fate?"

"That is a matter to be discussed"—Tarr winced as Aliss gently probed his wound—"at a later time. Do you know anything about the barbarian tribes to the north?"

"That is who attacked you tonight?"

Tarr nodded with effort. "What do you know of them?"

"They fight each other and have no honor."

"There is unrest among them?"

"Much unrest, and there are those who seek to expand their holdings—"

"This arrow must be removed soon," Aliss interrupted.

"In a moment," Tarr said. "There is one; he is large and powerful—"

"Like few men you have ever seen, and he wears a wolf's headdress?" Raynor asked.

"Like none I have ever seen, and aye, he wears the

head of a wolf," Tarr said. "With a single blow he pierced my arm with an arrow."

"He is the leader of the clan Wolf, not only because of the headpiece he wears, but because his attacks are vicious and he leaves few of his enemy unscathed. He rules his land and people with a strong hand, and none dare oppose him."

"I can understand why. When he lanced me with his arrow, the wolf's eyes in the headdress glowed like an animal set to devour his prey. I was lucky he caught only my arm."

Raynor grinned. "You were lucky, his weapon hit his mark. He speared your arm to let you know of his skill and intentions. He will return and the next time his aim will prove deadly."

"No more talk," Aliss said with a forcefulness that turned everyone silent. "This arrow needs removing now." She turned to Kirk before anyone could protest. "I will need your strength." She looked to Raynor. "And yours as well."

"We do not need our enemy's help," Kirk spat.

"Then tend your chieftain yourself," Raynor argued.

"I need no help," Tarr insisted.

"You think so?" Fiona questioned.

"I will do as I see fit," Tarr said.

"You will do as you are told," Aliss ordered. "Or you will chance losing all strength in your arm. Now drink this." She shoved a goblet in his face.

"Listen to her," Kirk said, looking from one twin to the other. "She knows of what she speaks. She has cured many of the clans' ills."

Tarr hesitated then reluctantly swallowed the drink. The arrow would be removed and the skin sealed with a fiery iron. Then there would be worry of fever. He himself had helped close wounds such as his.

"Do what you must," he said, and grabbed the arm of the chair, bracing himself for the pain. Kirk and Raynor lent their strength to him and held him firm.

Fiona stood ready to reach for the red-hot iron and Aliss wrapped a cloth around the arrow. With a skill that surprised everyone, she worked the arrow out of Tarr's arm inch by inch.

Tarr did his best to remain still, gripping the arms of the chair, gritting his teeth and fighting the pain that attempted to consume him. Sweat broke out on his brow and spread slowly over his entire body.

He refused to surrender to the intense pain, chasing away the blackness that rose up to swallow him. He would remain alert and rejoice in the pain for it meant he survived the battle.

His gaze locked with the twin holding the poker iron. He concentrated on her green eyes filled to the brim with fear and gut-wrenching pain. That she suffered along with him was obvious. She had to be Fiona, and he told himself to remember later to look in her eyes—for he might be able to tell the difference if he remembers this look.

He did not take his eyes off her not even when the arrow was finally removed.

The poker iron came next, searing his arm in two spots. Tarr groaned from the stinging flesh and, for a moment, almost gagged from the smell. His ordeal had finally ended and he rested his head back against the chair, his eyes still on the twin.

"Get him into bed. He needs to rest."

The twin he stared at spoke, though she grew blurry and his mind groggy. He was helped up and deposited in bed. His eyes closed of their own accord, even though he fought to keep them open as gentle hands touched his arm.

He did not want to sleep and appear weak. There were things he needed to see to, orders to give, the keep's safety to maintain, his clan to look after and . . .

"The brew Aliss gave him will have him sleeping until morning; we have work to do," Fiona said to Kirk. "Return Raynor to his room, then meet me in the great hall."

"I can help," Raynor offered.

Fiona shook her head. "You are a prisoner and Tarr will decide your fate."

Kirk smiled and did as she bid, closing the door behind him.

"Tell me he will be all right," Fiona asked of her sister.

"The arrow left no damage. We need only worry about fever."

"You will watch over him?" Fiona asked, gently brushing Tarr's hair off his forehead with her fingers. His brow was damp with sweat. She had watched him struggle to maintain his dignity and strength, refusing to scream or display any sign of weakness, and never taking his eyes off her.

"Your feelings for him grow."

Fiona bent down by the side of the bed and ran a finger over his warm lips. "I do not know why I feel the way I do. He shows me no such feelings in return, though when we kiss it is different. I can sense how very much he wants me. But then he is a man with needs. And I am a woman who needs love."

"Perhaps there is a common ground somewhere for you both."

"Love versus need?" Fiona said with a laugh, and stood.

"Need turning to love?" Aliss asked with a lift of her brow.

"I think it is in fate's hands."

"Then is it fate who brought us here?" Aliss questioned.

"We will have to wait and see," Fiona said, walking to the door. "I know not how or why I feel as I do about Tarr. I only know that when I watched the arrow pierce his flesh, it tore at my heart. For a brief moment I did not want to know life without him. The feeling and thought confuse me, and if this should prove to be love then it is very strange indeed, for there is more hurt and pain to love than there is joy and peace."

Chapter 13

A chill wind blew down from the north and many felt it was the breath of the barbarians bearing down on them, when it was simply a reminder of winter's approach.

Remnants of last night's attack, however, did little to remind them that the wind was harmless. Roofs bore holes from the fiery torches, fences were broken, their pieces scattered; the storehouse was ransacked, and the wounded lay suffering. Fear needed to be eased in the hearts and minds of the clanswomen and anger assuaged in the men.

The best way to do that was to keep everyone busy, and that is what Fiona had been doing since last night. She got not a wink of sleep; she was much too busy seeing to clan duties for a healing chieftain. She encouraged those in need and displayed confidence to those looking for leadership, which she did with ease and grace. And her efforts were met with appreciation. Several damaged roofs were already repaired, fences were being mended, stock being taken of the storehouse, and the wounded were finally finding relief from their pain, thanks to the brew Aliss had the women make and administer.

Fiona indeed had things well in hand most impressively by the time Tarr woke, when he was forced to eat breakfast by Aliss, made to wear a sling with her threat of death if he should remove it, and then before he left his chamber, warned he was not to overtax himself.

From the steps of the keep, Tarr stared in amazement at the amount of repair work that had been accomplished. He learned that guard posts had been doubled at his north borders and established along route so that any news of impending attack would be learned of in a more timely matter. He stood speechless.

"I tell you, Tarr, she—they—whoever commands in your stead is worthy of leadership," Kirk said. "She rallied the people, not waiting for someone to take command. With many in shock and still frightened, they were drawn to her courage and strength and followed willingly, and gratefully. I saw no reason to remind her she was not chieftain, for she certainly possessed the skills of a knowledgeable laird."

Tarr watched Fiona scoop a little puppy up that had peeked its head out of a barrel. She hugged the black pup to her and then deposited him in the lap of a little girl, Grenda, who looked to have spent the night crying. She laughed when the puppy licked her face and she hugged him tight. They were soon romping around together and other children joined in.

When Fiona caught sight of Tarr, she waved, smiled and hurried over to him.

"I need to help with the thatching," Kirk said and took off.

Tarr was glad for the time alone with Fiona. He had begun to believe more and more that it was Fiona he had spent his days with, had kissed so often, and looked so forward to seeing.

She *had* to be Fiona; he could not be wrong. Though just a feeling, it was a feeling that overwhelmed him. Then there was that lopsided smile of hers, which was not always visible and which lead him to believe that perhaps a distinction did exist between the twins.

"Feeling well?" she asked.

"Some pain but nothing unbearable." He noticed that she wore the same garments as yesterday, and understood then that it was the twins' habit to alternate their daily skirts and blouses, while continuing to wear identical garments. Just another way of fooling the eye. "Did you sleep at all?"

"No time," she said, and pointed to several roofs and the storehouse. "Some work required immediate attention."

Tarr looked around at the damage that had been done and the remarkable work already completed.

"Should you be up and about so soon?" she asked.

Concern not only filled her voice but her lovely green eyes as well. Had he not seen worry in the other twin's eyes and concern for his well-being?

Fiona answered her own question. "If I were chieftain, nothing would stop me from seeing to the defense of my clan."

Those words and the conviction with which they were issued is what he had wanted to hear from the woman he would call wife. From what he had seen, she was a fine example of a woman, more than capable of being his partner and seeing to the clan's needs with skill and confidence.

"You did well in my stead, and I am grateful."

Fiona stood tall and with a gracious bow of her head said, "It was an honor."

His glance returned to the damage the village had suffered and he shook his head. "Something does not seem right here."

"I thought the same myself."

"What did you think?" Tarr asked, eager to know if their thoughts were similar.

"It appears as if the attackers searched for something."

Tarr nodded in agreement. "They were after something specific."

"Or perhaps *someone* specific. They torched the cottages. Why? To force their target into the open?"

His brows drew together. "Who would be of such importance?"

"To barbarians," she added.

He turned slowly, looking over his people. "I cannot imagine them wanting anyone here."

"What of Raynor? Could they want something of him? He seemed to know about this barbarian leader of the Wolf clan."

"It is a thought."

"What will you do with Raynor?" she asked.

"You worry over him?" Tarr snapped, annoyed at her concern.

"I am curious," she said with a shrug.

He realized that it was his own concern he had heard. She did not sound as if she truly cared one way or the other.

"I will talk more with him and then decide his fate."

"Have you warred much with him?"

"Skirmishes more than anything."

"Would he seek this Wolf leader's help?" she asked.

"He is too proud, and besides Raynor is a warrior with an honored reputation. I cannot see him joining with barbarians."

"If this Wolf leader did not find what he came for, will he look elsewhere or return?"

"The very question on my mind," Tarr responded. "His search was mostly of the village, torching the cottages so that anyone inside would flee."

"And the storehouse was ransacked—"

"As if he thought someone hid inside."

"He kept his distance from the keep," Fiona said.

"Meaning this person would not reside in the keep."

"Or so he would think."

Tarr winced, the force of the pain in his wound causing deep wrinkles at the corner of his eyes.

"You do too much," she snapped.

Even though she sounded like she scolded, Tarr knew that her gruffness was out of concern for him.

"I do nothing but stand here and talk with you."

"You should be sitting," she argued.

"While my clansmen work?"

"Then go inside where you cannot see the work being done," she ordered, pointing her finger at the keep.

"I do not take orders from you." He tried to sound affronted, but his laugh did him in.

"You think not?"

"Do you know your eyes blaze like fiery emeralds when you grow angry?"

"You will not put me off with pretty words." She tossed her head up with a smile and stepped away from him, then shouted loudly for all to hear: "Your chieftain needs rest so that he may fully recover from his wound and lead you once more. I told him that we can do fine without his assistance right now. What say you all?"

"The twin can handle it, go rest," shouted one man.

"You are not needed now," yelled a woman.

"We trust the twin," called out another man.

More voices joined in until Tarr was forced to return to the keep, a smiling Fiona watching him walk away.

A cold rain was falling when Tarr woke from a sleep that he had no intention of taking though it had claimed him as soon as his head had rested on the pillow. He winced when he moved his arm; it turning to a gentle smile when he saw that one of the twins sat in a chair beside him, her head resting on her shoulder while she slept soundly.

He stretched his legs, which ached from battle, though he would admit it to no one, and as he eased himself up to sit at the edge of the bed, watched her sleep.

Her mouth hung open slightly and a soft snoring purr

spilled out. Her arms were crossed over her midsection as if she held herself up, and a stripe of white cloth held the ends of her braided hair together where it lay over her shoulder. She had changed into her green skirt and yellow blouse, the ties at her breasts stretched taught over her ample breasts.

He had thought on her breasts and how they would feel in his hand, soft and supple, and how he would enjoy rolling his tongue around her nipple until it was hard and he could suckle it gently.

He thought to reach out and touch her breast ever so lightly, but he recalled her warning that he should touch no place that would belong to her husband. But he was to be her husband, and those intimate places belonged to him.

But which twin would he touch?

He reached out and stroked her soft cheek with his finger and she sighed. Encouraged, he traced her warm lips with delicate strokes, the tip of his finger faintly brushing over the tip of her tongue.

She moaned softly and lifted her head, her eyes remaining closed, then he leaned over to steal a kiss.

A finger pressed suddenly to his lips stopped him; he grinned as best he could, the finger remaining tight against his mouth, then he attempted to speak.

"Awiss. You Awiss."

She laughed at his mumbling and freed his lips.

"Fiona would have been eager to kiss me."

"Would she now?" She leaned forward, her full chest leading. She ran her tongue over her lips. "Then I will just have to kiss you."

Tarr backed away from her.

"Do you not want a kiss?" She moved toward him.

Her chest was near in his face, her breath warm against his cheek. He reached out and grabbed her with one hand behind her neck and swung her toward him. They landed sitting on the bed; their lips locked tightly.

"What is this?"

The shout tore them apart, though they remained sitting beside each other.

"I work without rest and you two play?"

Tarr stared at the twin as she marched in and stopped in the center of the room. She wore the same clothes she had worn since the battle and looked exhausted from her endless efforts to secure the safety of his land and people.

He turned with a start to stare at the twin beside him. Had he made a mistake and kissed the wrong sister? He turned back to look at the twin who had entered the room? Was that Fiona?

"What have you to say?" the twin asked, planting her hands on her hips.

He stood and looked from one to the other. "That this charade must end."

"Then tell us now that if one weds you the other twin will remain here and join your clan," the twin that stood said.

How easy it would be for him to concede, but that would mean surrender and defeat, not something he was willing to accept. His conditions had been made known from the beginning.

"My terms remain as stated. I wed one twin and the other returns to her clan."

"I guess you do not want a strong wife badly enough," the standing twin said.

The other twin stood and went to her sister's side. "Good luck in finding a wife."

"It will be my way," Tarr said sternly.

"We remain together," one said and the other agreed with a firm nod.

"What of your husband?" he asked and took a sudden step forward, the width and breadth of him appearing as if he were about to consume them both.

The women stood their ground and showed not an ounce of fear, their chins turned up stubbornly and their green eyes blazing.

"Your duty is to a husband, not to a sister."

"A wife knows of her duty to her husband. It is a pity you do not know a husband's duty to a wife."

They turned and walked out of the room, leaving a dumbfounded Tarr staring after them.

Chapter 14

"I tell you it is impossible to tell them apart," Kirk said, standing next to Tarr in front of the storehouse. "Though all clansmen agree either twin would make a good wife for you—" He coughed as if clearing his throat and his voice turned firm. "The clan has been talking."

"Have they now." Tarr rubbed his arm, now out of the sling over a week. It continued healing nicely, barely a twinge or ache, and the scarring much less than he had expected, thanks to the poultice one of the twins had applied when the wound had closed.

Kirk spit out the words rapidly. "Marry one and let the other remain with the clan."

Tarr turned a stern glare on him, but Kirk did not cringe or shrink back; Tarr had not expected him to. Through the years it was Kirk who always had the courage to say to him what others would not and make him see the error of his ways when he was being overly stubborn. He also had been there many times to help ease his burdens.

"I have given the matter thought."

"Then you have seen reason," Kirk said, looking pleased.

"Reason!"

Tarr's near shout had Kirk shaking his head. "I should have known you would be stubborn about this."

"I am being sensible."

"Hah! Stubborn and foolish is more like it. The twins are good for the clan, both of them."

"One will distract the other," Tarr insisted.

"I saw no distraction during battle or otherwise. They do what they must, and they do it well together. They would bring honor to our clan."

"They would spend too much time together."

"Perfect, then you will not have a wife who constantly harps at you. She will be busy with her sister," Kirk argued.

"Her duties are to me." Tarr pounded his chest. "And I will suffer no harping wife."

Kirk laughed. "You have much to learn, harping is inherent in all women."

Both men laughed.

"At least give it thought."

"Believe me I have," Tarr admitted. "While the twins can make me insane at times, I also respect the battle they wage with me to remain together. It takes courage to defy a chieftain."

"A mulish one at that."

"You need not remind me so often."

"You would do the same for me and you have when it came to Erin."

"It was obvious the woman cared for you and you completely ignored the signs."

"Perhaps you do the same yourself," Kirk said.

"What do you mean?"

"There are times one of the twins looks at you as—as"—Kirk threw his hands in the air—"the way a woman does when she is interested."

"You are sure of this?"

"Erin is, and women know women."

"I have been trying to discover a way that would help me distinguish one from the other. Just when I think I have it, I find myself right back where I started. They are too alike."

"I know what you mean. Though I think it is a good charade they play. They make it seem that both twins can heal and both are good with weapons, but"—Kirk shook his head—"I do not believe it is so. It is a fine ruse they play on us."

"I agree and that is why I am determined to discover which twin is which, then I will marry—"

"The one you care for?"

"I do not care—"

"It is me, Kirk you speak with, and we have spoken nothing but the truth to each other these many years."

"I am attracted to one," Tarr admitted reluctantly.

"You are not sure which one."

"As I said when I think I have just discovered which one is which, they play with my senses and then I am not sure."

"Watch their eyes, Erin says it is in the eyes that one sees love," Kirk said, his voice growing lower and lower. "Start now, for one approaches." Kirk stepped away. "I will see to the matter immediately." With a quick grin he was gone.

Tarr remained focused on the storehouse, hearing the footfalls grow closer.

"Feeling well today?"

He turned and felt as if he received a swift punch to his gut. She looked lovely, her round face freshly scrubbed and shining, her fiery red hair piled on her head with curls falling everywhere around her neck and face, her simple dress appealing since her blouse always hugged her ample breasts, and her eyes . . .

He took a moment to stare at them. They sparkled with life. Was there love there somewhere?

"You look as if you drift off," Fiona said.

Tarr shook his head. "I am fine, just giving thought to the storehouse."

"Strange, is it not?" she asked, walking over to the open door and peering inside.

He bristled over the absence of her touch. He had not wanted to admit it to himself, but he favored her touch, be it simple or more intimate. He liked when she touched him.

"That the storehouse was ransacked, but nothing was taken?" he asked.

Fiona turned with a nod. "I have wondered over it since the men informed me of it."

"Your conclusion?"

"As we had discussed, they searched for something."

"I still cannot figure out what or who they searched

for. We have nothing here of value to the barbarians. They did not rob from the storehouse or take any cattle. We were right; they look for someone."

Fiona agreed with a nod. "The clue here is that they kept their distance from the keep, which means whomever they look for is not worthy enough to reside in your keep. Perhaps a traveler has passed this way recently?"

"None that I recall, and I usually know when there are any strangers among us."

"We need to learn more about the Wolf clan."

"Agreed," Tarr said. "I intend to speak with Raynor at length."

"I will join you," Fiona said, and stepped next to him.

He did not think of denying her. He respected her opinion and ideas and he liked that she did not hesitate to join him. He could count on her no matter the circumstances, a worthy attribute in a wife.

They walked side by side and he unconsciously took her hand in his.

She smiled and it was as bright as the sun, and it filled him with comforting warmth. He squeezed her hand and returned her smile.

"I am glad you heal well."

"Miss my arms around you?" he teased.

"Aye, I do," she admitted freely to his surprise. "Why does that shock you? I like your kisses and your touch; it's your bullheaded nature that annoys me."

"Me, bullheaded?" he asked with mock astonishment. "I think it is you who is willful, which makes us a matching pair. And a good match I think."

"We shall see."

They entered the keep and as they climbed the stone stairs, Tarr stopped suddenly and yanked her into his arms. She met his chest with a solid thud, which caught her breath.

"I have missed you in my arms and, lord, do I hunger for the taste of you."

Instead of her lips he went to her neck and nibbled and nipped until her skin shivered with gooseflesh.

He laughed softly in her ear. "I love when you shiver against me."

He captured her response in his mouth, his tongue turning it to a gentle moan, and then she eagerly joined him as her arms swept around his neck and she returned his kiss with an urgency filled with passion.

He finally tore his mouth away and she went to rest her cheek to his shoulder; he grabbed her chin and tilted her head to look into her eyes. What did he see in the bright green depths besides the desire that raged there? Was that a gleam he had never noticed before? Or was it his own foolish thoughts hoping to see—what?

Love?

He released her chin and she again rested her head to his shoulder.

Why did he think of love? He had not given it thought at all. He was to do his duty and marry a woman who would bring honor to his clan. She would bare him fine sons and daughters and remain by his side throughout their life together.

Love had no place in his plans.

It was his turn to moan when she began to nibble and

nip at his neck. Her nips were full of fire and purpose. She knew what she did; she did it with intention. She pushed him to his limits and would soon push him past those limits.

Ever so slowly she traced his lips with the tip of her tongue.

"You play with danger," he warned.

"I am not afraid."

She sounded as if she challenged him, and that was all he needed.

He grabbed her around the waist, hoisted her up, and braced her against the wall with the strength of his body.

She gasped and he claimed her mouth roughly while his hand sought her breast with a firm squeeze. He thought she might protest, but instead she grabbed onto his shoulders and shared in his fervor.

He rubbed her nipple between his fingers until it hardened and then he lowered his mouth and nibbled on the hard orb until it had both of them squirming.

"Someone approaches," she said in a fearful whisper, and pushed at his shoulders.

He stopped and listened realizing she had repeated the warning several times before he could react. Now fully hearing the approaching footfalls, he released her to stand beside him.

A servant soon appeared and excused herself as she hurried past them.

Had their lusty liaison been obvious?

Fiona then noticed the wet stain on her blouse and her hand went to cover it.

"You will be my wife, we have done nothing wrong. The clan is proud we will join hands."

"That has not yet been settled." Concern filled her voice.

"It has. You are Fiona. I do not believe I kiss both twins and they respond the same way."

"How can you be so certain?"

He lifted her chin. "There is something about you that is different. I cannot tell what it is; I only know it is there and when I finally discover it, I will know which one of you is which. Then we will wed."

He sounded as if he commanded and she refused to be forced to wed. The choice would be hers or there would be no marriage. She would wed Tarr of Hellewyk only by her say so, not by his command or demand.

"You do not know me, if you think you can force me."

His laughter rankled her.

"You are already willing."

"There is a vast difference between lust and love," she informed him.

He chuckled. "Lust is a good start to a marriage."

"Lust does not last. Love does."

"Love can be learned."

His seriousness startled her. Could he learn to love her? Was she willing to take such a chance?

"Can it?" she answered honestly.

"Are you not willing to find out?"

She stared at him a moment for she had thought she heard a plea in his voice, or did she hear what she wished to hear? He did not really care if they loved or not. She fit the requisites he had set forth in a wife and that was all that mattered to him.

"Your silence means yes," he said.

"There is much to my silence that you do not know."

He reached out for her hand. "Confide in me. Tell me what lies in your silence. I want to be a part of it."

His offer stirred her heart even more, but she wondered if he truly understood what he offered her. To be willing to go to the very depths of her soul, to share all her turmoil and happiness was more intimate than making love.

She tested him. "You do not know what you ask."

He looked affronted. "I do not speak my words lightly. Talk with me. Share with me. I am willing to hear and to listen."

The idea of sharing her deepest emotions, her inner secrets with him, made her fearful and she stepped away from him, slipping her hand out of his.

"Do not put a distance between us."

"It is a distance we both forged," she said.

"Out of stubbornness."

Her smile surfaced slowly. "I will agree to that."

"Finally, we agree on something, which means we can begin to build a bridge where we both can meet in the middle. It will take work building this bridge for it must be sturdy; stubbornness is at least a starting point, but trust will be the firm foundation.

He was willing to work toward a middle ground for them both, instead of him dictating; it surely was a beginning.

"This plan of yours for building a bridge sounds good to me."

"I am glad you like it." He held out his hand.

Fiona reached out and took his hand, the first block in the bridge being forged.

Chapter 15

"Tell me of my men, Aliss," Raynor said, looking out the window at the now all too familiar scene. He had been a prisoner, by his estimation, near to two months—and that was far too long. He had fully recovered weeks ago and it was time to escape.

He turned to look at her. She stood silent at the table that served as her work stand. Herbs, pots, flasks, pestle and mortar were arranged neatly on the table with a large enough space left for her to work.

"I need to know where they are being kept."

She dusted her hands free of the herbs she worked with and wiped them on a cloth tucked in at the waistband of her brown skirt.

"I know why you hesitate and I attempt to honor your request of not knowing my plans, but I need this information from you."

"I thought you would—"

"Escape on my own?" He shook his head. "I cannot abandon my men, especially when you have told me that they have fully recovered from their wounds."

"That is why you have waited," she said anxiously. "I wondered why you remained."

He ignored her remark. "My men, Aliss."

She remained hesitant.

Raynor decided on a different approach. "Do you spend much time with my men?"

Aliss stared at him for a moment.

"A simple enough question."

She nodded. "I see them only when they are taken out of their cells and allowed the fresh air for a short time every few days."

"They must enjoy their brief reprieves."

"They sit and watch what goes on around them."

"I am glad to hear this, but tell me why have I not been given a breath of fresh air on occasion?"

"Tarr will not allow it."

"Yet he gives it to my men?"

She shrugged.

He walked over to her. "You could get him to agree to it for me, could you not?"

Aliss sighed, pulled the cloth from her waistband, and dropped it on the table. "Securing a bit of freedom for your men was one thing; trying to get it for you"—she shook her head—"impossible."

"I appreciate your efforts on my behalf. You have taken very good care of me and I am forever in your debt. I will never forget your kindness."

"Say no more," she insisted with raised hands. "I do not want to know your plans." She placed a few items in an already overflowing healing basket and walked to the door. "I am a healer, please make certain that in your absence you leave behind none who would require my skills."

She opened the door and saw Tarr and Fiona approach from the end of the hallway. "You have company."

Raynor nodded. "Thank you very much."

Aliss hurried down the hall with only a nod to her sister and Tarr as she past them.

"She appears upset," Fiona said, and turned to rush off after her but stopped and looked to Tarr.

"Go, she may need you," he said, and shooed her away with his hand.

"I will not be long."

"Be as long as necessary," he said, pleased that she had at least considered him before running off after her sister.

Tarr entered the room to find Raynor seated in a chair by the window.

"The days grow more chilled," Raynor said without looking at him.

"We are ready for winter." Tarr glanced around the room, walked to the door and opened it. "Have ale and food brought to us," he told the one guard, and closed the door.

"Have you decided what will be done with me and my men?"

"That is not why I am here. You know more about

this leader of the Wolf clan than I do. I have heard stories, thinking them mere myths, for I have not seen him in these parts."

"He handles the unrest in his lands north of Scotland. From what I have heard he rules much of the land and its people by fear. None dare oppose him. I heard he is called Wolf hence the name of his clan."

"What would bring him here?"

"I asked myself the same question," Raynor said. "If his plan had been to seize your land, he would have arrived with a massive amount of warriors."

"You say you chased him off the island, the Isle of Non. What was he doing there?"

Raynor stood, the ale and food having been delivered, as Tarr poured them each a tankard of ale. He gladly took one.

"That was even stranger. He was there with a minimum of a dozen men, and his presence discovered by sheer accident. We gave chase and they took off without a battle. I followed them to the border of my land to make certain they were gone."

"This Wolf does not sound as if he would be spotted by accident."

"Another thought of mine also," Raynor admitted. "Why, though, would he want me to know he was there? He plans something. But what?"

"Whatever it is I'll be ready."

Fiona caught up with her sister as she walked out the door of the keep.

"The day hints at winter, you should have a shawl about you," she admonished.

Aliss slowed her pace as they walked down the keep stairs. "I was in a hurry and not thinking."

"What troubles you?" Fiona took off her green shawl and draped it over Aliss's shoulders.

"Now you will be cold."

"I am fine," Fiona insisted, and took the basket her sister held, slipped her arm around hers, and led her to a favorite spot of theirs beneath a large tree near the meadow. It was a secluded enough for them to talk, yet they were not out of sight of the village.

"I think Raynor plans his escape very soon," Aliss said after sitting.

Fiona plopped down beside her. "I really do not think Tarr intends to harm Raynor and his men."

"Confinement wears on Raynor and I cannot blame him. I would go insane if kept imprisoned for any length of time in a solitary room." She shook her head. "That is not what is important. I think he will ask us to go with him when the time comes."

"This upsets you? Have you come to care for Raynor?"

"Nay," Aliss said firmly. "He is handsome and seems a good man, but I have no such feelings for him. I but worry about us."

"How so?" Fiona asked concerned.

"What will become of us? I grow tired of this charade, of watching how I act and what I say. I miss being able to fully concentrate on my healing, and I miss my identity. Some people call me Aliss, others refer to me as Fiona. How long must we continue this?"

"I think I am making progress," Fiona reported proudly.

"Truly?" Aliss asked surprised.

"Tarr has suggested we build a bridge where we can meet in the middle."

"That sounds promising," Aliss said excited. "Perhaps this will turn out better than we had expected."

"It is possible, but we must continue to have patience." She rubbed her sister's arm. "Can you do that awhile longer?"

"Of course I can. I was just feeling worrisome today."

"Raynor must do what he must; you have done all you can for him," Fiona said. "Are you certain, though, that you have not come to care for him?"

"I am certain. I have enjoyed his company. He showed interest in me and it was easy to speak with him. We shared stories of our youth and of my healing skills, and he knew I was Aliss—that I will miss."

"It will not be long before our identities are revealed, but we will do the revealing."

"I will have patience till then."

Fiona was relieved to hear the confidence in her sister's voice. "I think we will do well."

"I do like it here," Aliss admitted. "The clan has generously welcomed us and genuinely accepted us. It is as if we have always been part of the Hellewyk clan."

"I feel the same myself. They have not once treated us like outsiders."

"It would be a good place to call home."

"I agree," Fiona said. "It has been a long time since we have felt at home."

"Uncle Tavish did his best to make us feel welcomed."

"And Leith did his best to make us feel like outsiders."

"He was jealous of you," Aliss said. "He was jealous that his father talked more with you, his niece, than with his own son."

"That was because uncle Tavish knew his son was an idiot."

They both laughed.

Aliss spoke low. "Perhaps here among the safety of those who care for us we could begin to find out about our past."

"Mother warned us to be careful," Fiona reminded. "She was adamant about us trusting no one."

Aliss looked up at the blue sky dotted with white clouds. "Do you ever wonder who we really are, Fiona?"

Fiona followed her sister's glance, her eye catching a cloud in the shape of a large woman. "That I do. I wonder about the woman who would give her twin daughters away, and if she did it to protect us or because she did not want us."

"I wonder if she gave us names."

Fiona took her sister's hand. "Is that what has upset you?"

"It has been a haunting thought since we have begun this charade. We switch names that truly are not our given ones. The question then is, who are we?"

"There will come a day we will find out."

"Mother waited too long to tell us," Aliss said. "She barely had a breath left in her when she confessed that she was not our mother and that we were to be very careful and let no one know. She feared for us but could speak no more."

"Her last whisper was of her love for us," Fiona said, a tear catching in the corner of her eye.

"I will never doubt our mother's love. She showered us with it and I will be forever grateful that we were left with such a generous and loving woman to care for us." Tears clouded Aliss's vision and she wiped them away with her finger.

"It is this ruse of ours that has brought this all to light."

"Perhaps it is time that we discover our true identities," Aliss said. "We have spoken of it in whispers and secrets and now may be the time for us to begin our search."

"Let us settle this with Tarr first, and then we can pursue our past in earnest."

The sisters squeezed hands and kept them locked firmly as they always had done as a sign of reassurance. Together they would survive and they would let no one come between them.

It was late, the keep settled for the night, when Aliss was summoned to Raynor's room. He complained of severe pain in his head, and she hurried along the stairs having hastily dressed.

Suddenly a hand covered her mouth, cutting off any chance to scream. She was yanked into the dark shadows and pressed against a muscled body.

"It is me, I will not hurt you," Raynor whispered in her ear.

His words did not alleviate her fear; she remained tense.

"I leave now. Do you and Fiona wish to come with me?" He dropped his hand away from her mouth.

"No, we have not finished our work here, though I wish you Godspeed."

"You are sure?"

"Aye, Fiona and I have talked and it is not time for us to leave."

"I am sorry to hear that," he said.

A rag was shoved in her mouth and a sack draped over her head before she realized what had happened. Her arms were secured behind her back and she was hoisted up and flung over, she assumed, Raynor's shoulder. She heard mumbling, which led her to believe there was someone with Raynor, and with a shuffle of footsteps and a sudden burst of fresh air she knew they had left the keep.

Careful steps, quick stops, more mumbling, and cold air seeping through her light garments was what followed for what seemed like hours. Crunches of leaves and twigs went on from there, and she assumed they were traveling into the forest near to the keep.

She was not certain what this all was about; she was however certain Raynor would not harm her. He felt indebted to her, which would not allow him to see her hurt in any way.

Why Raynor saw fit to abduct her, she could not imagine, and when she had a chance to speak with him she was certain he would explain. That did little, however, to alleviate her concern regarding her sister.

Once Fiona discovered her gone, all hell would break loose. She would follow to the ends of the earth in search of her and then . . .

She cringed thinking of the punishment Fiona would serve on the person responsible for her abduction.

The man carrying her stopped abruptly and slipped her off his shoulder. He carefully removed the sack and the gag.

She stared at Raynor and waited in silence for an explanation.

"You will not be harmed," he said.

"I never feared I would be."

"I am pleased to know that you trust me."

"I said nothing of trust. I know you feel obligated to me for taking care of you and therefore would see no harm done to me."

Raynor nodded.

She waited again for an explanation.

"You will understand in time why I took you."

"Fiona will come for me."

He smiled. "I am counting on it."

Chapter 16

The horn sounded and Fiona sprang out of the bed, dressing with haste and reaching for the sword she kept tucked beneath the bed, close enough to swiftly grab.

It took her a moment to realize that Aliss was not in the room, then she recalled her being summoned to Raynor's room. She burst from the room on a run and did not stop until she was a few feet from his room.

There was utter chaos, warriors seemed to be everywhere, and she pushed her way through the sea of them and into the room. One guard lay unconscious on the floor and the other guard sat in the chair holding his head. Tarr and Kirk flanked the man. Raynor was nowhere to be seen.

"My sister," Fiona demanded loudly. "Where is she?"

Silence fell suddenly and all eyes turned on her.

"Raynor has taken her," Tarr said.

"How do you know this?"

Tarr pointed to the guard in the chair. "He heard part of their plans before he was knocked unconscious."

"*Their* plans?"

Tarr's face muscles grew taut and anger glistened in his dark eyes. "Raynor's men have escaped along with him."

"How?" Fiona asked incredulously.

"Raynor managed to attack the one guard while the other guard went to get Aliss. His men had already made their escape, though I still do not know how they managed to coordinate their plans. One joined him in the room while the other hid in the shadows outside the door. That is how he"—Tarr nodded to the guard in the chair—"learned part of their plans."

"To take one of the twins."

Tarr approached her with heavy footsteps. "Not one of you—the healer twin." He stopped in front of her. "Did he choose the right one?"

"You will rescue my sister!" It was a fierce demand that had all eyes spreading wide.

"Answer me." Tarr's demand was just as fierce.

Fiona stepped forward, nearly touching his broad chest. "It matters not which one of us he took. What matters is that you rescue my sister and waste no precious time arguing about it."

"I will have my answer before any rescue party is dispatched." Tarr folded his arms across his chest.

Fury churned inside her like a violent volcano about to erupt. Her sister was gone and the useless debate caused lost time and meant more distance between them and less likely the chance of catching them.

She turned as if she intended to leave the room and then swiftly drew her sword, pressing the point to Tarr's throat.

His men drew their swords after a moment's hesitation, her action startling them.

"My blade will pierce his throat before you reach me," she warned.

Tarr raised his hand to halt his men and all hands dropped off their swords.

"I will cut out your cold heart if you do not see my sister returned safely to me."

"Tell me which twin I rescue."

Fiona glared at him with heated eyes. She had no choice. She surrendered her identity or else . . . chance never seeing her sister again?

With a spiteful toss of her head she announced, "I am Fiona."

Tarr stared at her while he shouted, "Gather the men; we ride at first light."

"Why do we wait?" Fiona asked, her blade remaining at his throat, while his men began to file out of the room.

Tarr pushed the blade away with one finger. "Traveling on foot at night is difficult and foolish, since tracks are hard to detect. We will catch up with them fast enough. In the meantime we will prepare and be ready to travel and do what we must to rescue Aliss."

Fiona lowered her sword to her side. "I will go get ready to join you."

"You do not go with us."

"You cannot stop me."

He grabbed her arm, a path clearing for him as he shoved her out of the room and walked her rapidly to his room, kicking the door shut behind him.

"I can and I will, Fiona. You are a skilled warrior, but this time it concerns your sister—"

Fiona yanked her arm out of his grasp. "He took *my sister,* therefore it is *my battle.*"

He pointed at her. "Your anger may cause foolish actions and bring dreadful results. You will remain here under lock and guard if necessary."

She pointed right back at him. "I will not make foolish decisions and you better not try locking me away."

"You threaten me?" He took a step toward her.

She advanced on him with the same determined step. "If I must."

"Watch your tongue with me, woman."

"It is my tongue, and I will not change it to suit a husband. I will have my say whether you like it or not."

"Have your say, but you will not have your way," he said, his face close to hers.

"I will or you will rue the day you challenged me."

"There you go threatening me again."

"*I* will see my sister safe," she shouted at him.

"Aye, you will, for I will see to her safe return."

"Not without me."

He grabbed her around the waist and lifted her off the floor. "Stubborn fool, I will not let you risk your life."

Her blazing green eyes calmed in color and sadness drifted over her face. "I must; Aliss knows I will come for her. She knows nothing will stop me; not even you."

Tarr lowered her gently to the floor, his hands remaining at the curve of her waist. He stared at her for several moments, the fire leaving his dark eyes.

"You will obey my commands?"

"Aye, I will follow your lead."

"Your word on this?" he asked.

"My word."

"Then go ready yourself to join me."

She hurried to the door.

"Fiona."

She turned around before opening the door.

"No one takes what belongs to me without consequences. I had all intentions of rescuing your sister."

She nodded slowly. "It is good to know you are a man of honor."

They left at first light just as Tarr promised, fifty men went, and Kirk remained behind ready to follow with another fifty if necessary. There was, however, the defense of the keep to consider, and with the unexpected attack of the barbarians, Tarr was taking no chances. Warriors would be dispatched as necessary. If they could catch them before they got to Raynor's land it would be an easy capture with little fighting, and that is what Tarr hoped for.

Fiona rode beside him, rigid and alert, prepared to battle at any moment.

"You have sent men ahead to scout and see that we travel the right trail?"

"I have," he answered, knowing she meant no insult by questioning his leadership. She was concerned for her sister. He had realized the full extent of that concern when she had told him her sister would expect her. He had understood at that moment the inseparable bond that existed between the twins. A bond of love and honor; he had no right to force her to break.

"The signs have been clear so far?"

"Aye, they have, and I expect they will continue to be so," he assured her.

"Aliss will not be fearful; she is very brave."

"A trait that you share."

"Many think me stronger than Aliss."

She shook her head and he could see her eyes glaze with tears, though she would not spill a one. She was too stubborn.

"They are wrong; she is the stronger, far stronger than I."

He let her talk, her worry forcing her words.

"Our mother died in her arms," she blurted out. "She comforted her, shed not a tear, but spoke gently to her, letting her know we would be fine and that she would find peace in God's home. But it was peace our mother found in Aliss's arms. I stood behind her crying, not being able to control my tears. Aliss eased her suffering with her gentle voice and loving embrace, that is why she is an exceptional healer for she heals with her heart and soul."

"I have known no healer that heals as successfully as she does."

"She is an angel," Fiona said with a smile. "Our mother always called her, her little angel."

"What did your mother call you?"

Fiona laughed. "Bullheaded, mulish, pigheaded, willful, and some I dare not repeat. My willful nature surfaced early, and my mother could not quite understand a daughter who preferred stringing a bow to sewing a stitch. My father, however, encouraged my interests. What of your mother and father?" she asked.

"My father taught me what it took to be a chieftain. My mother . . ." He paused in an attempt to find the right words. "I know she loved me; she hugged me often enough, but I always felt she was unhappy, though she saw to her duties and was respected by the clan."

A rider approached, interrupting their conversation.

"The trail rears off around the next bend and it appears they picked up pace."

"Follow and report to me what you find," Tarr said.

"They pick up pace in an attempt to get to Raynor's land and safety," Fiona said.

"With his land bordering mine, there are a number of places where he can cross onto his land."

"And be close to his keep?"

"No, it is a good day's ride."

"Then longer on foot," she said. "You look troubled. What concerns you?"

He shook his head. "I have known no one who can sense my thoughts as you do."

"I see it on your face and in your movements. Now tell me."

He could see the same in her. It was odd how much alike they were and comforting to share that kindred spirit with her. He had never known that closeness with anyone and it puzzled him.

"Tell me," she said again.

"Raynor rears off sooner than I had expected. His keep is farther north—"

"His men could be waiting for him," Fiona said, her glance quickly darting to her surroundings.

"How would they know of his approach?"

She settled into a brief moment of silence before finding an answer. "His men could have been scouting the area since his capture."

"Waiting to see if he escaped."

"But why take Aliss, and how did he know it was Aliss he took?" Tarr asked.

"Raynor could tell us apart," she admitted.

"How?" Tarr shook his head at the heavens. "I do not believe he could tell you apart and I could not."

"Raynor claimed it was easy."

"When I get my hands on him he will tell me this secret."

A scout's approach silenced them.

The scout was quick to inform Tarr. "Horses, they were met with horses."

They camped for the night with no fire's light to chase the chill and to alert no one to their presence.

Fiona sat braced against a large boulder, a blanket wrapped around her. She had worn her shirt, blouse, and a wool jacket of her father's, which she had kept for use when riding. Still she felt the chill of the cold ground creep through her clothes and send her shivering.

She watched the activity of the camp, the men moving more quietly than she ever expected from ones so large. The horses even seemed to know silence was expected of them. Guards were being posted and men settling in for the night with orders that they ride again at first light.

Tarr approached after talking with a few men, she watched him walk, his strides long and confident. He wore his plaid with a white shirt beneath. A night wind stirred his auburn hair so that it spread like the wings of a raven, and his handsome features appealed even more for his look was intense, with a spark of fire to it. A fur was draped over his arm and she silently sighed with the thought of its warmth, though shivered at the thought of him sharing it with her.

He settled down beside her, tossing the fur over them and tucking it around her before taking her into his arms for her to rest comfortably against him.

She did not object; she welcomed his warmth and the fur, and she smiled at the stir of desire his closeness caused in her.

"Comfortable?" he asked, resting his one arm just beneath her breasts.

"Very," she said, and snuggled into him.

"You know we will wed upon our return."

"We will discuss it," she said on a sigh.

"We will do well together," he said as if all was settled.

She lifted her head to look at him. "Kiss me."

He laughed. "You are not a shy one."

"I like when you kiss me and you have never kissed me knowing me as Fiona."

He looked baffled. "Have I ever kissed Aliss?"

Fiona laughed. "She would never kiss you."

"Why?" he said as if insulted.

She moved closer to his lips as she spoke. "She does not care for you." She ran her lips across his. "I do like the taste of you."

He grabbed her chin. "Once we share this kiss, Fiona, you are mine forever."

"Promise," she whispered, her warm breath fanning his lips.

"Damn, woman, but you tempt my soul."

She laughed, licked her lips in a slow circulating motion, then leaned in and ran her tongue over his lips in the same lusty manner.

His teeth captured her tongue in playful nips, and they were soon lost in a long lingering kiss that seemed to go on forever and ever until finally Tarr reluctantly ended it.

"Any more of this and our first coupling will be here on the cold, hard ground."

Her green eyes blurred with passion. "A tempting thought."

"Too tempting. Now, go to sleep before you get us both in trouble."

She sighed like a disappointed child.

"Go to sleep," he repeated firmly.

"I will have you," she said with a yawn, and closed her eyes.

He smiled and hugged her. "That you will, Fiona."

Chapter 17

Not a human sound could be heard as Tarr's men waited silently for orders. They sat on their horses at the edge of the stream that divided Tarr's and Raynor's lands, prepared for whatever was necessary.

Fiona kept a steady eye on the other side, grateful for the near end of autumn, the foliage not being as dense. She watched for signs of Tarr's return.

They had arrived at the stream a few hours after dawn, and at first it appeared as if they had followed a bogus trail. Two trails had been picked up on the other side and were being investigated when suddenly Tarr was summoned.

Fiona had wanted to go with him. She had a feeling it had something to do with her sister. Why else would he be summoned? He had insisted she remain behind and had cautioned her about following him.

He had stationed two guards on either side of her before he had left, letting her know he would not be long. But it had been too long, *much too long*. Something was not right; she could feel it.

"He takes too much time," Fiona said, looking to John, the larger of the two guards.

"He told us to wait on his return. We wait."

Fiona knew not to waste her time arguing with him. He would do what he was trained to do, follow his chieftain's orders.

With each passing minute her concern grew, and when early morning turned to early afternoon it was obvious something was terribly wrong.

John appeared the one in charge, for if one warrior dare move from their position his look alone would stay the man.

"We cannot continue to remain here and do nothing," Fiona demanded. "Something is wrong. Tarr would have returned by now."

She was surprised when he agreed with her.

"Aye, you are right." He looked to the man beside her. "Patrick, tell the men to prepare. We cross the stream."

Fiona almost sighed with relief, though instead she sent him a firm nod, acknowledging his wise decision.

The men were ready and eager, the horses impatient, and John's hand poised ready to give the order to cross when James, one of the warriors who had gone with Tarr, walked out of the woods and waved for them to cross.

John did not hesitate; he lowered his hand, signaling the men to cross. Fiona knew as he did that the warrior would have died before calling them into a trap. It was a matter of honor with a Scotsman.

James approached John, walking between his and Fiona's horse. "Raynor's men have taken Tarr." He then turned and looked to Fiona. "The message is that you are to come alone to Raynor's keep if you want to see Tarr and your sister."

"Fiona goes nowhere," John said firmly.

Fiona sent the man a scathing look. "That is not for you to decide."

"My orders were to protect you. I cannot do that if you ride into our enemy's hands. Raynor sets a trap, and I will not be fool enough to send you into it."

"If Raynor wanted Tarr dead he would be. It is obvious he wants something from us and I want something from him—Tarr and my sister alive and well."

John mumbled beneath his breath, Fiona hearing an oath or two while he scratched his bushy mustache.

"What you are telling me is that we have little choice."

"Now you understand."

"What I do not understand," John argued, "is how do I protect you."

"You don't; I protect myself." Fiona slipped off her horse. "I will need more weapons and a means to strap them to me. Raynor will expect me to be armed, and I do not want him to find all my concealed weapons."

John ordered the men to dismount, then he and James helped ready her.

"How much time do I give you before I strike?" John asked, strapping a knife to the under part of her forearm while James worked at her ankle.

"No more than an hour. That should be enough time to convince Raynor to free the prisoners."

John and James stopped what they were doing and glared at her.

Fiona glared back. "Raynor kidnapped my sister and then he had the gall to take Tarr. Do you think I go to reason with the fool?"

"You said 'convince,'" James replied.

Fiona drew the knife from the sheath attached to her arm. "A sharp blade convinces nicely."

John shook his head. "I would doubt your ability if I had not seen your skills."

Fiona returned the blade to the sheath. "Good, then you will have no cause to worry. Now, get the men mounted, we ride to Raynor's keep."

"We will remain a strong force for Raynor's men to see," John promised as they rode.

"Send one of the men to Kirk to advise him we may need more men, but he is to do nothing until word is received."

John followed her orders without thought of objecting, and she was pleased that he trusted her decisions and respected her command.

It was a couple of hours before they reached the keep and Fiona knew it would not be difficult to take it even with the few men they had. The keep was not fortified with a surrounding wall and was constructed of more wood than stone, though it appeared that construction was about to begin on something. Stone and felled trees were stacked in piles around the keep.

"Take note of the men positioned in the trees and

how the men as well as the women are armed," Fiona said at their approach.

John nodded. "A broom or rake can serve well as a weapon."

"They are ready to defend their home if necessary. Be prepared."

They were stopped on the outskirts of the village and Fiona was waved on.

"One hour; no more," John reminded.

Fiona nodded and rode her horse forward.

Two warriors halted her mare at the steps of the keep and while one handled her horse, the other told her to follow him.

Fiona was fully alert to her surroundings. She could tell that much in the village was newly built and the people protective of their homes and land. Cattle were plentiful and grazed in the field to the right of the keep and beyond. Garments also appeared newly stitched, and Fiona wondered if Raynor had suddenly acquired wealth.

A small empty room preceded entrance into the great hall and Fiona was immediately relieved when she saw Aliss standing beside Raynor speaking with him. She, however, was not happy to see Tarr shackled to a chair near the huge fireplace.

His scowl and intent glare told her he was ready to kill someone, and probably with his bare hands since his knuckles were white from being so tightly fisted.

Her presence seemed to annoy him, and she thought he most likely assumed that she was foolish for walking into the enemy's hands. He would learn differently soon enough.

No servants milled about, though a bounty of food was spread on the dais table and the few tables that lined the room.

"Welcome to my home," Raynor said with a smile.

Fiona approached him, satisfied that they were the only ones in the hall, the warrior who had escorted her there having left as soon as they had entered. It seemed too easy, the brief thought invaded her head as she reached out. Instead of taking Raynor's offered hand she pulled the knife from her sleeve and had it at his throat before he could retaliate.

"Aliss, release Tarr," Fiona ordered.

"Tarr is not being held prisoner and neither am I," Aliss said, and walked over to her sister's side.

"Tarr is shackled to a chair," Fiona said bewildered.

"Only because he refuses to listen to reason," Raynor attempted to explain while the blade remained at his throat.

Aliss placed her hand on her sister's arm. "Let Raynor go; he means us no harm."

Fiona had no reason to doubt her sister's words. She moved the blade away, though kept the knife firm in her hand. "What goes on here?"

Raynor stepped a safe distance away from her, rubbing his throat. "I wish all of you to be guests in my home." He saw Fiona's confusion. "I could not very well invite you to my home while being held prisoner by your soon-to-be husband. And I doubted Tarr would accept my invitation once I escaped, so I had no recourse but to take Aliss with me. Which guaranteed you would follow."

"I am listening," Fiona said, "but I will listen better if you release Tarr."

Raynor walked over to the shackled man. "Will you give me your word that you will be reasonable and listen to what I have to say?"

"Where are my men?" Tarr asked Fiona.

"They wait on the outskirts of the village. If they do not hear from us within the hour they will attack."

"Your men are invited to join us and enjoy the food I have had set out for them," Raynor offered.

Tarr stared at Fiona and she knew his thought. He was concerned with her safety; she however was not. She was confident in her ability to protect herself and her sister. She gave a slight nod, letting him know that she thought Raynor's proposal safe.

"I will listen," Tarr said gruffly.

Raynor released him and he walked over to Fiona, rubbing his wrists. "You have done well."

"Did you doubt I would?" she grinned and poked him with her elbow.

He slipped his arm around her waist and pulled her next to him. "Never."

He spoke with such heart that she pressed her cheek to his and held it for a moment, enjoying the feel of his warmth mingling with hers. Then reluctantly she squirmed out of his arm and turned to her sister.

They hugged.

"I knew you would come for me," Aliss said, her wide smile letting all know how glad she was to see Fiona.

Fiona sent Raynor a heated glare. "You have explaining to do."

He spread his arms. "Gladly, come sit and enjoy the food."

"My men could use nourishment," Tarr said.

Fiona understood that he brought his men in for added protection, but then Raynor did not object. He welcomed them, which meant he spoke the truth. He intended none of them harm.

"First, I wish to know why we have been brought here," Fiona said, having waited long enough for an explanation.

Tarr did not object.

Raynor smiled as though overjoyed. "I wish you to meet my parents, who are on their way here and should arrive in a few days."

"Why your parents?" Fiona asked, completely confused.

"Let me explain it all," Raynor offered eagerly.

"That is a good idea," Fiona said, "since I grow tired of this game of cat and mouse you seem to be playing."

"It will all make sense," Raynor said, and hurried on with the telling. "When first I laid eyes on Aliss I knew, and when you appeared"—he shook his head as he laughed—"you were how I imagined you would be. That was why it was so easy to tell the two of you apart."

"Easy?" Tarr asked as if the man was insane. "They are identical in every way."

"They are as different as night and day," Raynor insisted, "especially when you know what to look for."

Tarr pointed to Raynor's head. "That wound to your head has done damage."

Raynor patted the spot. "It has healed miraculously due to Aliss's skills."

"What do you mean what you imagined I would be?" Fiona asked.

"Your look, your strength, your stubbornness." Raynor smiled. "You are so much like her."

Aliss and Fiona glanced at each other.

"Like who?" Aliss asked cautiously.

Raynor walked over to the twins. "Do you remember that night I grew impatient to see again and forced my eyes open?"

"You screamed out in pain," Aliss said.

"It was not only the pain that caused my reaction. It was seeing your face that shocked me." He placed his hand on her arm. "I mean no insult. You are as beautiful as I knew you would be."

"There you go again," Fiona said. "Can you finally explain this so we know what you are talking about?"

Raynor took each of their hands. "I have waited long for this moment. This day when I am finally reunited with *my twin sisters*."

Chapter 18

"Brother?" Fiona questioned, and looked to Aliss.

Aliss reached out to her sister and Fiona grabbed her hand.

"I know how shocking this is for you both, but believe me when I say I am thrilled to have found you," Raynor said. "Please take a seat at the dais and give yourself a chance to consider the startling news." He turned to Tarr. "Let your men know all is well and invite them to feast at my tables."

"Half my men will join me here and the other half will make camp."

"Then I will see that food is sent to them." Raynor left, promising a swift return.

Tarr went to Fiona's side. "Discuss nothing until my return."

"You doubt his claim?" Fiona whispered.

"Is there reason he could speak the truth?"

"Aye, there is."

"Then I wish to hear all, so that this can be settled reasonably." With swift strides he was gone.

Aliss moved closer to her sister's side as they rounded the dais to sit.

"Mother warned us about trusting," she whispered, taking a seat as Fiona took the one next to her.

"We have Tarr's protection and I am curious, are you not?"

"Of course I am. Can you imagine meeting our true parents and having a brother? It is almost as if we are dreaming."

"It was no dream but a nightmare when I discovered you gone," Fiona said, annoyed. "If Raynor is our brother, he could have found a better way of letting us know."

"My absence forced you to divulge your identity," Aliss said regretfully.

"Your *kidnapping* left me no choice."

"Perhaps it is for the best," Aliss suggested. "I see in your eyes how you feel about Tarr."

Fiona cast a heavy sigh and rested back against the chair. "Is it that obvious?"

"To me, because I know you so well."

"I think I am falling in love with the stubborn man," Fiona grudgingly admitted. "But do not ask me why, for I cannot tell you. It simply makes no sense."

"Love never does, or so I have heard."

"Falling in love is downright agonizing. One minute

he is the most wonderful man in the world, the next minute he makes me mad as hell."

Aliss smiled. "But the question is, can you live without him?"

"Of course I can," Fiona snapped. "But do I want to?" Her sigh was even heavier than before. "No, I do not. Oh, how pitiful I sound."

"I think it is remarkable." Aliss smiled. "And I am so very happy for you. It is what you wanted."

"To be loved, but does *he* love *me*?" Fiona shot forward in the chair. "Or does he simply want a brood mare."

"I think you have grown on him."

"Like a boil that blisters."

The twins laughed.

"Think how wonderful this all really is, Fiona. You are falling in love and I believe Tarr is falling in love with you, though he is probably as bullheaded about it as you are and"—Aliss's smile grew—"and we may have found our true parents."

"You really think Tarr loves me?"

"How could he not? You have overwhelmed him."

"I truly have," Fiona said with pride. "Sometimes he does not know what to make of me."

"Which probably makes him all the more interested in you."

Fiona suddenly glared at Aliss. "Here I am babbling like a fool about Tarr when I should be focusing on the news of our parents."

"That is all right, love interferes with everything. It cannot be helped."

"I should be more concerned with the matter of our parents than loving Tarr."

"Why?" Aliss asked softly. "Love rules the mind, heart, and soul—and, presently, Tarr is first in all of them, as it should be. The issue of our parents will be addressed and settled with Tarr by your side."

"Your side too," Fiona insisted. "He had all intentions of rescuing you whether I threatened him or not."

"I never doubted that Tarr *would not* rescue me."

Fiona stared at her perplexed.

"Tarr is a chieftain, a man of considerable honor. Many believe him hungry for land and power, but is it not that very hunger that actually provides and protects his clan? He could not allow me to be abducted and do nothing, even if I was not the twin he would marry; his home offered me protection and his home had been violated. Honor would have him seeking revenge."

Fiona shook her head. "I was so angry and frightened finding you gone that I gave no thought to his reaction, only my own."

"A trait we both share, for I was fearful for a moment that I would never see you again."

"That would not happen," Fiona all but hissed.

"I wonder now what will happen? Will our parents be as loving as the parents we thought were ours? Will they want our return? Demand our return? Will we be given a choice?"

"It changes much."

"More than I think we realize," Aliss said, and nodded toward Tarr marching into the hall, sword strapped to his side, sheathed knife tucked into his belt, looking ready for battle especially with twenty of his warriors following in behind him.

Fiona smiled with pride.

"He will protect you against all odds," Aliss whispered.

"And I him."

Raynor returned as well, having seen to Tarr's men.

"Time to talk," Raynor said, extending his hand for Tarr to proceed him to the dais and motioning the men to enjoy the food at the tables. Tarr took the seat next to Fiona.

Raynor sat beside Aliss. "You can tell them apart now, can you not?"

"It now appears easy to tell who is who," Tarr admitted. "I do not understand how I could not have seen the obvious differences before. How did you?"

"There is a slight distinction in their voices, and once I saw them it was easy for me to see my father Oleg in Aliss and my mother Anya in Fiona. But you will see for yourself what I mean. My parents will be here in a few short days and I *request* that you visit with me until then."

Tarr looked from one twin to the other. "This is your decision; I will abide by it."

"We are grateful for your understanding," Aliss said.

Fiona gently rested her hand over his and squeezed. "Thank you for giving us this time."

Tarr moved his hand over hers and held it with a tender firmness. It was a message to Fiona that he had no intention of letting her go.

She grinned, placing her other hand over his and patting it, letting him know that it would be her choice. Then she looked to Raynor. "Tell us of our family and how we came to be separated."

"Our father Oleg is a Viking chieftain and our mother Anya is the daughter of the laird of the clan Blackshaw, who has passed on, leaving the leadership of the clan to me, his only grandson.

"I was eight when you were born and a very proud older brother. I would guard you when you slept, my hand on my trusty wooden sword."

The twins smiled.

"There was to be a large festival celebrating your births, and everyone was busy preparing for it. Mother kept you close by at all times, especially Fiona, she was the more demanding babe."

Tarr grinned and Fiona poked him in the ribs.

Raynor's smile faded. "It was only two days until the celebration. There was much going on and in the frantic pace of it all, you both disappeared. It was an easy enough abduction since the slave Shona, who helped during your birthing, simply walked off with you. No one thought to stop her; all assumed she was tending both of you while mother was busy. It was not until mother went to feed you that it was learned you were abducted.

"A search was made but to no avail. It was believed she had to have had help, for she disappeared too fast being on foot. Days later it was learned the Shona somehow made it to the shores of Scotland. Father did all he could to find you. He and mother never stopped searching. Any mention of twin girls anywhere and father would investigate.

"When Blackshaw land became mine, I alerted my men to look for twins wherever we went, and then one day I received information that Tarr of Hellewyk was to wed a twin of the clan MacElder."

"You never meant to attack my keep," Tarr said. "But why attack us on the road if you meant no harm?"

"Your scout saw our approach and assumed the worse. He raised sword against us and signaled an attack. I had no time to explain, nor a chance to catch a glimpse of the twins. But that is all done now; what matters is that I have found my sisters."

"Why would the slave abduct us?" Fiona asked.

"We have wondered the same these many years," Raynor said.

"You never found out who helped her?" Aliss asked.

Raynor shook his head. "We found nothing."

"How did a slave have such liberties as to walk freely with the babes?" Tarr asked.

"Shona, the slave, had been with my father's people since she had been young. She was an aging woman and seemed content with us. There was no thought that she would betray us. My father still cannot believe that she would do such a thing, and he has held firm to the belief that Shona made certain the twins would be cared for and not harmed."

"You think harm was meant us?" Fiona asked.

"We do not know."

"No harm will come to them now," Tarr stated boldly. "They are under my protection."

Raynor made no comment, though his eyes narrowed.

"If Shona meant to protect us, would she not have

separated us for safety reasons?" Aliss asked.

"Shona often made mention of a prophetess's words that the twins should never be separated. That could be the reason she kept you together."

Aliss turned to Fiona. "Mother repeatedly warned us that we were always to remain together."

Fiona agreed with a firm nod. "She was adamant about it."

"Tell us about your parents," Tarr said.

Aliss spoke up with a soft smile lighting her lovely face. "They were good people. I still find it hard to believe they were not our true parents."

"I am glad you had a good couple to look after you," Raynor said, "and while it dulls the pain of your absence, it does not make up for the years I have missed being with you."

Aliss reached out and took her brother's hand. "I can only imagine the pain you and our parents of our birth suffered, and I can understand your joy in this reunion, but it is different for me and Fiona."

"We knew only our adopted parents, and their love," Fiona said. "Then ten years ago on our mother's deathbed she confessed the truth. We were not hers or our father's daughters. She had little breath left in her, her body ravaged by disease, so her words were sparse. She told us that if anyone learned the truth, we would be in danger. She warned that we were always to remain together."

"The slave must have confided in her," Tarr said. "And with her dying breath, she continued protecting you."

Fiona looked at him confused. "What do you mean?"

"She chose carefully what she told you, knowing she had little time left. In keeping you ignorant of your plight, she thought to keep you safe. She gave you just enough to warn."

"What were your thoughts when you heard this news?" Raynor asked.

"It frightened us," Fiona admitted, recalling how Aliss had huddled in her arms and cried. She had not; she knew at that moment she would protect them both for as long as they lived.

"But it sent Fiona into action," Aliss said with pride. "She sent a message with a passing cleric to our uncle Tavish, our mother's brother. While we waited for him to come get us, she took care of all the outside chores, splitting wood, harvesting the last of the plants, tending the animals, repairing the thatching on the roof, and hunting small animals for food while I tended to the cooking and mending. She intended that we be prepared if our uncle did not arrive before winter set in."

"We discussed what mother had told us," Fiona said, "and agreed to keep it our secret as mother had warned. It felt strange for us to think that the two people we loved so dearly and believed we were a part of were not truly our parents."

"And we wondered who our parents were and if they did not want us," Aliss said.

Raynor was quick to speak up. "Now you know the truth. Your parents loved you with all their hearts and were devastated by their loss."

"It is good to know that," Aliss said.

"And it was good to know that our uncle Tavish

wanted us," Fiona said. "Of course he believed us his nieces. He welcomed us wholeheartedly into his clan, announcing to all we were his sister's daughters, which made us MacElders. We knew we could never confide our secret to him in chance of losing our only home."

Memories of those first few nights with the MacElder clan were the catalyst for Fiona's determination to be independent and self-sufficient. Each night Aliss would cry in her sister's arms, afraid that their uncle would discover the truth and cast them out of the clan. And each night Fiona would grow more determined in protecting her. She started adding to her already learned skills on their second day with the clan, insisting that her uncle teach her all he could. He had obliged and not dismissed the young girl with the willful spirit.

"Did not your true identity haunt you?" Raynor asked.

"When we grew older we discussed it more," Aliss admitted. "But where was there for us to start? We knew so little and we were warned of danger."

"It was better left alone for the moment," Fiona said, and smiled. "Besides we now have the truth and need not worry about searching."

"You have finally come home," Raynor said. "And I *will not* lose you again."

"Fiona is mine," Tarr declared. "Aliss may remain with her family."

Raynor disagreed. "Whatever arrangements you made with the MacElder clan concerning Fiona, is no longer valid. She is as free as Aliss in her choices."

"I will not argue this with you," Tarr said as if it settled the matter.

"No, you will not. My father will deal with you." Raynor grinned. "He will determine who his daughter weds."

"*No one* but me determines my fate," Fiona said, her bright green eyes daring anyone to disagree with her.

"Yes, you are just like mother," Raynor said with a hardy laugh.

Tarr stood, shoving the chair away from him with his leg. "Fiona, I wish to speak with you alone."

Raynor rose slowly and stepped away from his chair.

Fiona jumped up between them, spreading her arms out from her sides to keep them apart. "My decision."

Aliss cleared her throat loudly enough to get their attention. "I believe there is a question here that has been left unanswered."

The three stared at her perplexed.

"If Fiona and I were in danger those many years ago, and mother warned us to keep our identities secret, does that mean when it is learned we have been found our lives will be in danger again?"

Chapter 19

Raynor and Tarr had attempted to reason that, after all these years, surely the danger to the twins had past, besides no one but Tarr and Raynor knew their true identity. Just to be safe, extra caution would be taken, meaning the two intended to keep close watch over the two women.

Fiona walked with Tarr to the Hellewyk encampment.

Night had fallen and with it a sudden chill wind.

Fiona drew her green wool cloak around her and regarded Tarr out of the corner of her eye. He obviously was disturbed and she understood why. His plans to wed her had just come crumbling down around him.

"The weather is set to change," she said attempting to make conversation.

Tarr nodded but said nothing.

He was handsome even in deep thought; his brow knitted tightly, his eyes narrowed, and his shoulders were drawn back expanding his already wide chest.

Aye, he was quite a man, and she was not certain that she was ready to give him up. He had potential as a husband, though bullheaded; he could be fair. He cared deeply for his clan and saw to providing more than adequately for their safety and welfare, which meant he would do no less for his wife and children.

Then there were his kisses.

She smiled to herself. She loved when he kissed her. She felt more alive when he kissed her, as though she suddenly emerged from a cocoon and was seeing and feeling the world for the very first time. And it was brilliant, filled with marvelous sensations and exquisite thoughts. She also found that she missed him when he was not near. She ached for the simple touch of his hand in hers or their frequent walks and how they would talk away hours. She was beginning to realize just how good they were together, and that made a good start for a solid marriage for sure.

Sure.

She had to be sure. She did not want to regret her decision.

With little time left to them before her parents arrived, she decided to be direct. "You are troubled over the change this brings to your marriage plans."

Tarr stopped and looked at her, his expression potent. "This changes nothing."

Her eyes widened considerably. "You think not?"

"I know so."

"And why is that?" She all but snapped, disappointment spawning anger in her. She had hoped he would see reason and give her a choice.

"I believe you will honor the arrangement made by your cousin for you are a woman of your word. Though the MacElders are not your people, they cared for you when care was needed, and I do not think that you will dishonor them."

"I did not agree to this wedding."

"So you say, but you knew that when your identity was discovered you would do what was expected. And now that you know of your true parents, Aliss will have a home, which settles all problems."

Fiona stood speechless for a few moments, and actually, if she had not, she probably would have reached out and punched the fool. Finally she said, "You are an idiot." She turned and started walking back to the keep.

A firm grasp of her arm halted her.

A stinging glare warned him to release her.

He refused, and with a sharp yank she landed against him. "Then you wed an idiot."

Her smile was slow and sly. "We will see."

"Do not think you can win against me," he warned.

"I do not *think*," she spat. "I know! And if you were not such an idiot you would *know* as well."

A rebellious yank of her arm and she was free to return to the keep.

This time Tarr did not stop her. He watched her storm off, her steps more of a stamp then a shuffle. She was angry, but then so was he.

He finally knew her identity. But discovering that she is not a MacElder at all does invalidate the agreement, not that he would admit it.

He intended to wed Fiona. She belonged to him, at least he wanted to believe she did—or did he *need* her to belong to him? He turned and instead of entering his campsite, he wandered off on the outskirts in the dark until he plopped down by a boulder to rest.

He had never equated love and marriage. Marriage was a duty, as he witnessed between his mother and father. He did not remember ever seeing his parents embrace; they lived separate lives and there had been talk that his mother had left his father's bed after he was conceived.

That his mother had loved him he had no doubt, but she had not loved her husband, and so Tarr grew up believing that love was not necessary to a marriage. He had thought love a fleeting emotion, there one moment gone the next, too elusive to hold on to and too complicated to explore.

He shook his head and rested it against the hard rock. Why had he given love so much thought lately? It seemed to plague him, nag at him relentlessly.

His mother had once told him that love could be felt with the heart. It could bring joy and it could bring pain, but it would not matter for you would never want to let it go.

How would he feel if Fiona was taken from him?

A wave of pure anger washed over him and as it receded, an awful ache settled in the pit of his stomach, not a sickness ache but one that could not easily be defined nor would he want to try. He only knew he had no want of it now or ever.

If he felt this strongly about losing Fiona did it mean . . . ?

Several oaths flew from his mouth, and he punched the ground beside him. Had he fallen in love and not even realized it?

You are an idiot.

Perhaps Fiona had been right, he was an idiot.

He stood and looked to the keep. He had some thinking to do, some conclusions to reach. Some—

He threw his hands up in the air. Who was he fooling? He had fallen in love and was too stubborn to admit it to himself let alone Fiona. And why should she believe him now. She would think his declaration of love a ploy in an attempt to get her to wed him.

Now what was he to do?

Persist in his usual fashion and demand his agreement with Leith MacElder be honored? Then let her learn of his love for her later. Or attempt to make her see reason now? They were made for each other, both being bullheaded, quick-witted and exceptional warriors.

Tarr had no idea what he would do. He knew only one thing. Fiona would be his wife.

Fiona entered the keep mumbling to herself and looked to find a place of solitude, a nook or cranny so that she could be alone to think. She found it in a small barren room kept warm by a fire that burned in the hearth.

She stood before the fire warming her chilled hands,

her thoughts on Tarr. With so much news to digest, news that concerned her, she remained focused on Tarr. He invaded her thoughts day and night. There was not a moment she did not think about him.

She knew she was falling in love with him.

Why?

That was a good question. There were many things she admired about him and a few things that displeased her, like the way he ordered her about, demanding she would be his wife.

She hugged herself.

She wished she knew what determined love, how to define it, and why love seemed more complicated than simple.

She had been freed of wedding Tarr; the choice being left entirely to her.

What did she do now?

"What is it you want of me, Fiona?"

Fiona turned as Tarr entered the room and her breath caught in her throat, though she refused to let him see her excitement. It surely had to be love. What else could explain the odd sensation that consumed her every time she saw him? Besides, she was still annoyed with him, but she was happy that he had followed her.

"Do you know?" he asked when he reached her side.

"We agreed to attempt to understand each other—"

"How can I understand you if you do not talk and share your feelings with me?"

"You do not even *try* to understand my feelings with regards to my sister," she accused.

"You want me to disregard my decision and appease you?"

"Is that difficult?" she asked. "If it would remove a stumbling block to our being wed, why not?"

"As my wife your duty is to me."

"That has nothing to do with my sister."

"You will forever spend time with her," he argued.

Fiona's eyes rounded like full moons. "You are jealous of my sister."

"I am not."

She smiled and poked at his chest. "You are."

"You will ignore your duties with Aliss around."

"Aliss's healing keeps her busy. You have seen that for yourself."

"Are you telling me that if I agree to allow Aliss to remain with the Hellewyk clan, you will wed me?"

"No."

Tarr threw his hands up in the air. "You do not know what you want."

"I do too," Fiona said, her hands going to her hips. "I want a man who will love me, allow me to be me, not dictate to me, and will accept my sister. That is not very much to ask."

"What will you give a husband in return?"

"Love, respect, and devotion."

Tarr stared at her a moment, then reached out to take her in his arms.

She stepped out of his reach and held her hand out to prevent him from approaching her. "Your touch does not allow me to think rationally."

He smiled and advanced on her.

"No," she said firmly, and moved away from him. "It would be easy to get lost in your arms, but I cannot. It is important to me that you understand how I feel."

"Then the truth of the matter is that I would have to love you if I wish to wed you."

"I look for true love, not a love you conveniently discover to suit your need."

He shook his head. "You cannot be serious. If I did love you, how than could I ever convince you of it?"

"That is for you to determine."

Chapter 20

It was early, the sun having yet to rise, when Fiona crept silently through the keep to emerge in the great hall as a servant added fresh logs to the hearth. The dry logs caught quickly and the fire was soon blazing, sending heat scurrying out into the dank hall.

Fiona cozied up on a bench at a table nearest to the fireplace. She pulled her green wool shawl around her shoulders and knotted it at her breasts to keep warm, then tucked her feet along with the hem of her brown skirt beneath her crossed-legs on the bench.

The servant promised to return with hot cider, letting her know a cold rain fell hard outside and she would do well to remain warm by the fire.

The few of Raynor's clan she had the opportunity to meet she liked. They seemed hospitable and friendly, though a few warriors regarded her with skeptical glances. She did not blame them, for she would have done the same herself.

Fiona thanked the servant profusely when she placed a steaming tankard of cider in front of her and a wooden bowl piled high with bread that appeared hot from the hearth. A pot of honey was the last item left.

She eagerly reached for a piece of bread and stopped, her hands returning to the heated tankard. She thought herself hungry, but now . . .

Her chaotic thoughts had her stirring all night. She slept little and when she had, it was a restless sleep. Fearing she would disturb her sister with her twisting and turning, she left the bed, dressed, and thought food might ease her anxious state.

Her stomach presently thought otherwise. It rumbled, flip-flopped, and fluttered until she felt as if she could not eat a thing. She could not blame it only on her situation with Tarr. Being honest, she would have to admit she was concerned with meeting her parents.

How would they be? How would they feel about Tarr and his demands? And would they have demands of their own?

"Troubled thoughts?"

Fiona jumped and almost toppled off the bench, Tarr's firm grasp preventing her fall. They stayed as they were, gazing into each other's eyes, a million thoughts and questions caught in a single unacknowledged space and time. Instinct prevailed and they instantly joined in a kiss, ignoring all else around them.

Simple and sweet. Tasty and lingering. Trembling

and aching. Needing and wanting. Their kiss spoke volumes, they parted reluctantly.

"Join with me?" she asked, and shook her head as she corrected, "join me for breakfast?"

He brushed his lips faintly across her cheek to her ear. "I would gladly agree to your first offer, the time and place your choice. Until then . . ."

He left her side to walk around the table and sit opposite her.

The servant appeared from out of nowhere, startling them both as she placed a tankard of cider in front of Tarr and a pitcher, steam rising from it, between them on the table. She was gone as quickly as she had appeared.

"Tell me what troubles you," he said with earnest as he slathered a piece of bread with honey.

To Fiona's surprise he handed it to her. She took it with a gentle awkwardness. "Thank you." He actually seemed concerned not only that she ate but with her thoughts.

He waited, fixing himself a slice of bread and honey.

This man really cared for her, she thought, then brushed it aside. Was it what she wanted to think, or was she seeing a side of him she had not noticed?

"I think on my parents."

"The ones you are to meet?"

"Both," she said with sadness.

"You loved the parents that raised you."

She smiled. "Oh, yes, very much. They were so good and so loving to Aliss and me. And they taught us the value of family love."

"I envy you."

She stared at him perplexed.

"Why do you envy me?" she asked. She caught uncertainty in his eyes and reminded, "Last night you asked me to share with you my feelings; you must then do the same if we are ever to build that bridge to meet in the middle."

"You are right. I cannot expect you to give and me not to return in kind." He acknowledged his own words with a sanctioning nod. "There was a distance between my father and mother that I thought common for married couples. I came to think of marriage as a duty with love far removed from it."

Fiona shook her head and tore a piece of the bread off, suddenly feeling hungry. "Marriage is made stronger by love."

He hesitated. "I am beginning to realize that."

Fiona took a swallow of the cider, the piece of bread caught in her throat, though perhaps it was his reply that had lodged the lump there. Was he implying that he had reconsidered his concept of love?

He continued. "I admit, though reluctantly . . ."

She smiled.

"That love could prove to be a mighty weapon."

Fiona chewed her bread heartily while nodding rigorously.

"It is forged with patience, consideration, kindness, and most of all unselfishness."

Fiona wanted to sigh at his loving and tender words, but she remained wide-eyed and alert as if his every word was a declaration, but then was it not? Had he realized what they shared? Did he know that their souls were one and that their hearts beat to an exact rhythm? Or was he placating her to convince her he loved her so that they could wed?

"I admit there is much I do not know, but I am willing to learn," he said, and reached out to take her hand sticky with honey. "Tell me your thoughts on your parents."

He unselfishly maneuvered the conversation to her concerns, and it more than touched her heart, tempted her soul.

"I do not think of them as my parents."

"I would feel the same."

"You would?"

"Of course. Suddenly you learn that you were abducted from parents who loved you, yet you were raised by people who also loved you. How do you love strangers who love you?"

"I have thought on that all night. Am I expected to love strangers, to feel for them as I felt toward my parents, the couple who raised me? And yet it was not their fault Aliss and I were abducted. How, then, can I blame them, for they must have suffered greatly."

"It will take time," Tarr said.

Do we have time? Fiona thought. He allotted her time to visit with her parents, but then she would return home with him.

Or would she?

If she did, it would be as his wife.

"Time seems to be my enemy of late."

"Your enemy is my enemy; we will combat it together." He raised her hand and licked at the honey on her finger. "Sweet. Is it Fiona I speak with?" He teased with an endearing smile.

"You have tasted, you tell me," she challenged, while her stomach suddenly flip-flopped and her arms crawled with gooseflesh.

"I must taste again."

Not a good idea, Fiona.

She ignored her own warning, smiled, and wiggled her finger in his face.

His laughter was barely audible as he brought her finger to his lips and licked slowly, as if savoring the flavor of her. Several long lingering licks later he said, "There is a tartness there."

"Are you sure?" she asked, her flesh tingling at her finger, up along her arm and crawling slowly over her neck.

He leaned over the table. "If I dare taste you again, it will not be your finger my tongue licks."

Fiona yanked her hand free as if his words scalded her.

"We will join." He stood and spoke before she could deliver her usual response. "It is your choice when."

He delivered a stunning blow to her without raising his hand. She was too shocked too move, too shocked to watch him walk away. His words stirred in her mind like a whirlwind unable to settle.

He had suddenly changed the tactics of their skirmish. It would not be he who forced their union but she. So he thought.

He was an idiot.

Or was she?

Would she finally surrender to him?

Or would it be what she wanted?

"Are you all right?" Aliss asked, taking the seat where Tarr had sat.

Fiona nodded, shook her head, nodded again then shook her head adamantly.

"Tarr passed me in the same confused state," Aliss explained. "His response, when I expressed concern for him, was identical to yours."

"Really?" Fiona asked, perking up.

"He shakes his head harder than you."

"It is his own fault."

"Why do I doubt that?"

Fiona glared at her sister. "You take his side."

"I do not think sides exist in this matter. I think you are both stubborn and refuse to see the truth."

"What truth?" Fiona demanded.

"That you both love each other."

Fiona was ready to give a quick response, instead her mouth dropped open.

"It is obvious."

"Truly?"

"Raynor even made mention of the way Tarr looks at you."

"How does he look at me?" Fiona asked anxiously.

"Like a love-sick puppy," Raynor said, joining them at the table. "If the man were not my enemy, I would feel sorry for him."

"He cannot be your enemy," Fiona said curtly. "For then I would have to be your enemy too."

"You put this man before your brother?" Raynor asked incredulously.

"I do." Fiona was unyielding.

"It must be love," Raynor said with a laugh.

Fiona leaned across the table. "If we had grown up together, I imagined I would have clobbered you more than once."

"You wish."

"I know—"

"And I—" Aliss interrupted—"would have continually settled your foolish disputes."

"While we both protected our little sister," Raynor said like a pompous older brother. "Lord, but it feels good to sit here and talk with my sisters this way."

"It is strange to learn we have a brother," Fiona admitted.

"I can understand. It will take time for you to grow accustomed to me. But please understand that I have missed you both these many years and that I feel I *reunite* with you."

"We were mere babes when we vanished," Aliss said.

"True, but I was your older brother and loved you from the day you were born. My love did not tire and grow old or dissipate through the years. On the contrary it grew in strength and determination to find you and return you home. When word came of the twins Tarr was bringing to Hellewyk, I dared to pray for a miracle." He grinned proudly. "And I got it."

"Attention was drawn to us because of Tarr," Fiona said.

"Aye, I had heard no word of the twins of the clan MacElder before that," Raynor said. "I had passed through that clan years before but saw no twins."

"We had yet to arrive," Aliss said.

"I missed you by a few months according to what you have told me of your mother's passing." The sadness that had marked his tone turned cheerful. "Now we are together again, and we have much absent time to make up for."

"While that is true," Aliss said, "there is Fiona's situation to consider."

"I agree it must be addressed, but it must wait until mother and father arrive."

Fiona bristled. "I will make my own choices."

"I never doubted you would. I only ask that you wait on our parent's arrival."

"It will not make a difference in my decision," Fiona insisted.

"You never know," Raynor said.

Chapter 21

Tarr and Raynor stood as Fiona entered the great hall for supper. Her face shined from its recent scrubbing, her brazen red hair fell like wildfire to her shoulders, and a green shawl was knotted at her waist and hung over her hip.

She weaved her way through the trestle tables and collapsed in the chair between the two men.

"Where is Aliss?" Tarr asked.

"She is finishing up after a lengthy delivery, though mother and babe are doing fine," Fiona said.

"She must be exhausted and hungry," Raynor said. "I have heard the delivery took all night."

Fiona reached for a chunk of cheese. "I will see that she eats and rests."

"And what of yourself? You helped your sister," Tarr said.

"I took my leave right after the delivery, which is why I am refreshed, feeling good and starving." Fiona reached for a piece of succulent lamb and continued reaching until her plate was piled high.

"The clan talks of Aliss's skills and hopes she remains here with us," Raynor said, "though I have heard mumbles from your warriors, Tarr, that the healer belongs to them."

Fiona stared at Tarr, a smile tempting the corners of her mouth. Tarr appeared to ignore her obvious pleasure over the news.

"I heard they boasted of her talent." Pride rang in Raynor's voice as he continued. "Telling tales of how she healed several of their warriors and clan members, and of course they spoke of how she defended me when I could not defend myself."

"We may just have a war on our hands over Aliss, especially now with her saving Ellie and her son's life and—"

"Where Aliss resides is her choice," Tarr interrupted, shocking Fiona into abrupt silence.

She stared at him, his words echoing like a distant thunder in her mind. Had she heard him correctly? Had he just removed the major stumbling block to their joining? Did he really mean that Aliss could remain with the clan Hellewyk, which meant they would not be separated? Had their talk last night caused him to reconsider?

"Since the sisters refuse to be separated, Aliss will remain with the Hellewyk clan," Tarr said confidently.

Fiona ignored the talk between the two men. Her

mind was fixed on Tarr's change of heart. He would allow Aliss to remain with her. Had he done this out of love for her? Did he truly wish to see her happy? Or had the change in circumstances forced his change of heart? Or did his heart have nothing to do with the reversal of his decision; was he merely being practical?

Her stomach plunged and she cursed the affects love, or the uncertainty of it, had on her appetite. One minute she was herself and could eat, the next she could not put a morsel of food in her mouth. She would wither away to nothingness if this were not soon settled.

The subject was changed and she was finally able to eat in relative peace, not the amount she usually ate but at least enough to satisfy. As the evening drew to an end, the hall growing empty, Fiona began to gather food to take to her sister.

"Several women have offered to bring Aliss food," Raynor informed her.

Fiona stopped filling a wooden bowl. "I know my sister's tastes, and besides she would expect no one but me to bring her nourishment."

"And do not fill the bowl so much," Tarr said. "Aliss eats little and she will not appreciate you trying to force food on her."

Fiona held a chunk of black bread in her hand and stared at him. It was the second time this evening he had startled her. He was actually being considerate of Aliss and again she questioned his motives. Was he actually concerned for Aliss or was he merely attempting to seduce her into believing he cared?

Damn, damn, damn, this love game.

Fiona held her tongue, fearful of lashing out at Tarr for confusing her. Instead she allowed him to help her wrap the bowl in a linen cloth a servant provided, place it and a jug of cider in a basket, and walk with her, after a good-night to Raynor, to the cottage where Aliss kept vigil over the mother and newborn.

"Winter draws near," Tarr said, and took off the wool cloak he had donned, draping it over Fiona's shawl-covered shoulders as they left the hall and walked slowly through the village.

His hand lingered a moment, a brief moment at her shoulder, then fell away, but his touch was enough to spark her body—and she cursed her emotions for responding so easily, but then her body forever responded to his touch, simple or intimate, it did not matter. Her blood soon fired, her flesh tingled between her legs, and she grew moist.

She wanted him.

Why?

A stupid question. She loved him.

Or could she be only curious?

Idiot.

She fought with herself, and who could possibly emerge victorious when one battled with oneself?

"Something troubles you?" Tarr asked, reaching out and, with a little struggle, taking the basket from her.

Fiona shrugged. She was surrendering to this man more and more. She needed no one to carry things for her. And yet—it seemed so natural to let him.

"You do not answer me."

"I am thinking," she snapped.

He simply looked at her patiently waiting for her to reply, which annoyed her all the more.

"Why the change of heart?" she demanded, stopping in the middle of the village, thankful it was late enough for all to be snug inside their cottages.

His brow knitted.

"Do not play the fool. You know what I speak of. You suddenly decide that Aliss can remain with your clan. Why now?"

That he was uncomfortable by her confrontation was obvious. He looked off into the night sky, moved uneasily in place, and then reluctantly turned to glare at her.

"I realized you and your sister belong together."

"Now? This moment in time, when there is a good chance I need not heed the agreement reached between the MacElders and the Hellewyk clan? How convenient for you."

"You think I do this to keep you?"

Fiona wanted to shout *yes, yes*, tell me that you would do anything to keep me; tell me you love me. Instead she challenged him. "Do you?"

She watched him struggle with his response. He drew his broad shoulders back as if in defense, his head went up, his eyes narrowed, and his lips appeared stuck together purposely, preventing him from answering.

Suddenly he dropped the basket to the ground, reached out, grabbed hold of her shoulders, and yanked her against him, claiming a kiss before she could object.

His grinding kiss jarred her senses. He demanded, expected, insisted—and what did she do?

She surrendered willingly, melting into his kiss that robbed her of any sensible thought or reason. His tongue proved an awesome weapon and one that she had no desire to combat. With a thrust and a jab he had completely captured her, and she did not mind the capture, she relished it.

Her arms went up around his neck and they were soon locked together like two crazed lovers unable to let go, feared letting go, could not possibly let go.

The kiss heated along with their bodies until suddenly Tarr pushed her away and held her at arm's length. They stared at each other, their passion still stirring their souls.

He shook his head, turned, and walked away.

Fiona remained where she stood—She had to. Her legs had not stopped trembling—and stared at his retreating back. When he was finally out of sight, her footing more firm, she reached down, grabbed the basket, and walked to the cottage alone.

Tarr sat at a table in the shadows away from the few people lingering in the hall. The servants busily cleaned the tables, preparing to settle the keep for the night. He declined the pitcher of ale offered to him by a servant rushing by.

He wanted to be left alone, swallowed by the shadows so that he could wallow in his frustration.

"Fiona is a handful." Raynor plopped down on the bench opposite Tarr.

"I prefer solitude," Tarr all but growled.

"Why? To try and make sense of Fiona?" Raynor laughed. "It will not work."

"You talk as if you know your sister well, and yet you have not seen her since she was but a tiny babe."

"Fiona was never tiny. She was larger than the average babe. The women who helped with the birthing gossiped about how the first twin's size gave my mother a difficult time. And once out, she wailed and demanded and refused to be quiet until she was finally placed at her mother's side."

"She remains demanding and infuriatingly stubborn to this day," Tarr said in one long frustrated breath.

"Then why wed her?"

"Because I foolishly fell in love with her." He pounded the table with his fist. "There I have admitted it. I love your bullheaded sister. Why? I have no idea." He threw his hands up in the air. "She questions what I say and do. She challenges me constantly. She wields her sword with the same damn strength she wields her mouth, and she sets my blood to—" Tarr stopped abruptly and shook his head. "Like a fool I confide in my enemy."

Raynor's eyes crinkled at the corners and his smile looked ready to burst.

"Laugh again and I shall silence it with a fist to your face."

Raynor clamped down hard on his lips while his eyes sparkled with merriment.

"You think this funny? I hope that one day you meet a woman who is ten times more chaotic than your sister."

Raynor's humor vanished instantly. "Bite your tongue, and wish no such prickly woman on me."

"Fiona is not prickly." Tarr's fist slammed the table

once again. "She has a good heart and is caring, though she demonstrates it oddly at times. And she is adamant in protection of her sister. I sometimes wonder if that is why she skilled herself in weapons and fighting."

"She has protected Aliss since birth," Raynor said. "The gossip was that Fiona made it easy for Aliss to follow her grand entrance into the world. Aliss cried little as a babe, and when she did, Fiona would wail endlessly until Aliss was placed beside her. They would quiet, then cuddle next to each other."

"I will not see them separated."

"That sounds like a warning," Raynor said.

"Nay, it is my pledge to protect them both."

"I never doubted you would and that protection may be more necessary than you know."

Tarr lowered his voice. "What do you mean?"

"It may be just my own fear of losing my sisters again, but I worry. If someone wanted them gone so many years ago, what will happen when that person discovers they have returned?"

Chapter 22

Fiona felt trapped, not only in the keep but also by her thoughts. The day was blustery with a strong wind blowing from the north and bringing with it a chill that tasted of a winter's storm.

Everyone around her seemed content, settled in routines. Aliss slept exhausted from tending new mother and her son. Raynor was nowhere to be found and Tarr . . .

"What do I care about him?" she mumbled to herself.

She had come to the conclusion that while she had wanted to love, hoped to love, she was actually inept at loving. She had expected it to be a much easier process, and it had been nothing but angst since the beginning. And had that changed any?

"No," she near shouted, then recalled her sister was asleep and she did not wish to disturb her.

Then there was the fact that Tarr had occupied her thoughts almost all day and then some since he had also managed to invade her dreams.

She wanted him out of her head and she wanted her heart to stop aching. Aware of her stubborn nature, she knew she was probably causing herself more worry than necessary, but she could not help it.

She wanted Tarr to sweep her up in his arms like a gallant knight and proclaim his love for her. That he was a warrior unskilled in gallantry made not an ounce of difference. That she was being obstinate made not an ounce of difference. That she should see and accept him for who he was made not an ounce of difference.

She would have love and she would have it her way.

She shook her head. Good lord, she sounded like a spoiled child, but then did she not have a right to love and not just settle? She realized how unreasonable she could be at times; she could even irritate herself, but her stubborn nature had seen her through many difficult times. Or perhaps those difficult times created her obstinate nature.

Whatever the cause, she had to be true to herself or she would surely be disappointed.

Annoyed at her frustration she did what she had not done in some time. She dug into the small satchel she had brought with her and pulled out a pair of tan leggings and brown shirt.

With a quick change, she was wearing male garments. She twisted her hair up and pinned it to the top of her head, yet not all her massive curls could be contained. Most protested and fell in a frenzy around her head and shoulders.

She grabbed a brown wool cloak off the hook before leaving the room and hurried down the steps and out of the keep, straight for the stables that housed her mare.

In no time she had her saddled and walked her to the edge of the village.

"We are going to fly across the meadows, lassie."

She broke into a run as soon as she mounted the mare, flying by Tarr's encampment at top speed.

"Someone is in a hurry," Raynor said from where he sat in front of the campfire.

Tarr stood abruptly. "She wears men's garb and she is going to break her neck at that speed."

"She sits a horse more securely in men's garb, and from what I have seen, Fiona looks to be an excellent horsewoman."

Tarr ignored Raynor's comment and, tossing away the half-eaten biscuit in his hand, he headed straight for his stallion. He mounted the horse and was off after Fiona before Raynor could get to his feet.

"This day should prove interesting," Raynor said, and walked toward the keep.

Tarr misjudged Fiona's riding expertise. He had thought to catch up to her without difficulty. He trailed behind her much farther than was to his liking. She maneuvered her mare with such grace and skill that she appeared to travel on the wind itself. He should have known better, having seen her skill firsthand and admiring it on many occasions.

He was not certain if he should be angry with her, worried that she would break her neck at such speed or take pride in her talent. She appeared in an intent pursuit, and he decided to see where it took her. He tempered his stallion's pace to keep chase.

Her blazing red hair broke free of its confinement and raged like wildfire around her head while the wind caught her cape and made it appear like giant bat wings. From behind she looked as if she were a demon racing anxiously over the land in search of souls.

She finally slowed her pace and, with a strong hand, lead her snorting mare in the direction of a small brook bordering the north end of the meadow, keeping the excited horse from drinking until she calmed. Then she slipped off her and permitted her mare to approach the stream.

"You could not catch me?" She laughed when Tarr caught up.

"You ride as if being pursued."

Fiona turned, slipping her cloak off and tossing it over her saddle. "Am I? Being pursued, that is."

For a moment fear rushed over him. He thought on Raynor's comment that the twins may still find themselves in harm's way. Quick enough he wondered if it was he himself in question.

Did he pursue her? Was that why he was so hasty to follow her? Was he trying to catch her? He had assumed she was his from the very first day he had arrived at clan MacElder. Realization had finally struck that Fiona belonged to whomever she chose.

His answer came with a smile. "The choice is yours."

Her green eyes twinkled with merriment. "Finally you realize that."

She walked away from the horses, Tarr joining her.

"I needed a reprieve."

"From?"

Fiona shrugged. "Myself, though I dare not admit it."

"Then I did not hear it."

"It is hard not to hear me when I speak." She laughed at herself.

He defended her. "I admire your tenacious strength."

"Tenacious strength." She nodded. "That sounds better than stubbornness."

"It takes strength and courage to survive in this world."

"It also takes strength and courage to love in this world."

"You can survive without love," he said.

"Can you?" She stopped, planting her hands on her hips. She waited for his answer.

"Love is not a necessity in life," he said annoyed, uneasy speaking with her on something he was just beginning to experience. He felt like a novice warrior, weapons in hand but without the practice to use them.

"It most certainly is."

"Why?" He damn well, once and for all, wanted a sensible explanation to the recurring question.

Fiona plopped down on a grassy knoll and patted the ground beside her.

Tarr accepted her invitation.

"Love binds, it is something you can always count on."

"Duty does the same thing," he counted. "Without as much dread."

She chuckled and drew her legs up to wrap her arms around them. "Duty is a necessity, love is a choice. You are free to choose with love, with duty you are honor bound."

"Is it not your duty to wed me?"

"If given the choice which would you choose, duty or love?"

Weeks ago he would have answered quickly and without doubt. Now, however, he hesitated.

"You think on your answer. There is hope for you yet." She laughed and patted his outstretched leg. "A marked improvement since first we met."

"I will admit I have learned something these past few weeks."

"I am impressed."

He liked the way her green eyes sparkled with a mischievous playfulness. She was so very full of life, ready to take a chance, ready to defend, ready to love—and the hell with what anyone thought.

"Tell me what it is you learned," she encouraged.

He shook his head. "That just when you think you know everything, you know nothing."

"You can always learn."

"It might take time."

"I can be patient when necessary," she said.

He picked at the grass between his legs, keeping his eyes on his busy fingers. "I am a warrior accomplished in battle and duty. I do what must be done, too much thought could prove fatal. I must have faith in my judgments and see that my edicts and decisions are carried through without question. It means the survival of my clan."

"Strong sons are also necessary to your clan's survival."

He looked at her and for a brief moment pictured her

round with his child. It sent a rage of emotions cursing through him, the most powerful being his overwhelming need to protect her and his unborn child.

"Say nothing," she warned with a raised hand. "Your thoughts remain the same. I am nothing more than a brood mare to you."

"That is not true," he argued.

She propelled herself to her feet and looked down at him. "Then what is the truth?"

He searched for the right words, elusive as they were. Unable to form an adequate response, he jolted to his feet. "I care for you."

"Care? Care?" she yelled and threw her hands up. "My horse *cares* for me."

"I care enough to follow after you when you foolishly don a man's garb and ride at a speed that could kill you."

She glared at him, her green eyes smoldering. "You think me foolish because I wear garments that allow me to sit a horse more safely?"

He reached out but stopped himself from grabbing her. "You can be the most frustrating woman."

"The problem is that I am too intelligent for the likes of you."

Tarr grabbed her arm. "If you are so intelligent, why is it that you will wed me?"

"I have not agreed to marry you," she reminded him curtly.

His laughter made known he disagreed with her, and it spiked her temper.

"I will not marry the likes of you."

He brought his face to hers. "But you will, and you know why?"

She looked ready to spew a hundred or more oaths at him, yet she remained tight-lipped.

"You want me. You have wanted me from the first time we kissed. And what you want, Fiona, you make sure you get."

She jerked her arm violently and a pain tore through her shoulder. She refused to acknowledge the ache to herself or him.

"I will not let you go. We will wed and I will satisfy that lust I see rage in your heated green eyes. And you will give me sons and I will always care for you and protect you."

Her nostrils flared, her chest heaved, and her hand fisted at her side.

"Even now in your anger you want me," he challenged. "Deny it! Go on deny it!"

Her face molted with fury and her lips disappeared in her mouth, she pressed them so tightly together.

"Damn you for stealing my heart," he growled before forcing her mouth open with a forceful pinch of her cheeks, then robbing her of breath and sanity with a kiss that demanded, begged, and harassed.

Her surrender did not come easy; she struggled but not with him, with herself. The instant he kissed her, he could sense her urgency to respond in kind. But her pride had her pushing at his chest, sparring with his tongue, and squirming in his arms.

He refused her mercy, turning the kiss to an erotic blend of taunts and teases that soon had her crazy. Her hands grasped his shirt and tugged and pulled demanding he give her more, and he did.

His hand slipped down to her backside and he

squeezed the firm muscles, urging her closer and closer to him.

He tore his mouth free needing air. "Mine," he whispered as he nibbled along her ear. "You are mine."

He felt as if he were kicked in the chest, she shoved him away from her with such force. He stumbled briefly reaffirming his footing quickly and immediately grew concerned when he saw her wince in pain, her hand grabbing her shoulder.

"What is wrong?"

"Nothing," she said. "Everything," she yelled, and hurried to her horse.

He followed. "You are hurt."

"Leave me alone." She swung herself up on her mare and the pain ripped threw her shoulder, stealing her breath and blurring her vision.

"Fiona," Tarr said with worry.

She stared at him, and in the next second toppled off her horse in a dead faint.

Tarr caught her in his arms and tried to revive her. When she would not wake, he placed her on his horse, holding her steady as he mounted behind her. He called her mare over, grabbed her wool cloak off the saddle, and draped it around her.

He looked to Fiona's mare and, assuming she must have been trained to follow, simply said, "Let's go, lassie."

He took off and the mare kept pace.

He entered the village with a roll of thunder and a rush of gray clouds overhead. His men and Raynor's men were quick to give a hand, and he was soon entering the keep.

Raynor rushed forward.

"She is hurt," Tarr said, and mounted the stairs quickly, Fiona appearing no burden in his arms.

She moaned as if in dire pain.

"I take you to your sister," Tarr said, and turned down the corridor to see Aliss leaving her room.

Her eyes widened in fright and she rushed forward. "What happened?"

"I am not sure," he said. "She was fine one minute and then the next she appeared in pain, then fainted."

"Get her in bed," Aliss ordered, hurrying ahead of him to open the door. She tossed the bed covering back for him to lie her down.

Tarr was as gentle as possible, but Fiona yelped with pain as he placed her on the soft bedding.

Fiona finally opened her eyes, seeing Tarr's face first. "Go away."

"What pains you?" Aliss asked, drawing her sister's attention.

"My shoulder."

Aliss nodded and slipped the brown shirt off her shoulder.

Tarr winced at her drooping shoulder. "Some of my warriors have suffered such an injury."

"What do you do?" Aliss asked.

"My mother taught me how to move the shoulder back in place."

"Then you have done it before?"

"Aye, but it is terribly painful. The strongest of my men faint from the hurt," Tarr said, concerned for Fiona's fate.

"Good, then you can adjust her shoulder."

"You do it," Fiona snapped, and regretted her slight movement.

"Tarr is stronger than I, which means he will be faster and it will be less painful for you."

"I do not care," Fiona said.

"I do," Tarr and Aliss said in unison.

Raynor stepped forward. "Tell me what to do and I shall do it."

"No!" Again Tarr and Aliss spoke simultaneously.

"It is my choice," Fiona insisted.

"Not this time," Tarr said, and stepped forward.

Fiona glared at him.

"I mean you no pain," he said, apologizing for the suffering he was about to inflict on her.

"Worry not, I can withstand the pain."

Tarr took a deep breath and as his hands reached for Fiona's shoulder, her eyes followed him. He met her defiant eyes with a sense of relief. This was one time she would benefit from her obstinate nature.

After examining her shoulder gently he asked, "Ready?"

"Be done with it," she urged.

He obliged, and with a sudden quick snap her shoulder was in place.

Fiona gritted her teeth and squeezed her eyes shut for a moment before springing them open. She glared at him with fury.

"With my tolerance for pain I should birth sons for you without difficulty. Now get out of my sight. I hate you!"

Chapter 23

"You drive the poor man insane," Aliss said, ladling them each a bowl of cabbage soup from the iron pot in the hearth before joining her sister at the small table in their bedchamber.

"You take his side now?" Fiona accused, and eagerly lifted the bowl to taste the potent smelling soup.

"Careful it is hot and your question deserves no answer."

The steam drifted over Fiona's face as she placed the bowl on the table for the soup to cool. "He cares for me. *Cares!* What about love?"

"Perhaps he expressed his feelings the best he could."

"There you go defending him again." Fiona grimaced at the ache in her shoulder.

"Your shoulder will mend fast enough, but I can't say the same for your unbending heart."

"You are my sister, you should be agreeing with me."

"I will not agree to foolishness," Aliss insisted. "I see how Tarr looks at you and I also see his confusion. His life has been devoted to his clan. His choice in a wife was with his clan in mind. Enter a crazy woman who turns his world and his heart upside down, and you have a man who is completely lost."

"I am not crazy." Fiona's voice faltered almost as if she questioned herself. It was followed by a lazy yawn.

"Finish your soup, then it is to bed and rest."

"I do not mean to demand," Fiona said, pushing her near empty bowl aside.

"I know," Aliss said, and walked over to nudge her gently out of the chair. "You need to sleep to let your shoulder heal, and rest will also help you think more clearly."

"I told him I hated him."

Aliss heard the quaver in her sister's voice, which meant tears were close at hand, though Fiona had not shed a single tear since the day after their mother died. She did not even cry the day they buried her.

"You were in severe pain and not thinking straight."

"I *felt* the hurt in his eyes."

"It was probably your own pain you felt," Aliss said, hoping to ease her sister's guilt as she helped her into bed and pulled the blanket over her.

"Nay, this pain was different. It was as if I could feel it down to the very core of me, and it lingers there waiting."

"For what?"

Fiona strained to keep the tears that pooled in her

eyes from falling. But they rolled slowly out as she whispered, "Hope."

Aliss sat with her sister while she slowly cried herself to sleep. Of course the potion she had added to her soup had helped in inducing her slumber. But she needed a good solid night's rest, and knowing Fiona she would have had a fitful sleep without it.

Besides this was a good time to speak with Tarr.

With a tuck of the blanket around Fiona, and after extinguishing a few candles, she silently crept out of the room.

Tarr looked anxiously at Aliss when she appeared in the hall and stood suddenly at her approach. "Fiona?"

"Is sleeping soundly and will remain so throughout the night."

His wide shoulders sagged with relief.

Raynor stood and pulled out a chair for her to join them.

"I was hoping to speak with Tarr alone."

Raynor obliged her. "My solar is a more private place for you to speak."

Aliss thanked him and followed Tarr to the solar. It was a small room with a generous fire in the hearth, keeping it comfortably warm. A narrow wooden table looked as if it served as a desk, and several chairs took up most of the space. Candles added a faint glow.

Tarr moved two wooden chairs nearer to the fire and waited for her to sit.

Aliss intended not to mince words, but Tarr spoke first.

"Fiona hates me."

He sounded devastated, as if he had just lost his best friend. Aliss reminded herself never to fall in love; it simply involved too much trouble and heartache.

"Fiona does not hate you," she assured him.

He turned to stare at the flames, her words not assuaging his worry.

She studied his profile. He was a man of fine features, and she appreciated the way he kept his long auburn hair so clean and shiny. Sitting near him she could smell its freshness. It hinted of fresh rain on a summer's day.

He was also a man of considerable strength, his tall frame carrying much weight, and yet there was not a soft spot on him. His shirtsleeves were rolled up and his thick forearms were pure muscles. His hands gripped the arms of the chair and while large and powerful, she had seen tenderness in those hands when he had cradled her sister in his arms and hugged her tightly to him.

If she had doubted that he truly cared for Fiona she did no more. She had seen the concern in his eyes, the worried expression on his face, and the gentleness of his touch. This man did not just care—*he loved* Fiona.

"It is not always easy dealing with my sister."

"Fighting raging battles has been easier."

She laughed. "It is good you retain your humor. You will need it"

Tarr released his grip on the chair and leaned back shaking his head. "I thought my plan simple. Pick a woman and wed her. I felt I had much to offer a woman, a strong clan for her to join, a man who would protect and respect her." He shook his head again. "Then I met your sister."

Aliss reached out and patted his shoulder. "Then something happened you did not expect."

Tarr stared at her, his look one of disbelief.

"You fell in love with Fiona."

He leaned forward and dropped his head in his hands. He raked his hair with his fingers as he swung his head up and rested it back against the chair. "I have no idea how it happened or when. And I still question myself. Is this love or lust?" He paused, his dark eyes round with confusion. "Then when she was hurt—" His confusion turned to distress. "I never feared as I did when Fiona toppled off her horse into my arms, and I never prayed as hard as I did while I rushed back to the keep."

"Sounds like love.'

"Really?" he asked anxiously.

She realized that he looked to her to confirm it for him, but who was she to know of love?

"What does your heart tell you?"

"It is more of my stomach that speaks."

She smiled.

"I cannot eat, and when Fiona turns stubborn my stomach knots. You are a healer," he said as if just realizing it. "You can give me something for my aching stomach."

"Advice is what I can give you."

He seemed disappointed, but then he shrugged. "Anything if it helps."

"Fiona has seen to our care since our father died. Our mother had turned ill soon after and was bedridden until she passed. I tended her while Fiona saw to the care of the fields, hunted food, made repairs to the cottage, made certain there was peat and logs for the fireplace, and protected us."

"She was but eleven years, how could she protect?"

"With sheer stubbornness and a sharp tongue," Aliss said and smiled, though it instantly faded. "And a tenacity to survive." She turned silent for a moment, recalling the painful memories. "After mother died, I cried terribly; Fiona cried but once right when she died. She kissed our mother, prepared her for burial, then dug her grave. She dug straight through the night, wanted it deep like father's grave, so that no man or animal would disturb her.

"I wanted to help but she insisted that I sit with mother, that she was not to be left alone. When it was finally done, the wooden cross staked in the ground, the prayers spoken, she turned to me and held out her hands. They were raw and it took weeks for them to heal."

Tarr winced at the thought. "Your uncle came then and she had to worry no more, right?"

"Fiona intended to take no chances of us ever worrying about surviving on our own again. When we arrived at the MacElder clan, she immediately befriended the bowmaker and begged Uncle Tavish to let her learn bowmaking. She also discovered that an old warrior known for his swordsmanship lived as a hermit in the woods. Many thought him a myth, but Fiona searched those woods until she found him. At first he chased her away, yelling at her that he wanted nothing to do with children. But she persisted, and he soon relented they became friends. It is because of him she is skillful with a sword.

"Fiona did what was necessary for us both, and the only thing she has ever asked for herself is to find a love as strong as our parents'."

A catch in her throat paused Aliss, and her shining green eyes warned of tears.

"Fiona loves you. I hear it in her voice when she speaks of you. I see it in her eyes when she looks at you, and I feel her joy when she returns from having spent time with you." She paused purposely this time and reached out to place her hand on Tarr's forearm. "And I think you feel the same about her. You are both lucky to have found such a strong love. Do not let pride or foolishness stand in your way."

"You are telling me to fight for her."

Aliss nodded, fighting back her tears.

"But I must fight Fiona to win Fiona."

Aliss smiled and let one tear fall. "She is so very obstinate. I fear she will lose you and will always regret it."

Tarr patted her hand and grinned. "Thank you for telling me all this. And do not fear Fiona is mine and will always be mine."

"I am glad to hear you say that, for then I will worry no more. I know you will be good to Fiona and patient with her."

"Patience, you will need to remind me of this every now and again," Tarr said with a laugh and stood, holding his hand out to her. "Suddenly I am hungry, will you join me?"

She took his hand. "I would be honored."

"Nay," he said, his expression serious. "It is I who am honored that you join the clan Hellewyk, and proud I will be able to call you my sister."

A tear fell as they walked out of the solar. All would be well now. Her sister would be happy and so would she. Life was good.

"I am famished," Fiona said as she and Aliss entered the great hall the next morning. "You were right, rest was what I needed."

"I wish to speak with you," Tarr said, stepping out of the shadows and grabbing hold of Fiona's arm.

"Can it not wait until after I have eaten?" Fiona stretched her neck so that she could glimpse the table heavy with platters of steaming food.

"It is important."

"Oh, all right, but it better not take long." She walked off with him not having noticed the wink he sent Aliss. "Do not eat all the honey bread," she called over her shoulder to her sister, then sent Tarr a heated glare. "This better be urgent."

He drew them into a small alcove off the hall and took her hand. "I love you."

Fiona stared at him and shook her head. "You love me?"

"Aye, I love you and thought it time I told you."

Her eyes crinkled at the corners. "You have only suddenly realized this?"

"I am not certain when I realized I loved you."

"Yesterday you simply *cared* for me," she reminded. "Now suddenly today you love me?"

"You do not believe me."

Fiona folded her arms across her chest and glared at him.

"I do not lie," he said vehemently.

"No, you conveniently discover you love me just before my parents arrive."

He gritted his teeth. "I love you."

"Simple enough words to say. Why do you love me?"

"Why?" Tarr threw his hands up. "I have no idea why I love a bullheaded wench like you."

"Oh, you give me gooseflesh when you talk that way to me," she mocked.

He grabbed hold of her good arm. "How does this sound? I love you in spite of your pigheaded nature and I am determined, in spite of your pigheaded nature, to love you until the day you die."

He kissed her before she could speak, forceful and hungry as if he were trying to solidify his words by his actions.

He pushed her away when he was finished and stomped off.

Fiona stood alone for a moment, her fingers faintly tracing her swollen lips. They pulsed from his kiss and ached for more.

"Damn him," she mumbled, and marched into the great hall in a fury. She looked around, and catching no sight of Tarr she hurried over to the dais where her sister sat alone. "Where did Tarr go?"

Aliss pointed to the door.

Fiona debated. Did she follow him? Why, though? What else could she say to him that she had not already said?

She looked to Aliss.

"The decision is yours," Aliss reminded.

Fiona sighed and hurried out the door.

She looked over the village, trying to see where Tarr had gone. She finally spied him talking with one of his warriors.

She had responded badly to his declaration of love, though she could not help question it, coming so soon after their discussion. How could she believe he truly loved her?

She kicked at the stone near her foot. He had expressed several times how he had not felt love was necessary to marriage, so why should she believe his change of heart now?

This love thing was not what she had expected. She had expected to meet someone, fall in love, wed, and be happy. She had suffered nothing but angst since meeting Tarr. But then she had not expected to fall in love with him.

"Have you chased after me to apologize?"

Fiona looked up to see Tarr standing a few feet away. She was about to snap at him when she thought better of it. She held her tongue.

"Love is new and strange to me, Fiona. It caught me off guard, quaking the ground beneath me, and I am still trying to find firm footing. It makes no sense to me, and the more I attempt to define it the more confused I become. So all I can say to you is that I love you and I'll keep saying it until you finally believe me."

Fiona stared at him.

"Do not tell me that I have struck you speechless?" Tarr asked with a laugh.

"I think you have," she said surprised.

"Good, then you will think on what I have told you

and hopefully reach the same conclusion that I have—that I love you."

He had declared his love for her several times in a short span of time. Did he truly mean what he said?

"Doubt it if you will," Tarr challenged, "but I do not."

A shout drew their attention and Raynor waved to them. "Our parents have arrived."

Chapter 24

"I do not know if I am ready for this," Aliss said to her sister while they stood on the steps of the keep watching a procession of impressive warriors enter the village.

Fiona took her sister's hand. "We have each other. That is all that matters."

Tarr walked up from behind. "You also have me."

Raynor paced at the bottom of the steps, looking about ready to burst with excitement. Though he appeared a potent warrior in a dark brown leather tunic and leggings, he seemed more a young boy eager to reunite with his parents.

The warriors divided to the left and right before reaching Raynor. Then finally, two horses approached and on them rode a man and woman. The woman's eyes rounded when she spotted Raynor, and she rushed to dismount.

Raynor hurried forward and helped her, though she needed none. She was on the ground, her arms stretched out, before Raynor could reach her.

The woman was stunning, her height equal to Fiona's. Her hair was dark like her son's and plaited in a braid that hung over her shoulder. She wore a simple though elegant gown of a heather color with a rich purple cloak draped over her shoulders. She was slim, and though she had to be at least twenty years older than Fiona, she showed little signs of an aged woman.

The man walked up behind her and Raynor stepped around his mother to greet his father with a bear hug.

He was several inches taller than his wife and there was no doubt he was Raynor's father, they looked so much alike. Traces of gray, heavy at his temples, ran through his darker shoulder-length hair. His dark eyes were framed with a mixture of worry and laugh lines, which added to his fine features. And love and pride shined in his eyes when he looked at his son.

With their reunion finished, the man took the woman's hand and they followed Raynor up the steps.

"Aliss," Fiona said, and stretched her hand out.

Aliss joined hands with her sister and they stood together as one.

Raynor was all smiles as he made the introductions. "May I present *our* parents, Anya and Oleg. Mother, Father, this is"—he bowed his head—"Aliss and"—he pointed—"Fiona."

Tears shimmered in Anya's eyes, and it took her a

moment to speak. "I know I am a stranger to you both and I cannot expect you to think of me as your mother, but in time I hope . . ." Her voice faltered.

Aliss went to her and took her hand. "It is an awful tragedy to lose a child, but a miracle has been granted us. It would be foolish of us not to be grateful and take joy in what has been returned to us."

A single tear dropped from Anya's eye. "You have the quiet strength of your father, and you are so very beautiful."

"Then is it your candor that I possess?" Fiona stepped forward.

Oleg smiled at his wife. "She truly is your daughter."

Fiona knew she must introduce Tarr and chose a simple introduction. "This is Tarr of Hellewyk."

Tarr paused a moment before stepping forward.

Fiona knew he waited to see if she intended to explain that they were to wed, but she could not offer him that courtesy, her decision yet to be made.

She was not surprised when he clarified his identity.

"Fiona is to be my wife, and I am pleased to meet her parents."

Oleg and Anya looked ready to greet him warmly when Raynor stepped in.

"There is much for us all to discuss. Let us retreat to the great hall to feast and talk."

Aliss walked beside her sister, slowing her step for Fiona to keep pace with her and let the others walk ahead.

"Be careful you do not regret your actions," Aliss whispered.

"Until I come to know these people I cannot treat them as my parents."

"You know it is not Anya and Oleg of whom I speak. Tarr stood beside you—"

"When it was not necessary."

"He was there for you," Aliss snapped.

Fiona stared at her, surprised by her outburst.

"He is trying, Fiona—"

"What is he trying?"

"To love you, if only you would let him."

Aliss stomped ahead, leaving her sister behind, and walked up beside Tarr.

Aliss never got angry with her. They had had their disagreements, but never had they been angry at each other. The thought upset Fiona and the more she thought, the more upset she got. This was all because of Tarr who had not wanted Aliss around in the first place, and now she defended him?

She marched forward. This was his entire fault. He was using her own sister against her to make certain he got what he wanted. He would probably use her newfound parents as well.

Not if she could help it.

She entered the hall prepared for anything.

"Please, Raynor, a table in front of the hearth where we may keep warm and converse more easily with everyone," his mother said, slipping her cloak off for a servant to take.

The servants got busy moving one of the trestle tables and benches lengthwise in front of the hearth. Soon platters and bowls of food were being placed on the table along with pitchers of wine, ale, and cider.

Anya sat with her back to the fireplace with her husband on one side and son on the other.

Aliss took the end of the opposite bench and Fiona scooted in beside her, leaving the other end for Tarr. The space was tight between the two, Tarr sitting closer to her than she would have liked, but there was little she could do about it.

His thigh rested against hers, solid and strong. She thought to squeeze closer to her sister, but the warmth of him felt good. His heat penetrated her skirt, sinking deep into her flesh, sending a sensation of comfort coursing through her.

Another thought to add to her already upset thoughts. Here she was annoyed with him yet comforted by him.

His hand slipped beneath the table. He splayed his hand on her thigh just above her knee and squeezed a few times before his fingers drifted slowly up her thigh, kneading her flesh lightly as he went. He stopped with his thumb dangerously close to being intimate when, in a second, his hand reappeared on the table.

What did he think he was doing tempting her under her parents' very noses?

Or was he reassuring her?

Fiona was glad conversation got underway. Her body tingled like it always did when he touched her and her thoughts turned lusty.

Damn him.

"Your names are not your given ones," Anya said.

Fiona was quick to comment. "They suit us fine."

"The people who raised you were good to you?" Oleg asked.

"*Our parents* were simple farmers with generous hearts and provided us with a loving home," Fiona said. "We miss them to this day."

"We have missed you these many years. Your absence left not only an emptiness in our hearts but in our home," Anya said, and glanced at her husband, who took her hand. "There has not been a day that has gone by that we have not thought of you both. We worried if you were well, hungry, alone, alive . . ." She barely whispered.

Fiona felt Anya's pain. Once when she was very young, Aliss had wandered off and was missing only for a short time, but the fear that had gripped her heart had pained her like none she had ever known. She could only imagine what Anya had suffered when they had been lost to her. A pain beyond description, no doubt.

Oleg continued in his wife's stead. "We searched endlessly for you, but to no avail. We did not want to believe you dead, so we prayed and kept hope alive in our hearts."

"And our prayers were answered," Anya said with joy.

"A toast!" Raynor raised his tankard. "To reuniting with family."

Everyone joined in and soon laughter and talk spread easily around the table.

When the conversation paused, Oleg took the opportunity to say, "Tell me of this marriage that is planned between Fiona and you, Tarr."

Fiona smiled at him. "Aye, tell *my father* about this proposed wedding."

Tarr did exactly that, outlining in detail the arrangements made with Leith of the clan MacElders.

Fiona admired the confidence and courage he showed. He did not falter in his explanation nor offer excuses as to why the arrangement should be honored. He was impressive in his strength and determination, and even had Fiona believing that they would wed.

Oleg cleared his throat and he and his wife joined hands before he spoke. "Having just found our daughters after all these years, we had hoped to have time to get to know them and share in their lives. A wedding would prohibit that—"

Oleg paused to glance at his wife.

Fiona moved in restless annoyance at the thought that this man she did not know would dictate to her. It was Tarr's firm hand to her thigh that stilled her and calmed her frustration, at least a little.

"Though I have been absent from my daughters' lives all these year, through no fault of my own, I feel compelled to attend to my fatherly duties. I would never expect my daughters to marry against their wishes, so therefore if Fiona wishes to wed you, then I give you both my blessings. If she does not wish to wed you, then I will see to it that she gets what she wants."

Fiona spoke before Tarr could. "I appreciate your support, but I have taken care of myself and Aliss these many years and will continue to do so."

She shot Aliss a glance, knowing without a doubt she would concur with her.

Aliss did not disappoint her. "I agree with my sister."

"You possess the patience of a saint when dealing

with your sister, Aliss," Tarr said teasingly. "I should have fallen in love with you."

"Love?" Fiona asked on a screech. "You claim to love me to get what you want, a wife and a brood mare."

"I must love you to put up with your foolishness."

"Foolishness?"

"You heard me," he said, his face close to hers. "A brood mare may have been what I first wanted in a wife, but no more."

"Are you telling me you do not expect me to bear your children?"

"Nay," he said. "I always wanted children and I want those children to be *ours* conceived out of love, not out of duty."

"How romantic," Aliss sighed.

"Be quiet," Fiona ordered.

"Fiona is right," Anya said. "Tarr should explain further."

Oleg shook his head. "The man has explained. He loves her, what more do you want of him?"

"Why has he suddenly changed his mind?" Anya demanded, looking to Tarr.

"Aye, why?" Fiona repeated her mother's query.

"I have no answer," he said with a shrug, "except that I love you. When did I fall in love with you? I cannot say. It simply happened—"

"And shocked you," Fiona said accusingly.

"Aye, it shocked me," Tarr admittedly freely. "I knew nothing of love. I was too busy learning to be a good chieftain, my father demanded it of me. I had no time to consider love, and besides, a marriage would be arranged. It is the way of things."

"Not for me."

"So I have learned."

"So I am a fool for wanting to love the man I wed?"

"I thought you were," Tarr said. "I thought I offered you much and that you were not only foolish for not accepting my generous offer but selfish." Tarr pressed his finger to her lips to keep her silent. "I learned differently as time went on, and the more time we spent together the more time I wished to spend with you. I discovered I admired and respected you, *and* the ruse you perpetrated. In my eyes you were an adept warrior woman capable of anything, and as I made all these surprising discoveries, along the way I also fell in love with you."

She shoved his finger off her lips. "How convenient!"

"Aye, for us both," he said, and leaned close enough for their noses to touch. "There is much more that I wish to say to you but not here in front of everyone."

"Why?"

"There are some words meant for your ears alone."

"Give him a chance," Aliss urged from beside her.

"Aye, I agree," Oleg said. "Talk with him."

Fiona looked to Anya. "Have you no opinion?"

"I reserve my opinion for a later time."

"I agree with my father and Aliss," Raynor said. "Be fair and talk with Tarr privately."

Fiona stood. "I will give you but a few minutes."

Tarr stood, grabbed her hand, and pulled her along behind him. "That is all I need."

Chapter 25

They made their way to his bedchamber and Fiona hesitated at the door.

"It is the most private place and the place most likely we would not be disturbed," Tarr said.

Fiona agreed by entering his room. She went to the window, though not for the view of the meadow. Rather, to put distance between them. She would grant him his few minutes, hear what he had to say, but no more. She would not allow him to touch her, and least of all kiss her. The thought itself made her anxious.

"Speak and be done," she said more sharply than intended, and faced him with arms crossed over her chest.

"Is there any point?" he asked calmly, to her surprise. "Your mind seems set. Would what I say make a difference?"

"I said I would listen."

"But would you hear?"

He stood just inside the closed door not having moved since he entered. She had expected him to approach her, attempt to touch her, but he had not. This calm control of his sometimes infuriated her for it usually meant he would have his way.

A warrior's way.

Did he look prepared to battle?

The silent question irritated her for it reminded that it was she who was ready to battle, to defend against him. She could convince herself of it easily. There were signs; he stood blocking the door and any escape, his body was rigid, every muscle taut and prepared to attack.

But then she looked into his eyes and they told her a different story. There was a desperateness in them, a plea of sorts and an ache that—

Would you hear?

She felt a catch in her throat. Were her own words caught there? She cleared the lump as she said, "I will hear you."

He walked to the center of the room, a few feet from her. "Will you? I know you have a right to doubt I speak the truth, but how will you ever know if you do not shed that heavy shield you keep around your heart?"

She stiffened in silence.

He took another step. "Nothing penetrates it, not truth, not passion, not love. How, then, can you truly feel anything? You tell me you wish to know love, and yet how do you expect love to pierce your defenses?"

She tightened her arms to her chest.

He approached her slowly. "You took on the burden

of protecting you and your sister after your parents' death. You refused to rely on anyone, trust anyone. How, then, could you think to love?"

His words were a direct hit to her heart. *Where, then, was her shield?*

"We are much alike, you and I, which is why I think we love so passionately. How it happened, when? I do not need to know. I only know that I love you. If you ask me why I love you—"

He shrugged and smiled. "I would give a different answer each time. At this moment I love you because you stand firm, unafraid to listen, your arms shielding your heart, your green eyes filled with uncertainty, your soft lips tempting me."

He shook his head as he stopped a few inches from her. "I love you, Fiona. I know not how else to say it, but simply, and those three words I will say to you everyday of our lives together."

He reached out and gently took her wrists, pried her arms away from her chest. "Marry me, Fiona. Marry me because I love you. Marry me because you love me."

Her body was rigid from holding herself so stiffly, and she stumbled as he drew her into his arms.

"I will always be there to catch you if you should fall," he whispered in her ear. "And I know you will do the same for me, for we love each other."

A tear trickled down her cheek as she looked into his eyes and he kissed it away.

"I cannot promise I will kiss all your tears away, but I will promise that *I* will never make you cry and I will never let you cry alone."

She did not hesitate to kiss him; she needed to kiss

him, to know that this was not a dream. His lips were warm and welcoming and so very gentle.

He eased his lips away to say, "I love you, believe that I love you."

A faint brush of his lips over hers had tingles racing through her and she eagerly captured his lips for a more fervent kiss.

As the kiss heated so did Fiona's body and she grabbed at his tunic, wanting desperately to rip it off his body and feel his naked flesh.

She refused to end the kiss, her need for him growing more potent as their bodies pressed tightly to each other.

Finally Tarr grabbed the back of her wild red hair and yanked her head back, freeing their lips. "Keep this up, Fiona, and it will end in my bed."

Her answer was to reach for his lips.

He gave them to her, grabbed her around the waist, she wrapping her legs around him as he carried her to the bed. They fell down upon it as one, she on top of him and he tugging at the ties to her blouse.

Her breast finally fell free and his mouth caught her nipple. She gasped, her head falling forward to rest on his forehead as he teased her nipple unmercifully with his tongue. Her hair fell around them, concealing the intimate act. She straddled him while he feasted at her bosom, sending a rush of power through her, firing her desire beyond reason.

She shifted her body until it fit against his potent erection and then she rubbed against him until she was wet.

He grabbed her backside and yanked her skirt up.

His fingers squeezed at her bottom then hurried forward to touch her wetness. She yelped at the shot of passion that hit her like a bolt of lightning, and she moaned as his fingers played with her.

"You're mine," he said, his free hand grabbing her around the neck and pulling her mouth to his. "Always mine."

His words suddenly hit her like a splash of icy cold water to her face and she tore free of his grasp and flew off him to stand, nearly breathless, at the end of the bed.

"What is wrong?" His own breath was labored.

She shook her head and, realizing her breast hung free of her blouse, she slipped it in and with shaking hands tied the strings tightly.

Tarr sat up and Fiona backed away.

He remained still. "Tell me what is wrong."

She continued to shake her head and fled the room, leaving him sitting on the bed stunned.

Fiona raced up the flight of stone steps, praying Aliss was in their room by now, but she found Anya sitting in the chair near the hearth instead. Her frantic entrance had Anya jumping up and once she saw the tears in her daughter's eyes, she held her arms out to her. Fiona did not hesitate, she rushed into them and released her tears on her mother's shoulder.

When Fiona's tears were finally spent, mother and daughter sat on the bed together, Anya's arm remaining firm around her daughter.

"The talk did not go well with Tarr?"

Fiona sniffled. "I am a fool."

"We are all fools when it comes to love."

"He does not love me."

"Why do you think that?" Anya asked.

Fiona wiped at her red swollen eyes as she spoke. "He attempted to convince me with simple, thoughtful words then while he—"

Anya patted her hand, understanding what she could not say. "Intimacy is natural between those in love."

Fiona sighed. "He said *always mine*, which meant he thought I belonged to him since first we met. He does not love me, I am but chattel to him, no more."

"I can see why you doubt him."

"You can?" Fiona asked with a breath of relief.

"Of course. You want to trust him completely, and how can you? He lies."

Fiona's eyes rounded. "He does not lie. He is a man of his word. A true warrior."

"Is he now?"

"Aye, he protects his clan with pride and strength and provides well for them, which is why he sought a marriage with me."

"Then you are his chattel."

"A good marriage was necessary for his clan's survival," she defended

"He told you this?" Anya asked.

"Repeatedly. He was honest with me from the very beginning."

Anya squeezed her daughter's hand gently. "Then what makes you think he is not honest with you now?"

Fiona's mouth fell open.

"Raynor spoke of Tarr in the message he sent informing us of finding you. They were few words, but those words painted a picture of a man who spoke the truth and honored his word. It is not Tarr you doubt, Fiona. It is yourself."

Anya brushed back the hair in Fiona's face. "I was like you, brash and outspoken." She laughed. "Oleg would say I still am, but my nature was driven by fear. Fear of not being loved, since most young men showed little interest in me."

"None showed interest in me."

"That is because we are strong women, and it takes a man of great strength and patience to love such special women. I doubt Tarr understood you when first you met."

"He did not even know who I was, Fiona or Aliss." Fiona smiled. "He did tell me he admired my skills and courage, more than once."

"He began to discover your true worth. Only a man of equal strength can do that, a man that does not fear the discovery but embraces it. I think Tarr has embraced all he has learned about you and is proud to love you."

"I am a fool." Fiona hung her head.

Anya lifted it. "Love is being foolish, foolish is being in love. All is forgiven when love is true. Do you love Tarr?"

"With all my heart." Fiona near wept. "It frightens me how much I love him and I worry that—"

"He will not love you as much?"

Fiona nodded.

"Tarr is a man of his word, Fiona, if he tells you he loves you, believe him."

"He told me to believe him and he told me he would tell me he loved me every day of our life together."

"How beautiful and unselfish, for I tell you there will be days he may feel differently," Anya said with a laugh.

"Tarr loves me," Fiona said as if accepting it for the first time.

"Know it in your heart and it is so."

"My heart has known and accepted it far longer than I have."

"Then tell him this," her mother urged.

"He must think me a fool." Fiona grimaced. "I called myself a fool before leaving him."

"Do not worry. He probably thinks himself an idiot."

"Why?" Fiona asked surprised.

"Because he sits now wondering what he did wrong."

"He did nothing wrong."

"But he thinks he did, and he berates himself for it and wonders how he can make it right."

"I hurt him," Fiona sighed.

"It is not the first hurt and it will not be the last," her mother advised.

"He told me he would never make me cry."

Anya laughed. "Oh, dear, sweet daughter, as much as he believes that he will not make you cry, he will, though not intentionally, and he will be distraught by your tears and seek to make it right between you. It is inevitable; it is love."

"Does love bring more grief than pleasure?"

"That is up to those who love."

"I have brought grief to our love," Fiona admitted with reluctance.

"Then it is time to turn it to pleasure."

Fiona looked doubtful.

"Patience with yourself. This is all new to you, and it will take time to understand. Let your heart lead you and forget everything else."

"That is easier than it sounds."

"Let go of the fear, Fiona, and it will be much easier than you think."

"The fear has kept me cautious all these years."

"You need it no more," her mother said gently. "You have me and your father now. We may have failed once to protect you girls, but I give you my word we will not fail again."

Fiona smiled. "You are telling me that if you thought Tarr no good for me you would stop this marriage."

"Immediately. Oleg and I want what is best for you girls even if it means losing you to a husband when we have just found you."

"Our parents were like that, putting Aliss and me above their needs."

"You do not know how happy it makes me to know that you both were loved. I feared you might have suffered a harsh life. I am glad, so very glad you had loving parents." Anya sniffled. "Though I cannot say it does not upset me that I missed all those years with you."

It was Fiona's turn to comfort. "We have many more years ahead of us, and between Aliss, Raynor, and me you will have many grandchildren to spoil."

Anya kissed her cheek and whispered, "Do not keep me waiting."

Fiona hugged her. "I am anxious."

"I would bet that Tarr is eager."

"What if he thinks me insane?"

Anya grinned. "Insanely in love with him. Go to him with nothing but love on your mind. Let no doubt enter your thoughts, and be ready to love him with all the passion your heart holds for him. Believe me when I say your actions will be enough. There will be no need for talk."

"Thank you," Fiona said with a hasty hug, and hurried out of the room before she lost her courage.

Chapter 26

Fiona rushed into Tarr's room, slamming the door behind her so hard she could have sworn she shook the entire keep.

Tarr remained as she had left him sitting on the bed.

He stood when she did not move and they stared at each other, both questioning with their eyes until Tarr stretched out his arms to her.

She flew across the short distance and would have knocked him over had he not braced for the impact and glad she was that he did, for his arms wrapped around her and held her against him with a strength that assured he would never let her go.

She looked up at him and he shook his head.

"No words this time. This time I show you how much I love you."

Love him, just love him.

She smiled and turned her head to the bed.

He smiled along with her as he lowered her to the bed, but before he joined her he shed every piece of clothing he wore and his nakedness left Fiona breathless.

He was magnificent, big and solid and confident as he crawled over her.

"Your turn."

He took off each of her garments slowly, his fingers stroking her naked flesh as he went along. Short strokes, long strokes, lazy strokes, and quick strokes until Fiona moaned, "Not fair."

His muttered laugh sounded more like a growl and when he nipped at her nipple then took it into his mouth to tease, she knew he had no intentions of playing fair.

But then neither did she. She had no qualms about being adventurous in a game she had never played before. She only knew she wanted to fully participate. She slid her hand over his chest, down his stomach that was warm and hard, and stopped suddenly when he squeezed her breast and suckled her nipple like a man enthralled with the taste of her.

She groaned at the passion stirring in her and her hand inched down slowly until she was able to grasp hold of him. He was silky smooth and rock hard, and he pulsated in her hand. The feel of him empowered her like never before, and she did not want to let go.

She massaged the length of him and he brought his head to rest against hers.

"You know not what you do, lass."

"Teach me," she challenged, and rubbed him against her own heat.

He threw back his head and moaned like nothing she had ever heard before, and it fired her blood even more.

"Keep that up and this will be done before it starts," he managed to say on a quick breath.

She released him, not wanting this time between them to end too soon.

As soon as she did, he moved down between her legs and tasted her, sending her passion soaring while her hands grabbed hold of the pillows and squeezed. She tossed her head from side to side as his tongue did oh-so-deliciously nasty things to her.

She begged him not to stop and he did not; he continued tormenting her until she almost cried from the pleasure he was giving her.

Then he stopped and she whimpered. He lifted her legs over his shoulders and slowly entered her. She was eager for their joining and tried desperately to draw him closer.

"Easy, lass, I do not want this to be painful."

She glared at him with blazing green eyes. "The pain will be a welcome relief to this torture."

He laughed. "God love you, Fiona, for being such a passionate woman."

"Then feed my passion, husband-to-be."

"You will wed me, then? Of your own free will?"

"Aye, aye," she cried in surrender, and moved against him. "I love you, Tarr."

He grabbed hold of her backside and with a careful thrust entered her.

"More," she pleaded.

He gave her all of him and she reached out.

He leaned down over her and together they joined in

a matching rhythm. She latched onto his broad shoulders and moved with a wanton abandonment that pleased her and had him basking in her eager response.

He took her mouth, his tongue mingling, urging, teasing hers, and matched her movements with equal eagerness.

She tore her mouth from his, her breathing quickening as she rose toward climax.

He quickened his pace and she moaned loud and long, and he rode her hard and furious.

It hit her like a giant wave washing over her again and again until she thought she was drowning.

She heard him groan and clasped him tightly to her, the last ripples of pleasure racing through her to slowly recede quietly in the distance.

He rolled off her to lie beside her, his hand reaching out to take hers.

She held firmly to him, needing an anchor, afraid she would drift away with the ripples. It took several minutes before her breathing returned to near normal, then she turned to look at him.

"I had not thought coupling this much fun."

He laughed and moved to lie on his side, bringing her hand to his lips for a kiss. "I am glad you think it is fun. This way you will wish to do it often."

"Very often," she said seriously.

"I will make sure of it," he promised her.

"I will too."

"Then it is a slew of children we will be having."

"I will give you as many as you like."

His smile faded. "You truly wish to wed me, Fiona?"

"Aye," she said joyously, and planted a wet sloppy kiss on his mouth. "I do."

"Good, then our children will be conceived of love."

"Lots and lots of love and we should wed as soon as possible."

"I agree, but I wish to wed at my residence so that my clan can join in the celebration. Of course, your parents must be present."

She sat up quickly. "We must inform them of our intentions to wed."

"Now?"

"They will be relieved to know all is settled between us."

"Later." He said and urged her down beside him with a firm hand. "I have waited long and patiently for this moment, and I wish to lie here beside you and look at your beautiful body."

"I have never spent an afternoon in bed."

He grinned. "That is about to change."

She giggled and wrapped her arms around his neck, nibbling at his lips. "I do like the taste of you."

"You can taste me anytime."

"Be careful what you allow me. I may not get enough of you."

"Wear me out, lass, I care not." He laughed and pulled her on top of him.

She rested her head on his shoulder with a yawn, splaying her hand on his chest.

"It looks like it is I who have worn you out."

"Give me time to refresh and we shall see who wears who out."

"Rest, then, and I will take you up on that challenge."

"You will lose."

"Impossible, lass, I win either way."

Tarr and Fiona were sitting at the trestle table before the hearth the next morning when Aliss entered through the front doors of the great hall along with the first light of dawn.

"Where have you been?" Tarr asked with concern before Fiona could.

A yawn attacked Aliss, leaving her no time to answer.

"You have not slept," Tarr said, and stood to assist her to sit.

"I birthed a stubborn babe last night." Aliss sat with a grateful plunk on the bench, her green shawl slipping off her shoulders as she reached to pour herself a goblet of steaming cider.

Fiona did it for her. "It appears neither of us slept in our bed last night."

Aliss moved the tankard away from her lips and grinned so wide her eyes appeared to smile. "I am so very happy for you both."

"Fiona has agreed to wed me."

"What is this I hear?" Oleg said with excitement as he and Anya entered the hall followed by a smiling Raynor.

Anya rushed forward and hugged Fiona. "We have a celebration to plan."

"Your help would be appreciated," Fiona said, "though we wed on Hellewyk land."

"We could have a fine celebration here," Raynor offered.

"My thanks," Tarr said, "but we wed at my home."

"You do not leave yet, do you?" Anya asked anxiously.

"A week's time and then we leave, but you are welcome to come and visit at Hellewyk."

"What if Fiona remained here with us?" Raynor suggested. "She would have more time to visit with our parents and then we would journey with her to your keep."

To Fiona's surprise Tarr turned to her.

"What say you, Fiona?"

He was giving her a choice and his considerate gesture swelled her heart to near bursting. It also acknowledged that he understood her need for independence in her life, not something many husbands would allow, let alone value. Her husband-to-be was a special man and she suddenly felt grateful.

Her arm coiled around Tarr's. "I go with Tarr."

"Then Aliss can remain with us," Raynor said.

"She cannot," Fiona said curtly.

"Is it not her decision?" Raynor asked.

"I know her decision. She would not remain here without me. Right, Aliss?"

Aliss, her elbow on the table's edge, rested her chin in her hand and fought to keep her drooping eyes open. "What?"

"Dear lord, she looks exhausted," Anya said, and hurried to her side. "Come, dear, let me get you to bed."

Fiona nearly jumped out of her seat. "I will take care of her."

"It is all right, I will see to her," Anya said graciously.

Tarr reached up and tugged Fiona down beside him, forcing her still with a firm hand. "Thank you, Anya. Fiona and I have matters to attend to."

A protest hovered on her lips, but one warning look from Tarr told her she best save it for a more private time.

Then his dark eyes softened and shifted to Anya and Aliss.

Fiona's eyes followed and she realized what he tried to convey to her. Anya for the first time in twenty and one years was able to care for her daughter.

She felt a tug in her heart for the woman as she slipped her arm around Aliss and helped her up, all the while talking gently to her.

"I will have you tucked soundly in bed in no time."

Fiona watched the pair walk off and was surprised that she found herself close to tears. How Anya's empty arms must have ached for her twins. How horrible to always wonder if her babies were safe and cared for. She and Aliss had been spared such cruel suffering, never knowing their true parentage and having been lucky to be placed with good, loving people.

"This has not been easy for her," Oleg said, his voice quavering. "And my Anya is a strong woman, much like yourself, Fiona. Her heart has suffered greatly these many years, and I had hoped this reunion would heal it."

Fiona reached across the table and placed her hand on her father's arm. "You brought her to the only place she could heal. You brought her home to her daughters."

A tear slipped down Oleg's eye. "You have grown into a fine woman. I am proud to call you Daughter."

His words touched her heart and for a brief moment she thought of her own father, different in features from Oleg but similar in nature. Her father would expect her to honor and respect Oleg, and in her father's memory she would do that.

"It is with pleasure I give my blessings for you two to wed," Oleg said, looking from Fiona to Tarr. "The joy on my daughter's face tells me she is happy, and if she is happy then I am happy, but"—he waved a finger—"be prepared for frequent and lengthy visits from Anya and me."

"You are welcome anytime, and you are welcome to stay as long as you wish," Tarr said.

"He is a good man," Oleg said with a nod and a wink to Fiona. "A very good man."

"I think so," Fiona said, and ran her hand over Tarr's arm down to lock her fingers with his. He moved close against her side and she cherished the warmth and strength of him. He would love her, she was sure of it and feeling rather foolish for causing him and her so much angst. But that was behind them. Their future loomed large before them and she looked forward to everyday of her life with him.

Talked turned to the ordinary, and Fiona became restless listening to the men, though their conversation did not bore her. She, however, felt the urge to be outdoors, to feel the sun upon her face and enjoy the crisp fresh air.

Her thoughts had her hopping out of her seat and, with a quick kiss to Tarr's cheek, she said, "I am off, the bright day summons me."

She grabbed her sister's dark green shawl from where it had fallen on the bench, draped it around herself, and tossed the end over one shoulder, then out the door she went.

Tarr watched her go, his eyes remaining on the closed door, and after seeing that it remained closed, he turned to Oleg.

"I am concerned for the twins' safety."

Oleg nodded to his son. "We have thought the same as does my Anya. She fears leaving them alone."

That brought a laugh from Tarr and Raynor.

"God help the man who attempts to abduct Fiona," Tarr said.

"He will live to regret it," Raynor chuckled.

Oleg's words turned the room silent. "I myself do not worry about another abduction. My concern is for their safety. What if this time they want them dead?"

Chapter 27

Tarr watched Fiona pick heather alongside the women of the clan. Her cheeks were spotted red from the crisp wind that made its way down the sloping hill. A purple flower was tucked in her bright red hair, which resembled a mass of fiery flames kept aglow by the bright sun overhead.

She had not put the sprig in her hair nor did she collect the heather for the joy of it. She was not that type of woman, all flowery, soft, and gentle. She was a woman of great passion, tremendous strength, and courageous heart.

She would prefer to clean her sword, tend her mare, or string a bow, instead she picked heather for her sister.

He returned the wave she sent him once she spotted him standing there, then she resumed her task with a smile. He could not explain how or when this woman worked her way into his heart, or how she obtained permanent residence there.

He just knew he never wanted to lose her. He had expected little to change in his life when he took a wife; he was wrong and glad of it.

Fiona had filled an emptiness inside him that he had not known existed. His life had been a constant learning in preparation to lead the clan. His father had reminded him daily of his duties, including finding a woman who would bare him strong sons so that the Hellewyk clan would always prosper.

His mother had been a good woman and in her own way loving, though distant. That she had loved him he had no doubt, her quiet nature and gentle voice he would always remember, but strength?

If it was there he never saw it.

Fiona displayed her strength with pride, and he felt honored to love and be loved by such an extraordinary woman. His heart swelled and so did his passion. He had to laugh to himself. He had thought of his husbandly duties as a necessity. He grinned wide, a chuckle rippling beneath his breath.

It would be no chore but a pleasure to do his duties with a woman who found as much joy in making love as he did.

Tarr saw Fiona stop suddenly, glance his way and, after a few words to the women around her, she walked his way.

He waited with arms crossed over his chest and a devilish smile on his lips.

Her pace was unhurried, her hips swung in a

provocative sway, and her breasts bounced gently beneath her blouse with each step. Her hands went to the knotted shawl at her waist and she untied it as she approached him.

"Your eyes tell me you are hungry." She slipped her shawl over her shoulders to hide her fingers as they loosened the ties of her blouse. "I myself am famished."

Her nipple peeked at him from the edge of her blouse. "You seduce me here and now?"

"Aye," she said, her eyes turning wide, "and with much impatience."

He laughed and shook his head. "I got more than I bargained for when I chose you for a wife."

She poked at his crossed arms. "It is I who chose you, and lucky you are that I did."

"Aye, I am lucky that you love me."

Her hand came to rest on his arm. "Let me *show* you how much I love you. I want to taste you as you did me."

His eyes turned round and he leaned down close to her face. "If we were not standing in the middle of the village, I would scoop you up in my arms and rush you to bed."

She leaned closer. "Coward."

He threw his head back and roared with laughter, then with a swiftness that had her yelping, he swept her up into his arms and walked to the keep. Giggles and wagging tongues surrounded them, but Tarr paid them no heed. He was on a mission and nothing would stop him.

He pushed the door to his bedchamber open with his

shoulder and kicked it shut behind, then walked over to the bed and dropped her down on it. She scurried to her knees and reached out to help him undress.

"I want you naked so that I can touch and taste and—damn, my body tingles every time I touch you."

He grabbed her hand and placed it over the hard length of him. "This is what my body does every time you touch me."

She grinned. "Good, I like you that way."

She started stroking him, his thick muscle growing ever stronger with each lazy, tempting stroke. And when he went to move her hand away, she brought her tongue to him and stroked the cloth that covered him, nipping at him between tastes.

He groaned when she slipped his leggings down and as soon as he sprung free she took him in her mouth. There was no hesitation or repulsion, she feasted on him as if his flavor intoxicated her and she could not get enough.

A sudden rapid knock at the door tore them apart and Tarr hastily pulled up his leggings while Fiona scurried off the bed.

"An urgent message in the great hall for you," a servant called out.

"I will be right there."

Fading footsteps told them they were once again alone.

Tarr reached out and wrapped his arm around Fiona's waist and yanked her up against him. "We will finish this."

"Not soon enough for me."

He laughed and kissed her, and together they went to the great hall.

Raynor and Oleg waited near the dais along with one of Tarr's warriors.

"Shamus, what are you doing here?" Tarr asked as he approached.

"The Wolf has attacked the keep again."

"Damage done?"

"Minor with no lives lost, but the clan MacElder have sent word that they are being troubled by a bordering clan and ask for help."

Tarr turned to Raynor. "We leave within the hour."

"I and some of my warriors will go with you," Raynor said. "And do not bother to argue. You do not know who may lie in wait along the trail. And I want my sisters safe."

Tarr raised a brow.

"I lost them once, I will not lose them again," Raynor said in defense of his actions.

Oleg stepped forward. "Accept his help, please. I would feel safer knowing my son escorts his sisters. Then Anya and I will follow in a few days along with family so that we all may celebrate your wedding."

"I honor your request, Oleg, but once Fiona is my wife, I will see to her protection."

"As it should be."

Anya hurried to her husband's side. "I heard as I entered the hall. You cannot wake Aliss; she finally rests comfortably. Leave her with us, we will bring her."

"The decision rests with Aliss," Tarr said.

Anya turned pleading eyes to Fiona.

"Aliss would not leave me behind without a word and I would do the same for her."

Anya relented with a nod. "She will go with you; you two are inseparable, perhaps a cart so that she can rest?"

"A cart would slow us, but if Aliss is not strong enough—"

"Aliss needs no cart," Fiona said, irritated they should think her sister weak. "She is strong and will ride along with me as always."

She turned and marched out of the hall.

"She defends her sister like a mother cub," Raynor said.

"Well, what do you expect?" Anya snapped at her son. "She is the older one and feels responsible."

Raynor shook his head. "She is only ten minutes older."

Anya walked up to her son shaking her finger. "Those ten minutes seemed like ten years to me, and gives my daughter the right to claim the title of older sister and protector."

Raynor held up his hands in surrender. "Whatever you say, Mother."

"See that food is prepared for their journey while I go help my daughters."

Oleg grinned at Tarr as Anya left the hall. "I told you Fiona was like her mother."

Fiona hated waking her sister but as soon as she explained the circumstances, Aliss was out of bed gathering her things.

"I look forward to a permanent home," Aliss said on

a yawn, while she finished placing the last of her healing herbs that had been drying on the table in her basket.

"I will see that you have a fine room in the keep."

"You are happy; I can see it on your face." She smiled, pleased for her sister.

"Love is grand. You will see for yourself when you find it."

Aliss did not bother to reiterate her intentions to remain free of a burdensome husband. Fiona was set on her being as happy as she, so there was no point in disappointing her.

To avoid a confrontation she returned to her sister's previous remark. "About a room in the keep?"

"I would prefer my own cottage," Aliss said.

Fiona dropped the garment in her hand. "You want to live away from me?"

Aliss went to her, the shocked expression on her sister's face making her feel guilty. "It is not that. I wish time to work with my herbs and help heal those in need. It would be best if I had my own cottage, then the ill could seek me out day or night without disturbing you and Tarr. I would still be close by."

"Maybe you are right."

It was Aliss's turn to appear shocked. Her sister agreed much too easily.

"Tarr and I will need time alone. Your own cottage may be just what you need. After all I can see you any time I want."

Aliss giggled. "You enjoy making love with him."

Fiona hugged herself and grinned. "It is amazing, and more amazing I want him all the time."

"Then you do not need me in the way."

"You are right, that is why you shall have a cottage," Fiona agreed hastily.

"I had expected you to be stubborn about it," Aliss said, returning to her packing.

"I am feeling generous instead of stubborn."

"I think passion rules your decision."

The twins laughed as a knock sounded at the door and they both bid the person entrance.

Anya entered with teary eyes. "I came to help." She burst into tears.

Aliss and Fiona went to her and helped her to a chair.

"I am sorry," Anya said sighing heavily. "It is just that I have finally found you both and again you are taken from me."

"You will be with us in a few days time," Fiona reminded her.

"I know." She looked from one twin to the other, tears continuing to fall. "I just want to get to know you both. You are my daughters and I know so little about you. I had hoped sometime today we would talk and now . . ."

Fiona crouched down beside her. "I punched a little boy when I was six for pushing Aliss."

"He landed on his backside crying and I helped him up," Aliss said.

Fiona shook her head. "She forever tended people, even ones who did not deserve it."

Anya laughed and listened as her daughters' lives unfolded in story after story.

The door suddenly burst open and in walked Tarr followed by Raynor.

"Told you," Raynor said with a grin to Tarr.

"An hour," Tarr said to Fiona. "I told you we would leave within the hour and here you sit chatting."

Fiona walked over to him. "We are ready. We were waiting for you to finish."

"I have been ready and waiting for you in the great hall."

"It is you who has delayed our departure," Fiona accused with a grin.

Aliss approached the bickering couple. "Let us be on our way. I look forward to returning home. Is the weather good for our journey?"

She chatted endlessly as they left the bedchamber and entered the great hall, and did not stop until they had mounted the horses and were ready to leave.

Raynor rode over to her. "You must surely be winded by now, though your chatter did the trick. It got everyone moving without further arguing." He laughed.

"Hold strong to your humor, dear brother, for it is now your turn to mediate the loving couple."

His laughter ended abruptly.

They rode off leaving a tearful Oleg and Anya waving after them.

The journey was tedious and long, Tarr refusing to stop, insisting that they would travel straight through the night so that by midmorning they would be home. No one objected. It seemed as if the return journey was long overdue.

Aliss fought the yawns that frequently attacked her and the fatigue that racked her body. She did not wish to delay the journey, and besides she was looking forward to finally settling down to a normal existence. No more charade. No more worry of what was to become of them. They were together and they would stay that way.

Tarr finally relented and allowed them to stop for a couple of hours of rest, but Aliss felt as if she no sooner had closed her eyes than she was being shaken awake. She reminded herself that they would be home soon, that she would sleep the rest of the day and the entire night away.

Several hours after midday they approached the keep.

Aliss rode behind Fiona and Tarr, Raynor following at the rear with his men.

Aliss had kept her eye on the dark gray cloud that looked about ready to burst. It had trailed them for the last hour, and now the rumble of thunder in the distance convinced her the storm was about to descend.

They had arrived just in time, the thought of a blazing hearth and warm bed had her smiling. She was about to call out to Fiona when suddenly she was hit with great force on the side of her head, and as she toppled to the ground the world went black.

Chapter 28

The warriors' frantic shouts had Fiona and Tarr turning simultaneously, their hands reaching for their swords.

Fiona froze for a moment, her heartbeat stilled and her breath caught in her throat. Aliss lay crumpled and lifeless on the ground, her bold red hair covering her face. She shook herself into action and bolted off her mare. In seconds she was on her knees at her sister's side, her hands anxious yet hesitant to touch her.

She could be dead.

The dire thought froze every muscle in her body and tears crept into her eyes. She refused to surrender to either weakness and forced herself to gently brush her sister's hair away from her face.

She gasped. "Oh my God."

Tarr dropped to his haunches beside her and Raynor fell to his knees opposite them.

"An arrow has gashed her temple," Raynor said.

Tarr exchanged knowing glances with Raynor before he stood. "Tend her while I see to the culprit." He marched off.

Fiona shook her fear away and sprang into action. She began tearing the hem of her skirt. "I need to stop the bleeding and see if the wound needs stitching."

"Can you stitch?" Raynor asked, gently peeling away strands of blood-soaked hair from the wound.

"Not as good as Aliss, but sufficient enough." Fiona grimaced when she finally cleared the wound of blood enough to examine the gash. "The excessive blood has made it appear worse then it is. The arrow merely grazed her skin, the bone is not exposed."

"This is good?"

Fiona nodded. "The worry now is that it will fester. Aliss spent much time cleansing wounds; she felt it important."

"If it festers?"

"Fever usually sets in. Aliss does all she can to draw the poison out of the wound; sometimes she is lucky other times she is not."

"So what do we do?"

"Clean the wound with fresh water, bandage it and"—she choked on her words—"pray that she wakes up."

Tarr watched Fiona from a distance. He wanted to go to her, take her in his arms and absorb her pain. But she would not appreciate interference now while she tended her sister. She would expect him to see that whoever did this was apprehended and punished.

He had every intention of doing just that for the coward that did this was surely a fool to think that he could penetrate Hellewyk's borders, harm a member of the clan, and escape unscathed.

Tarr tempered his rage, losing it would do him no good. He must keep reason clear and his mind sharp so that he could outwit this man who dared to challenge him so blatantly.

"Shamus," he called out, and the young man hurried to his side. "Ride to the keep and inform Kirk of what has happened, also tell him that we require a cart and more men."

Shamus took off on his horse and Tarr's glance was once again drawn to Fiona. She hovered over her sister, protectively administering to her gently. That she feared losing her was obvious, and he suddenly regretted ever trying to separate them.

They possessed a special bond he had come to understand and respect. He would not force them apart; he would provide for Aliss as if she were his own sister. He would do this because he respected and admired Aliss and because of his love for Fiona. He wanted her happy and content, and that would not be possible without her sister's presence.

He directed his horse over to Fiona and as he approached he could see her hands tremble and noticed how she nibbled at her bottom lip in worry. She had bandaged Aliss's head and blood was seeping through the cloth.

Fiona's head jerked up and her green eyes implored him for help.

"I sent for a cart and more men. We will get her home safely so that she may heal."

"She needs to wake up," Fiona nearly shouted on the verge of tears. She glanced down at her sister. "Do you hear me, Aliss, wake up!"

Raynor stood and reached out to calm her but she rejected him, jerking her arm away.

"Nay, she will listen to me and wake up," Fiona shouted louder.

Tarr dismounted and approached her slowly. "When Aliss is ready, she will wake up."

"*She,*" Fiona pointed to her sister, "will wake up now." She pounded her fisted hand against her palm. "I insist. Wake up now, Aliss. *Now.*" Fear chilled her bones and she shivered. "She must wake up. Oh, God, please let her wake up."

Tarr went to her side, and though she tried to deny his comfort, pushing him away with flaying hands, she finally crumbled in his arms and wept against his chest.

"Quiet!"

The forceful shout surprised them all.

"My head hurts," Aliss said more softly.

Fiona was instantly at her side as was Raynor.

"An arrow pierced your skin and you still bleed," Fiona said, then hurriedly asked, "What do I do?"

"Stitches?" Aliss winced as she raised her hand to touch the wound. "If the bleeding does not stop soon"—she paused for a breath—"you will need to stitch the wound."

"I am not good with a needle," Fiona protested.

"Do what must be done." She took a breath. "I am weak and may not remain conscious long. Follow these instructions."

A shout sounded for Tarr that riders approached, and with a quick look to Raynor to watch over the women, he hurried off.

When Aliss finished, she barely had a breath left in her.

Fiona took firm hold of her sister's hand. "You will be fine, I will see to it."

She watched Aliss's eyes as they drifted shut.

"She needs rest," Raynor said.

"You reason while I worry."

"I try to look at this as Aliss would, and do what she would do. She did the same for me once and saved my life."

"Aliss knows what to do." Fiona shook her head. "I fear I do not know enough."

"She instructed you and I listened well. I can help you." He reached out and placed his hand over hers and Aliss's. "We will save our sister together."

"Forgive me. It will take time for me to realize I have a brother who truly cares."

"Do not worry," Raynor grinned. "I shall not let either of you forget it."

"Aliss will be all right," Fiona said with certainty, yet she wanted Raynor to confirm it.

He obliged with a hasty, "She will be her old self in no time."

Fiona turned a sad smile on her brother. "We both attempt to convince."

"Better than to think the worst." Raynor shook his

head, glancing down at Aliss. "The bleeding does not subside. You need to stitch the wound now."

"What has happened?" A shrill screech ripped through the silent chilled air.

Raynor and Fiona turned to see Anya rushing toward them. Her purple cloak flew out behind her and her green eyes were wide with fright.

Raynor stood shocked to see his mother. She immediately went down on her knees beside her daughter. "Mother, what are you doing here? Where is father? How did you get here?"

"Your uncle Odo arrived shortly after you left and he brought me here. I could not bear to be away from my daughters. Now tell me what has happened to Aliss."

"An arrow has grazed her temple," Fiona explained, and wondered over a sudden sense of hope and comfort that rushed over her. It was the same feeling she had gotten when she was little and her mother would tend her when she was sick or wounded. "She slips in and out of consciousness and has told us what must be done."

"Her wound needs stitching," Raynor informed her.

Anya looked to Fiona. "I am talented with a needle."

"Good, for I am not and this must be done now before she loses more blood."

Fiona fetched her sister's healing basket containing a cloth with her various size needles and threads and her pouches of herbs. She instructed Raynor to ask Tarr where the closest water supply was and to bring her a bucketful. Anya prepared her daughter by placing a blanket beneath her head, removing all hair away from the wound, then finally removing the blood-soaked cloth from around her head.

When all was ready, Anya kneeled over her daughter and with skillful hands and a gentle touch she began to stitch the wound.

Fiona remained beside her, dabbing at the wound between stitches as Aliss had taught her to do. Keep it clear of blood she would order Fiona when she had helped her. So with her sister's words strong in her head, she did as she recalled.

It was over and done in a few minutes, to Fiona's relief, and glad she was that her sister was not awake to feel the continuous prick of the needle as five stitches were made in her flesh.

The cart arrived soon after, and Tarr and Raynor saw to moving Aliss while Fiona and Anya cleaned up.

Fiona watched the men carefully, ready to bark her disapproval if they were not cautious with Aliss. She needed tender care and a watchful eye, which was why she intended to ride in the cart with her sister and—

Her thought was interrupted by a strong squeeze to her arm. Her glance drifted to her mother.

"I will ride in the cart with Aliss and watch over her."

A tug, sharp and fast hit her heart. She took care of her sister, no other did.

"Please," Anya pleaded softly. "Let me tend my daughter."

Tarr walked up to stand beside Fiona. "We are ready to leave."

"Mother will ride in the cart with Aliss," Fiona said, the tug at her heart now a dull, persistent ache.

Anya hugged her daughter. "I will take good care of her."

Tarr slide his hand into Fiona's and locked his fingers around hers.

She squeezed tightly. "Things are changing."

"For the better."

"Then why do I feel this ache that chokes my heart?"

"It has just been you and your sister for some time and that is no more. You have a mother, a father, and a brother, and soon you will have a husband. It will no longer be just the two of you."

His remark pitched her deep into her own thoughts, and she remained there as they journeyed to the Hellewyk keep. She rode beside the cart and watched Anya gently cradle Aliss's head in her lap to keep it from bouncing from the ruts and bumps along the dirt road.

She had wondered over Anya's sudden appearance. There was time for that later, when her sister was settled in bed. But then Anya would probably want to keep vigil at her daughter's bedside.

A shout alerted everyone that they neared the keep. When they entered the village surrounding the keep, there was a rush of activity as clansmen and women rushed to offer help and to see how badly their healer was hurt.

Prayers and well wishes were offered as they carried Aliss into the keep. Anya directed Tarr and Raynor to be gentle with her daughter, then chased them from the room after they had carefully placed Aliss on the bed. Anya fussed over her daughter, ordering Fiona to take Aliss's boots off while she heated water in the hearth.

"You will help me get your sister out of her skirt, but we will leave her blouse, the head wound must not be disturbed. Then I will bathe her as best I can and rid her of the dried blood. After you fix the brew Aliss told you of, you will then go eat and rest."

Fiona stared at the woman. "You order much like me."

Anya smiled. "You are my daughter." Her smile faltered. "I love you both very much and I want what was taken from me. I want my daughters, but right now it is Aliss that matters."

Fiona nodded and got busy doing as her mother instructed.

Chapter 29

Tarr was speaking with Raynor in his solar when Fiona entered unannounced and with barely a knock. He was expecting her, though her disheveled appearance made him realize the extent of her trauma. She had feared her twin would die and that was not acceptable to Fiona. She would give her life for her sister and that frightened him.

"Join us," he offered, filling a goblet with wine for her.

She grasped the goblet with both hands and took a generous swallow.

"Aliss is well." It was not a question for he knew the answer—Fiona would not be here if her sister was not resting comfortably.

Fiona nodded. "She rests peacefully and mother looks after her."

"And you?" Raynor asked with obvious concern.

"I want the bastard who did this to my sister."

Tarr smiled. He admired her tenacity and boldness. He reached out and placed a hand on her shoulder. "We will find him."

"Your word?"

"You have my word," Tarr said.

"Mine too," Raynor added.

"Good, for you know if I find him first . . ."

Her words trailed off. She did not need to finish, both men understood Fiona would have no trouble taking the man's life.

Fiona emptied her goblet and held it out to Tarr to refill.

"Have you eaten?" he asked, pouring more wine.

"This morning, I think."

She sounded unsure, and he could understand why. The past few hours were like a bad dream, best forgotten.

"I will have food brought for you."

"I am not hungry."

"You will eat," Tarr ordered.

Fiona took a swallow of wine. "You will not tell me what to do."

"I have every right to tell you what to do. I am to be your husband."

"I want no husband that issues orders."

"When the orders are best for you, you will obey."

"Did you say 'obey'?"

"Mistake," Raynor whispered to Tarr and with that he took his leave, closing the door quietly behind him.

A crack of thunder split the silence, followed by a

sudden pounding of rain against the windows. The sky had darkened considerably, it looked as if night fell upon the land yet it was only late afternoon.

The lone couple remained as they were, staring at each other, until Fiona broke the heavy silence.

"Do you expect obedience from me?"

"I expect you to be you," Tarr answered.

Fiona's shoulders slumped, she looked about ready to collapse, but Tarr's arms were right there to catch her.

"You need to bathe and rest," he said, holding her close.

"Do you tell me I stink?"

"Fiona—"

She looked up at him.

"Shut up."

"I want answers. Someone threatens Aliss and me."

"Leave that to me."

"But—"

"Later," he insisted. "We will discuss this later, when you are rested and can think clearly." He did not give her a chance to argue. He scooped her up into his arms and carried her to his bedchamber, catching a servant in the hall and ordering that a tub of water be prepared for her and food brought.

He no soon as placed her in a chair by the hearth than he was summoned to the great hall.

"Go," she said reluctantly. "I do not need you."

Tarr leaned over her, his hands braced on the arms of the chair. "You need me more than you know." He kissed her and hurried off, promising to return shortly.

In the meantime she tended herself, chasing away the servants who offered her help. She needed no one. She had taken care of herself and her sister since she had been eleven; she needed no one, not a soul.

She wrapped herself in a towel and crawled into bed exhausted from the day that seemed never ending. It should be night, she thought, so she could sleep and rest. It was not right to sleep during the day, though the sky did look more like dusk. There were things that needed attending to, like the threat to Aliss and her. She needed to give it her immediate attention.

She yawned and cuddled beneath the wool blanket, and in seconds fell asleep.

Tarr spoke briefly with Kirk in the great hall, issuing orders meant for their ears alone, before he hurried out of the keep to greet Odo and his men. They had met briefly when he arrived with Anya, but in all the excitement he had had little time to speak with him. When it was made known what had happened, Odo instantly volunteered to search the area for the culprit, hence his delay in arriving at Hellewyk.

Raynor was already greeting his uncle with a bear hug and a slap on the back.

Tarr took note of Odo's size, tall and broad with a full gray beard that seemed to swallow up his mouth. His gray eyes were sharp for a man whose weathered and wrinkled face made him appear well into fifty years.

He dressed like men from the north in furs and leather, and he spoke in a Viking tongue with Raynor, though switched quickly enough to the Scottish tongue on Tarr's approach.

"Your men are diligent, they went over our tracks," Odo said in lieu of a greeting.

Tarr held out his hand. "They obey orders."

Odo grinned and gripped his hand in a firm shake.

Tarr responded, his hand like a vise that refused to let go until finally Odo relented, easing his grip.

"You found nothing?" Tarr asked, directing Odo into the great hall where food and drink awaited him and his men.

"Not a sign or a disturbance," he answered, entering the hall and following Tarr to the dais. His men dispersed to the tables laden with food and drink. They stripped off their fur cloaks and hurried to feast on the inviting banquet.

Tarr took the center seat on the dais while Raynor and Odo flanked him.

As soon as drinks were poured and plates filled, Tarr asked, "Tell me what you know of the twins' abduction."

"There is not much to tell. One day they were safe in their cradles and the next day they were gone."

"What of the slave who kidnapped the twins?"

Odo shrugged. "I knew little about her private life, just that she spent most of her time tending to Anya, Raynor, or the twins."

"She cared for the twins?"

"Aye," Odo said. "She knew her place and her duty."

"Who else could possibly mean the twins harm?" Tarr asked.

Odo shook his head. "We went over the same questions years ago and found no answers. We could find no reason for the abduction. No one would benefit from the twins' disappearance. There simply was no reason for their abduction."

"There had to be a reason," Tarr argued. "And I intend to find it." Then he left Odo feasting with his men and Raynor, and met with Kirk in his solar.

"What have you learned?" he asked his trusted friend.

"Whoever does this, leaves no tracks."

Tarr frowned. "How is that possible? There are always tracks to follow."

"Not with this one. The men have gone over the whole area and have found nothing. They grumble amongst themselves, insisting it is a ghost who haunts the twins."

Tarr pounded his fist on the table. "It is no apparition, but a man of flesh and blood who *hunts* the twins."

"How do we find him if he leaves no tracks?"

"Every hunter leaves a track and we are going to find it."

Tarr crept into his bedchamber after giving further instructions to Kirk. Fiona was curled in his bed sleeping and he did not wish to wake her. He merely wished to make certain she was all right.

He went to the bed, slipping out of his shirt and tossing it to the floor as he went. He would change into a clean one for the evening meal. He tucked the strip of plaid that ran over his shoulder around his waist as he reached the bed.

Fiona was sound asleep and completely naked, the

blanket only partially covering her. One long leg and part of her firm backside lay exposed. Her bright red hair crowned her like a wreath of flames and her cheeks were rosy from their recent scrubbing.

"Beautiful," he whispered, and shedding his plaid and boots he crawled in next to her.

He only wanted to hold her, nothing more. He pressed his body gently to hers and draped his arm over her, sliding his hand beneath the blanket to cup her breast. She was warm and her skin soft and smelling fresh, and it felt so right to be there beside her.

He loved to touch her, but then perhaps it was because of the way she responded to his touch, eagerly and with a sense of excitement that flamed his own already raging desire for her.

She was a woman comfortable with making love and she was adventurous. She had not shied away from his nakedness or his eagerness to please her, and welcomed him and all he had to teach her.

She stirred and her hand joined his at her breast, forcing a gentle squeeze out of him.

He nibbled at her ear. "You are awake."

She wiggled her backside against him. "I was waiting for you to wake."

He trailed kisses down her neck, turning her skin to gooseflesh while his hand left her breast and drifted down between her legs. As his finger slipped inside her he pressed himself hard against her.

"Is that awake enough for you?"

"Mmm, not sure; let me feel that again," she laughed.

He bit playfully along her shoulder as his finger worked a magic that soon had her moaning with pleasure.

"Damn, but I want you," he whispered harshly in her ear, then flipped her around on her back and eased over her.

A sharp knock had them both holding their breaths until Tarr finally called out, "Who goes there?"

"Shamus. You are needed in the hall."

Fiona grabbed his arm and demanded in a whisper. "You will finish this before you go."

He grinned as he shouted. "I will be down shortly."

"Aye," Shamus acknowledged, and walked away.

"I would have liked to take my time with you."

"Tonight when every one is abed, for now"—she reached out and took hold of him and guided him into her— "fast and hard will do."

Tarr obliged entering her with a solid thrust that had her tossing her head back and moaning. Her moans grew as he plunged into her time and time again, and when he emptied into her she joined him, her head spinning, her heart thumping, and her body tingling with satisfaction.

He lay on his back a moment regaining his breath, his hand reaching out to take hers.

"That felt wonderful," Fiona exclaimed with a smile. "I do not even feel tired anymore." She hopped out of bed and stood with her hands on her naked hips. "I will dress and go see how Aliss is, then join you in the hall."

Tarr sat up, swinging his legs off the bed to sit on the edge. "We best wed quickly for you are bound to get with child soon."

Her hand rushed to cover her stomach. "How exciting to think that I could now be carrying your child." She hurried over and threw herself at him.

He caught her and they fell back on the bed together.

She snuggled her face against his. "I would be proud to carry your child."

"I am pleased to hear you say that, but I will worry endlessly about you."

She sat up on top of him. "Why? I am strong and healthy and I will push that babe right out."

His hands went around her waist as he laughed. "I bet you will, but I still fear—"

She poked him in the chest. "What do you fear?"

He pulled himself up so that their noses were touching. "I fear losing you."

Her hands ran up his arms to grab hold near his shoulders. "I am not going anywhere. You are stuck with me for a very long time."

"Promise?" he asked with desperation.

"Aye, I promise you, Tarr of Hellewyk, that I will live a long life with you, and when it is my time to go I will expect you to follow."

He placed a sweet gentle kiss on her lips. "I will follow you, Fiona, whether it is heaven or hell you go to."

She laughed, hugged him, and slid off him to kneel between his legs. "Mmm," she murmured, and slowly traced her lips with her tongue. "I wish we had more time."

He shut his eyes and ordered, "Get dressed."

She laughed again and did as he said, but not before running a hand over him.

Tarr kept his eyes closed. "Let me know when you are dressed."

"Coward," she teased, hurrying into her garments but sauntered to the door as she laced the ties to her blouse. "I am done."

He opened his eyes.

"Not with you, though. Tonight I shall have my way with you." And with another lick of her lips, she scooted out the door with a laugh.

Fiona did not stay long at her sister's beside. It was not necessary. Anya was fussing over Aliss like a mother hen tending a favorite chick. She had cleaned Aliss and combed her hair, tying it to the side away from the wound. A light blanket covered her and she checked her head at least three times for fever while Fiona spoke with her.

That she enjoyed tending her daughter was obvious, and that she intended to let no one interfere was also obvious, so Fiona left her to fuss.

She hurried down the stairs eager to learn why Tarr had been summoned to the great hall and grinning over what had delayed him.

Her grin soon vanished when she entered the hall to see the solemn faces on Tarr, Kirk, and Raynor, the three men present. A shiver ran through her, something was wrong and she worried that it had to do with her and Aliss.

She raced forward and took hold of Tarr's arm. "What is wrong?"

"The stable lad who took your mare to tend on your

arrival has discovered that your saddle strap has been slashed near through to the end."

Fiona stared at him for a moment, comprehension dawning like a bright rising sun that blinded then shed light.

She nodded slowly. "Then it is so, someone wants Aliss and me dead."

Chapter 30

The sun was rising though bleak clouds and a cold wind whistled past the window, reminding that the weather this far north was often unpredictable, bright sun one moment, freezing rain the next.

Fiona stood in front of the window watching the fast-moving clouds swallow the debuting sun, and wrapped her shawl more tightly around her naked body. She gave a quick glance over her shoulder to see that Tarr still slept, his large body sprawled across the bed. Of course if she were in the bed he would be wrapped around her. It was now like that when they slept; it was as if they were one, forever entwined.

She sighed and turned to look out the window once again. She had awakened just before sunrise, unable to sleep any longer; her mind heavy with thoughts and her heart weighted with sorrow.

Who could possibly want twin babes dead? They could harm none.

Raynor was in line to inherit the leadership of the Blackshaw clan, while the sisters would be absorbed into other clans once they wed. Perhaps their abduction was a spiteful act against Anya and Oleg?

She shivered and hugged herself as the drafty room took on a decisive chill from the relenting wind. She should return to the warm bed and the heat of Tarr's body, but she felt restless with her nagging thoughts and would only disturb him.

Normally she would ride her mare when she felt like this and had the need to clear her head. But she had given Tarr her word that she would not ride off on her own, and besides, it would be a foolish thing to do when she knew that someone hunted her.

She closed her eyes and shook her head. At the moment there was little to do but think and worry. She was good at thinking while worry irritated her, it usually set her into action. For this situation, she was not sure what type of action was called for, so she silently recited a prayer for her sister's speedy recovery.

Aliss could reason better than she, and would know what to do.

Her eyes sprang open as she was suddenly wrapped in strong arms and ensconced with Tarr in a warm wool blanket. He tugged at her shawl and she released it to drop at her feet. He drew her back against him and she welcomed his heat. It drifted through her body, chasing the chill away and toasting her flesh.

"You will make a good husband; you keep me warm."

He nibbled playfully at her ear. "I prefer you hot."

"Keep that up and you will ignite me."

He stopped after placing a kiss on her cheek. "Something bothers you. I can hear it in your voice. You and Aliss are safe, you have my word."

"How can we be safe when we do not know who pursues us? He could be in this keep right now, planning his next attack."

"If you believed that, you would be at your sister's side this instant."

"Anya would not hesitate to kill anyone who dared to threaten Aliss's safety. She will not lose her daughter twice. She is the best guard Aliss could have at the moment."

"You have not considered Anya a threat?"

"Briefly, but I dismissed it. You can see the pain she has suffered these many years in her eyes and the relief of finding us. Have you not determined the same yourself?"

He hugged her and pressed his cheek to hers. "We think alike and reach the same conclusions. We make a good match."

"It took you long enough to realize that."

"It took me?" he asked with an incredulous laugh.

"Aye, but I forgive you your stubbornness."

"My stubbornness?" His laughter continued.

"In time you will learn patience."

Tarr laughed, sputtered words that made no sense, then laughed again.

"It takes a strong man to admit his weaknesses."

When his laughter finally subsided, he whispered in her ear. "I have but one weakness—you."

She turned in his arms and took his face in her hands. "I love you, and do you know why?"

"Tell me."

She kissed him first, tenderly as if in gratitude. "Because you love me for who I am: stubborn, impatient, sometimes impossibly willful, but all of me—*Fiona*—and you often do it with a smile. That smile tells me how much you care." She pushed up at the corners of his mouth. "Even when it's barely a smile, I see it there and it fills my heart with joy."

Her fingers fell away as his smile grew freely.

"You make me happy; I cannot help but smile."

"And you make me happy, *more happy* than I ever thought possible."

"I have been told love does that to you, now I know it is true," he said, and kissed her.

She responded as always and they were soon laughing between kisses as they stumbled together to the bed.

A knock interrupted them.

"What do you want?" Fiona snapped irritated.

"Sorry to disturb," Raynor said with a chuckle from the other side of the door. "Aliss wakes and wishes to talk with you."

"She is well?" Fiona asked anxiously.

"Aye, but she is eager to see you," Raynor said.

"Tell her I will be right there."

Raynor acknowledged with, "I'll go to talk with my men. I will see you later."

Tarr dropped the blanket that held them together. "Go, your sister needs you."

"You will make a very good husband. I am glad I picked you."

He shook his head and dressed along with her.

"Come with me?" she invited as they left the bedchamber.

"Aliss asked for you."

Fiona took his hand. "We are one now; her summons would be for both of us."

"You are so sure?"

"It is how I would feel if Aliss were wed and since we are twins and think alike." She tugged at his hand. "Come. She is eager to see us."

Aliss was sitting up in bed, a white cloth wrapped around her head and not a speck of blood soaking through. Her cheeks were rosy, her eyes alert, and she was smiling.

"Fiona," Aliss cried out happily, "Mother is spoiling me."

"And happy I am that I can do it," Anya said and moved out of the chair beside the bed, leaving it for Fiona.

Fiona hurried to hug her sister. "You heal well?"

"Mother has done a good job tending me. She keeps the wound covered and clean, bathes my face with cool water to keep the fever away, and makes certain I drink the brew I instructed you to make. I feel good, though I still must be watchful and not do more than I should."

"Which is why she will remain abed a few more days," Anya said firmly.

"Who can tell me what happened?" Aliss asked. "No one has spoken of the incident to me."

Fiona had no intention of keeping anything from her sister. Ignorance of the situation would only prove dangerous.

Obviously Tarr felt the same way since he answered, "We believe the arrow was meant to kill you. We have also learned that someone cut the straps to Fiona's saddle, and if not found it would surely have meant her death."

"Fiona and I thought this might happen."

Anya did not look surprised. "We all worried over it."

"Has any progress been made in finding the culprit?" Aliss asked.

"It is like chasing a ghost," Anya answered.

"I do not believe in ghosts," Tarr said.

"They are real, I tell you," Anya insisted, and sat on the edge of the bed. "I saw one."

Fiona squatted down beside her mother. "What did you see?"

"Months after you girls disappeared, I woke one night to see Shona standing beside my bed. She told me the twins were safe and I should not worry. Then she was gone."

"She said nothing else?" Fiona asked.

Anya scrunched her eyes as if trying hard to remember, then all of a sudden her eyes rounded. "She made a sign in the air with her finger before she disappeared."

"What sign?"

"A protective sign, the sign Giann the prophetess would make on entering and leaving our home."

"Why would she do that?" Tarr asked.

"I assumed to protect us."

"Where can Giann be found?" Tarr asked.

"I do not know. She travels the land and goes from village to village. I have not seen her in many months, *though*," she said, startled by her own realization, "it is said she favors the Wolf clan."

"Not a friendly clan," Tarr said.

"But Giann is a generous woman. She goes where her skills are needed, perhaps if we let word out that her skill is needed here in Hellewyk, she would appear?" Aliss suggested.

Fiona stood and shook her head. "It could take time to reach her. We need information now."

"True, but it is worth a try," Tarr said. "Anya, who in your clan sought Giann's skills?"

"Many went to her."

"Anyone more than another?"

She thought, nodded, then slowly shook her head. "Odo spent much time with her, though it was more because he favored her, and not for her skills."

"Still, he may be able to tell us something that would help," Fiona said. "Was Giann around when we were abducted?"

"Nay, she had left before you girls were born, though she predicted the birth of twin girls for me."

"Did you seek her skill to help find us?" Aliss asked.

"Odo did. Giann confirmed it was the slave Shona who abducted the twins, and she said they were taken far away. That was all she could tell us before she took her leave. I had hoped for more and wished she would remain with us just in case she was needed. But she had other matters to tend to, and she was a free woman; we could not force her to stay. When next I saw Giann she told me you girls were safe, but refused to say any more." Anya grew upset. "You do not think she had something to do with the kidnapping, do you?"

"She knew more than she told," Tarr said.

"Why keep it from me?"

"That is a good question," Tarr said. "I will leave so that you three may talk." He hurried out of the room.

"Such a sudden departure," Aliss said, curious.

"I agree," Anya added.

"He is up to something and I intend to find out." Fiona fled the room.

Tarr braced himself against the wall at the top of the stairs and waited. He did not expect it to take long; Fiona should be following him in mere minutes. He heard her approach, though he had to admit she was quiet. Most would probably not hear her gentle footfalls, but his father had trained him to hear not only in the chaos but in the silence as well.

As she rounded the corner, his arm reached out and caught her around the middle.

"You set a trap," she accused, and shoved his arm away. "You knew I would follow because you are obviously up to something."

"You are angry that I caught you, not that I set a trap and I realized Giann is the key to this mystery? I wanted to speak with Odo about her."

"I have not been snared since I was young, and father taught me the skill of avoiding capture. You should have told me that."

"Why would he teach you such a thing?"

"It was a game to us, nothing more, and do not change the subject."

"Forget that for now, I think I have discovered something more important. It was much more than a game," Tarr said. "He was preparing you."

"Preparing me?" Fiona glared at Tarr. "That would mean—"

"He knew this day would come."

While the news surely must have shocked Fiona, she remained calm. "Why would he not have told Aliss and me?"

"You were probably too young to fully comprehend the situation."

"Keeping us ignorant of it certainly was not wise."

"Preparing you to defend and avoid capture was definitely wise," Tarr said, "and if you think back to what your parents taught you girls, they prepared you well for the future. One of you defends and the other heals."

"Then it can be assumed that the slave Shona confided the truth to my parents."

"I would agree with that. Raynor spoke to me of the love the slave had for him and the twins. She would do whatever was necessary to protect them," Tarr said and took her hand. "Let us see what else he can tell us of Shona."

"And Odo, we must speak with him about Giann," Fiona said.

Tarr turned to descend the stairs, but Fiona tugged him back.

"A kiss," she demanded with a smile. "I miss your lips on mine."

His hand grasped her cheek, his thumb stroking her lips. "There will be no other lips but mine on yours."

"I want no other lips but yours." She grimaced. "The thought of another man kissing me makes me ill." She poked his chest. "I would gut any man who attempted to kiss me and—"

He kissed her silent, and he did not relent until he felt her body melt against him. Then he tugged and nipped along her bottom lip and whispered, "Promise to let me protect you now and again?"

"Perhaps."

He nuzzled her neck, sending gooseflesh racing over her. "You will let me protect you or else . . ." He stopped nuzzling.

There was laughter in her green eyes when she looked up at him. "Do I detect a threat? Perhaps you think to keep your favors from me if I do not comply?"

"I did not say—" He gasped, her hand grabbing hold of his loins and stirring them to attention.

"A useless threat," she laughed, squeezing the hard length of him. "We both know you cannot resist me."

He grabbed her hand. "You play with danger."

She licked her lips. "I like danger."

That was enough for him. He grabbed her, swung her over his shoulder and turned to take the steps when he heard voices coming their way. He put her down reluctantly.

"We are not finished."

Her grin was wide. "You are right; I have just started."

She sauntered down the steps leaving him to stare at her swinging backside and grow more lustful as his imagination went wild.

She stopped, the voices near, and mouthed, *I want to taste you.*

He rushed to her side. "You will pay for this."

"Promise?" She laughed with delight and was still laughing when Raynor and Kirk came into sight.

Chapter 31

Fiona had not only teased Tarr but herself as well. She was ready for him, not just moist but wet and aching. When he had tossed her over his shoulder, her passion spiked like a flame to a dry log. He could not get her to his bedchamber fast enough to her way of thinking.

Unfortunately they never made it there, and now here she sat in the great hall at a trestle table near the hearth with Tarr beside her and Raynor and Kirk across from them, discussing what?

Damn. She needed to pay better attention, but her passion refused to abate. Of course, Tarr's leg pressing against hers did not help any.

It was only a leg, she told herself, but *damn, damn, damn,* if the heat of him did not penetrate her skirt or his muscle did not grow taut, relax then grow taut again. And why should all that excite her?

Because she wanted him so badly she could scream. Lord, did she enjoy making love with this man.

The clatter of tankards and pitchers being placed on the table interrupted her musings, and she silently scolded herself for getting lost in desire when there were more important matters to discuss.

"What do you know of Giann?" Tarr asked Raynor.

"That her predictions always prove true. Odo is more familiar with her than I am. She spoke with me only once, and her prophecy came true."

"She predicted our reunion?" Fiona asked curious.

"She predicted that *I* would find my sisters." He frowned. "Strange that I should just recall that she warned me to tell no one of this."

"This Giann knows much and yet she is out of our reach," Tarr said frustrated.

"That has never stopped you before," Kirk challenged.

"Odo could help us," Raynor suggested. "He knows Giann well."

"That I do," Odo said, entering from the shadows near the entrance to the hall.

"Sit," Tarr offered, "and tell me what you know of this Giann."

"I concur with Raynor," Odo said, and instead of sitting he stood near the hearth. "Her predictions always ring true as Raynor has proved."

"What had she told you of the twins' abduction?" Tarr asked.

"Not enough to offer any hope of finding them,

though obviously with her words to Raynor, she had known they would be found."

"Giann is the key to this mystery," Fiona said.

"Is it known where she resides?" Kirk asked.

Odo answered. "The Wolf clan is probably where you will find her. She favors the people there."

Fiona watched the way Odo's eyes shifted around the room, looking at everyone whether he spoke to them or not. He was a man much aware of his surroundings, and prepared. She noticed he made certain to stand with his back protected by the hearth and a weapon lodged in his belt.

"My brother and I have spent years trying to find the twins and when Raynor grew old enough, he joined us," Odo said proudly. He looked to his nephew. "I remember when he was eight and had practiced with a sword all day until his hands blistered. He informed me quite seriously that he intended to find his sisters and bring them home safely, then he would find the person responsible and kill him."

"My sisters are safe," Raynor said. "It is now time for me to complete the promise I made to myself. I will journey to the Wolf clan and find Giann."

"You will not." Fiona's tongue was sharp and adamant.

"Well, that does that," Tarr smirked. "You are not going."

"The choice is mine," Raynor said firmly.

"It certainly is not."

The voice was not Fiona's but it sounded enough like her, and Fiona smiled at her mother as she approached the table.

"I finally have my family all together and together they will stay."

"This is important, Mother," Raynor said attempting reason.

Anya looked to her brother-in-law. "You go, Odo."

Raynor attempted to protest. "I—"

Anya did not give her son a chance. "Odo is friends with Giann. It is better he goes."

"I will gladly go," Odo said, stepping forward.

A debate began to rage amongst the men as to who should go, with Anya insisting her son was not going. While the heated discussion continued, Fiona slipped away, though not before Tarr caught her eye and nodded, letting her know he was aware of her departure.

Fiona went to see her sister. Aliss was practical, always looking at all sides of a discussion and determining the best approach and solution.

Aliss was sitting at the table sorting through herbs. "Thank goodness it is you. I feared mother's return."

"Feared?" Fiona queried.

"Not real fear," Aliss attempted to explain. "Fear of her constant fussing and insisting I remain in bed. I need to move around and do something. I know when to rest and besides—"

"You do not like being the one who is ill."

"I abhor it. And to lie abed all day?" She shivered and shook her head. "I cannot abide it."

"I trust you know what you do so I will not argue with you."

"Oh, thank you so much, Fiona," Aliss sighed. "Someone who finally agrees with me. Sit and tell me what goes on."

Fiona plopped in a chair and watched her sister skillfully blend a variety of herbs that would eventually be used to make potions and salves. She forever worked to perfect her talent and expand her knowledge, seeking advice from the older women of the clans and determining whether it was myth or fact they shared with her.

That was probably what made her view everything with reason. With facts and sound judgment, Aliss felt solutions could be reached for all.

"It seems that this prophetess Giann may be the key to our kidnapping, which means it would be worth our while to speak with her."

"The problem is that she resides with the unfriendly Wolf clan, as mother mentioned." Aliss shrugged. "An easy solution to two problems."

Fiona shook her head. "Easy? Two problems?"

"This Wolf has something that Tarr wants, and it seems that Tarr has something this Wolf wants. An exchange seems the solution."

"That does make sense." Fiona sat straight.

"Simple things often do."

"What if this Wolf does not agree?"

"Then he looks for something Tarr would not be willing to give. Either way, Tarr will have gained knowledge of his enemy that he did not have before."

"Good point." Fiona reached out and began helping her sister sort the herbs.

"You do not think of going in search of this Giann, do you?"

"I gave it thought."

"Leave it thought," Aliss ordered. "It is not a wise choice."

"I determined that myself, but sitting here waiting for something to happen is not a wise choice either."

"You do not think we are safe here?"

Fiona stopped sorting and smiled.

"Do not think to lie to me."

Fiona's smile faded quick enough. "It was a fleeting thought."

Aliss chuckled. "You do not lie well."

Fiona looked affronted. "I can when necessary."

"Not really," Aliss affirmed, her chuckle having turned to a wide grin. "You are much too blunt and honest to lie."

"Well, being blunt and honest can get you into just as much trouble as lying can."

"There are times people do not want to hear the truth."

"Too bad," Fiona said. "It does no good being ignorant of the truth."

"It would seem that mother and father thought ignorance of our situation was best for us."

"I would think that too, except that Tarr pointed out how mother and father actually prepared us both for what we might face."

Aliss stopped sorting. "I never thought of it that way, but Tarr is right. Mother encouraged me to learn all I could about healing—"

"And father taught and encouraged me to defend."

"They knew our lives were in danger," Aliss said.

The twins grew silent, both lost in memories.

Aliss spoke after several minutes of silence. "Mother was insistent that we stay together until we marry."

"Actually she was insistent about us marrying. Remember how she would repeatedly tell us to find good husbands who would provide and protect."

"She would get so upset when I would insist I did not want to wed," Aliss said.

"She knew we were in danger and that husbands would protect us."

Aliss caught a yawn with her hand.

"You should rest."

"You are right. All this thought has made my head ache."

Fiona followed her sister to the bed and tucked her in. "I will make certain no one harms us."

"Father prepared you well to see to our safety." Another yawn had Aliss closing her eyes.

Fiona stood beside the bed watching Aliss drift off to sleep, her words repeating in Fiona's head. They echoed Tarr's, and a sudden thought came to her. What if she and Aliss were purposely taken to Peter and Eleanor, the parents who raised them? What if it was their purpose to prepare the twins for the future? What if this whole thing had been planned from before their birth?

Fiona hurried to find Tarr.

She discovered he was at the storehouse with Kirk and was about to rush out of the keep when her mother insisted she put on a wool cloak.

"You will catch a chill," Anya said, draping a green wool cloak over Fiona's shoulders. "The day is gray and cold."

Memories tugged at Fiona's heart. She recalled how her mother had fussed over her, made sure she had been warm, hugged her to her warm body when Fiona had been chilled. She felt safe and secure in her mother's arms, and there had been times she could not wait to feel them wrap around her.

How Anya's arms must have ached for those moments with her daughters.

"That is better," Anya said, closing the cloak over Fiona's chest. "Now you will be warm."

"Thank you, Mother."

Anya looked teary-eyed. "Go, perhaps later you will share some of Aliss's special brew of hot cider with me. She instructed me on how to prepare it and promised I would enjoy it."

"It is perfect for a cold day. It chases the chill out of the bones."

"Good, I will expect you later in Aliss's room so that we may share it all together."

"I will be there," Fiona said and almost turned to leave but stopped, stepped forward, and hugged her mother tightly. Anya returned the affection and Fiona could feel her reluctance to let go, and she understood it. The fear of losing her daughters would always haunt her.

"Until later," Anya said, and hesitantly turned away and hurried off.

Fiona watched her brave retreat and admired her strength. Aliss and she were actually lucky. They had a wonderful mother who raised them with love, and now they had another mother who was as equally wonderful and loving.

Fiona braved the gray day with a smile and went to find Tarr.

* * *

"You cannot mean to do this," Kirk said.

"What choice do I have?" Tarr asked, looking over his shoulder to see if anyone approached the storehouse. Once inside with the door partially left ajar for sufficient light and to watch that no one lingered about, he told Kirk of his intentions. He, Tarr, would go meet with the leader of the Wolf clan.

"Let someone go in your place."

"Who?" Tarr frowned, his own frustration annoying him. "I do not know who to trust."

"Anyone in the clan would—"

"Would not be received well by the leader of the Wolf clan," Tarr argued. "And while I believe I can trust Raynor and his parents, I will not chance that I may be wrong and place my future wife and her sister in the hands of those who wish them harm."

"So you go alone into the clutches of your enemy." Kirk shook his head. "I do not agree with this plan of yours."

"This Wolf attacks us but inflicts little damage. It seems he wants something from me and now I want something from him. We will see what can be agreed upon."

"I thought the man Odo agreed to go find this Giann."

"How do I trust him to do as he says?"

"Send some of our warriors with him," Kirk said.

Tarr shook his head. "I do not want secondhand information. I will hear the truth from this Giann, not through anyone else."

"Have Giann brought here."

"If she favors the Wolf clan, then they offer her protection. I will speak to her directly and learn the secrets that have been kept hidden all these years."

"At least take someone with you, do not go alone," Kirk urged.

"I would then be perceived as a threat; if I travel alone the leader will know I wish only to talk with him."

"This is not a good time for you to be away from the clan. There is the trouble with the MacElder borders—"

"You know that I have already dispatched a troop of warriors to help quell the disturbance along the borders and to show proof that the MacElder and Hellewyk clans unite. Your other concern for summoning me home pertained to the Wolf clan. You mentioned that they scout the area, which means another attack is imminent. My meeting with the leader may prevent that attack."

"Still, you place yourself in grave danger. At least take one other with you," Kirk suggested, then added quickly. "Take Raynor, two warriors from different clans would appear a possible truce."

The door suddenly swung open and Fiona stood hands on hips. "I go if you go."

Tarr rolled his eyes and shook his head. "I will not argue this with you, Fiona."

"Good, then we have no problem. I am ready to leave when you are."

"You are not going!"

"Then neither are you!"

Tarr marched over to her and planted his face in front of hers. "You will not dictate to me."

"Nor you to me."

"You will obey me on this."

Kirk cringed and slowly slipped out the door.

"Obey? I owe you no obedience."

"You will be my wife—"

"I am not your wife yet," she emphasized.

"You change your mind?" he challenged.

"A stupid question."

"Why?"

Fiona stabbed his chest with her finger. "Because I love you and just because you make dumb decisions, it does not mean I will stop loving you or love you any less. You can, however, count on me to let you know when you are foolish."

Tarr grabbed her face and kissed her lips. "I love when you tell me you love me."

"Do not change the subject."

He pulled her close and rubbed his body against hers. "I think we should finish what we started before."

"After this matter is settled."

He leaned down to nuzzle her neck but her hand stopped him.

"You go, I go. I will have your word on this."

"You know I cannot do that."

She pulled away from him.

He yanked her back, her outstretched hands preventing any contact between them.

"Let me protect you and Aliss."

"Not by placing yourself in danger."

"He wants something from me, I want something from him. We can trade."

"Aliss's exact suggestion," Fiona said.

"She sees reason."

"And I do not?" Fiona snapped.

"When you want to."

She surprised him when she threw her arms around his neck and squeezed him tight. "I could not bare losing you."

His arms wrapped around her waist.

She released her stranglehold on him. "Please, at least do as Kirk suggested, take Raynor with you. I know he would want to go. And please—" She hesitated, looking uncertain.

Tarr tugged at her waist. "Tell me what else you want of me."

She rested her forehead to his. "Wed me now."

Chapter 32

Tarr lifted her chin to tilt her head so he could look into her eyes. His breath almost caught when he saw the love that shined in them. It was potent and palpable, and he wondered why he had never noticed it before. Or had he never looked for it before?

He had only been interested in wedding her, not loving her. Much changed when he discovered he loved Fiona. He had to admit it was a grand feeling and one he would not surrender for all the world.

He kissed her gently, lingering in her familiar taste, then brushed his lips over hers before saying, "Your proposal touches my heart."

She smiled and laughed softly. "Never expected to hear such words from me, did you?"

"No, but I must admit it is good to hear."

She placed a tender hand to his cheek. "I want to be

your wife, Tarr. I will be a good wife. I will stand by you, care for you, protect you, and love you."

"And I will do the same, but tell me why do you wish to wed this day? Your family has yet to arrive and a celebration has yet to be planned."

Her hand fell away to rest on his chest. "I know not what any of this will bring, and I wish to be your wife if only—"

He grabbed her hand. "Do not dare say what I think you mean. Nothing will happen to you, I will see to it. I will *always* keep you safe."

She pressed her fingers to his lips. "I know your heart believes that, but we both know life is unpredictable. We never truly know what will happen. I want to be your wife. I would be proud to be your wife for a very long time, so I ask you again. Marry me this day so that we may begin our lives together as husband and wife."

He kissed her fingers and took her hand in his. "I would join hands with you this day, but the cleric who joins us before God and man will not be here for another three days."

"Then promise me you will not meet with the Wolf clan until after we wed."

"I want you safe."

"Wed me and I will be safe. Who would dare hurt Tarr of Hellewyk's wife?"

Tarr nodded slowly as if a thought dawned. "You are right. Whoever is responsible may think twice before attempting to harm my wife and sister-in-law."

"It is well known that anyone who threatens your clan would suffer your wrath."

"True, for many have seen the results of such actions."

"Then it is agreed?" Fiona asked hopefully. "We marry first?"

His laughter released his concern if only for a moment. "In three days time, woman, you become my wife."

They hugged and kissed and hugged some more until Fiona kicked the door shut, leaving total darkness to embrace them.

"We should finish—"

Tarr did not let her finish. His mouth settled on hers with a hunger that fueled both their appetites.

"This is not a place of secure privacy," Tarr said between kisses.

"Then make our coupling fast, for I will not be denied you again," Fiona said, and hoisted her skirt.

"I love your boldness." Tarr smiled and lifted her up to brace her against the wall, his hands firmly grasping her naked backside. With a bit of fumbling, laughter, nibbles, and kisses the pair joined swiftly.

"Shhh," Tarr warned in a whisper when her moans grew loud.

"Your fault," she mumbled, and buried her face in his shoulder.

Her moans vibrated against his flesh and excited him all the more, so did her fingers digging into his back urging him deeper and deeper inside her until . . .

He groaned in deep silence as he climaxed minutes after her, and when he went to release her, she hugged him tightly.

"Not yet, I love the feel of you inside me."

Her words shivered his soul. How had he gotten so lucky to fall in love with such a unique woman? He had no answer but he intended to cherish his special gift every day, and love her with all his heart.

Voices and footfalls drawing near broke them apart and had them hurrying to straighten their garments. They opened the door, not wanting to surprise anyone who should enter and saw that the women whose voices they had heard had already passed by.

They smiled, grasped hands, and strolled toward the keep. Nothing at the moment could disturb the joy they shared. They were deeply in love and nothing could take that from them.

Fiona was eager for the evening meal, not that she was hungry, though her rumbling stomach reminded otherwise. She was eager to see Tarr. The day had grown busy once it was discovered Tarr and she would wed in three days. The cook pestered her with questions of what she wished served for the wedding feast, several clanswomen offered help in stitching her wedding dress, which she had not even considered, and then there was talk of decorating the hall.

She had finally managed to escape to visit with Aliss and Anya, and was relieved when after complaining about the problem that her mother volunteered, with excitement, to handle it all.

"I just want to wed," she had told Anya.

Anya had insisted the wedding was not only for her and Tarr, but also for the clans. It was an important event that needed proper attention.

And Fiona gladly handed full responsibility to her mother.

Anya had also surprised her with a newly stitched dress. It was dark green and made of the softest wool Fiona had ever felt. Pale yellow embroidery done in the finest stitching trimmed the low neckline and the edge of the sleeves.

She had hugged her mother and hurried off to wash up and put the dress on for supper. She had wanted Aliss to join her in the great hall, but she declined admitting she was not feeling up to the task.

After making certain her sister was all right, only tired and continuing to recover nicely from her wound, she had rushed to her bedchamber to ready herself.

She felt like a princess descending the stairs, the green dress fitting her body perfectly, curving in at her waist, falling nicely over her hips down to her feet. And the wool was so soft and warm against her skin.

Her hair had to match in elegance, so she had returned to Aliss to see what could be done. Her mother had taken charge and had swept her hair up on her head, secured with two combs. She pulled several strands loose to fall around her face and neck and claimed it a work of art when she was done.

Aliss had agreed, telling her sister she had never seen her looking so beautiful. She then teased her about the faint blush that tinged her cheeks and the brilliant sparkle in her green eyes, and what of her lips so ripe with the color of a blossoming pink rose. She was more than beautiful Aliss had insisted; she was gorgeous.

She felt gorgeous and could not wait to see Tarr's reaction.

She entered the great hall, which was filling with men and women who came to share the evening meal. Blackshaw and Hellewyk clan alike mingled and appeared comfortable with each other.

Tarr stood near the dais talking with Raynor. He had yet to spot her and that was all right for she enjoyed the sight of him. Tall, broad, and strong like the claymore he wielded with such ease and might. His stance was one of pride and he wore his plaid in the same manner. His auburn hair hung down his back and he wore a braid down the side that had been plaited with a strip of his plaid.

He was a fine man with extra fine features, and he belonged to her.

Raynor saw her before Tarr and his surprised expression had Tarr turning.

She kept walking toward him, smiling. His blank look remained and she wondered if he was blind or if her appearance did not appeal to him. Then he shook his head as if clearing it, and she realized for that brief moment he had not known her.

His admiring smile grew slow and steady until it spread across his face, and his dark eyes? They looked as if they wanted to devour her.

She giggled beneath her breath and hurried to him turning round to show off her dress. "You like my new dress? A gift from mother."

He grabbed her around the waist with his arm. "You look stunning." His other remark was a whisper meant for her ears alone. "You tempt my soul, woman."

She kissed his cheek, empowered by what a simple

dress could do, and made a mental note to speak to her mother about stitching other dresses.

"I second his opinion," Raynor said. "I always knew my sisters would grow to be beautiful, but I never imagined such depth of beauty."

Fiona went to her brother and kissed his cheek. "Thank you for the compliment."

"It is the truth," he insisted.

Fiona joined the two men in talk and drink, enjoying a goblet of wine. She felt safe, secure, and happy here with her family. She only wished Aliss could join them, but she was not alone, mother had refused to leave her daughter's side, and keeping good company with Aliss: they were busy and content planning her wedding.

Odo entered the hall suddenly, his expression worrisome. He walked directly to Tarr, paying no one else attention.

"What is this I hear you wed my niece in three days' time? You should wait upon my return."

"Where do you go?" Tarr asked.

"To seek Giann as we agreed."

"We agreed to discuss the matter further before any action was taken."

"I cannot sit around and wait when my nieces' lives are in danger. Giann will speak with me."

"But will she tell you the truth?" Tarr asked. "It seems that Giann knows much but says little, and I wonder over her chosen silence."

Odo fisted his hand at his side. "I will find out once and for all, I promise you."

"I believe it is I who needs to speak with Giann."

"The Wolf clan will not let you cross their borders."

"They will let you?" Tarr asked doubtfully.

"Blackshaw is no friend to the Wolf clan," Raynor said.

"I have my ways," Odo insisted. "This wedding must not take place yet. You must wait."

"We have waited long enough. Fiona and I will wed in three days time."

"What of your father?" Odo asked of Fiona. "Do you not want him present at your wedding?"

"He will be. He arrives late tomorrow or early the next day in time for the ceremony and celebration, and he brings the cleric who will wed us."

Tarr slapped Odo on the back and shoved a tankard of ale at him. "We celebrate the joining of powerful clans. We will deal with the other matter the day after the celebration."

Odo accepted the ale, but his taut expression belied his words. "To my niece and her future husband Tarr of Hellewyk, may you know only happiness."

They all drank to the toast and when done, Odo was quick to excuse himself, explaining that he had to inform his men they would not be leaving just yet.

"He is not pleased with the news," Fiona said after she, Tarr, and Raynor took their seats at the table on the dais.

"He is a man of action," Raynor said. "It disturbs him to sit by and do nothing when trouble brews. He was the one who organized the search parties after your abduction. Father was distraught and mother"—he shook his head—"she insisted on going with Odo to search. He promised mother that he would be relentless in his pursuit and find you girls."

"He must have been upset returning empty-handed," Tarr said.

"Upset? He was furious. He had no choice but to rest the horses and the men; they were exhausted and could not continue. He kept a vicious pace for months until finally father ordered him to cease. Odo argued but father made him see reason. It was not that he wanted the search to end completely, but it would be wiser to plan a steady, continuous search alternating men."

"How long did that go on?" Fiona asked.

"It never stopped. Different areas were searched."

"I do not understand how the twins were not found," Tarr said. "The area where they resided was only a week or two journey from your home. Odo must have covered that area."

"He did but no twin babes were seen."

"Did he consult with Giann on locating us?" Fiona asked.

"I am sure he did. He trusted her word."

"I was thinking earlier," Fiona said, "that no one would benefit from our disappearance, and that it cannot be determined it was a vengeful act. What if our abduction was planned to protect us until we could return prepared?"

Raynor shook his head. "But for what reason? Prepared for what?"

"We, Aliss and I would be the reason and prepared for what I am not sure."

"Are you suggesting that this was planned before your birth?" Tarr asked.

"Yes, and it is because of you I thought of this."

"How?" He shook his head, realization dawning. "Your father. He taught you to defend and survive."

"And mother taught Aliss to heal should either of us need it."

"You mean that you and Aliss were purposely placed with the couple who raised you?" Raynor asked.

"It makes sense when you add all the pieces together," Fiona explained. "You tell us that Shona the slave who abducted us loved and cared for us. She would not want to see us harmed and she would want us to survive."

"Or know the reason you both needed to survive," Tarr said.

Raynor shook his head. "You are confusing me yet I see where this makes sense, and how it all points to Giann."

"She would be the one who would have known the twins' fate," Tarr said.

"And the reason why it was necessary for us to survive and one day return."

"Then you think she enlisted the aid of Shona?" Raynor asked.

"She would need someone she could trust with the twins," Tarr said. "Someone who would protect them even at a risk to her own life."

"Shona would have done that," Raynor confirmed. "Then they would need someone to teach the twins."

"Enter Peter and Eleanor, the couple who took us," Fiona said. "Who I am sure must have known Giann."

"Why this elaborate plan?" Raynor asked. "Why not

just tell my parents and"—His abrupt silence had him looking from Fiona to Tarr. "She did not trust my parents."

"Not necessarily," Fiona said. "She may not have thought them capable of protecting us."

"Mother and father would have died protecting you both."

Fiona shook her head slowly. "I do not think that was to be their fate. Perhaps Giann protected more than Aliss and me."

"Giann knows we will come for her, that is why she resides with the Wolf clan," Raynor said.

"My thought as well," Tarr admitted. "That is why you and I shall go alone to the Wolf clan to speak with Giann."

"We tell no one of our plans."

"Kirk knows," Tarr admitted.

"He will say nothing; he is a friend," Raynor said. "Which I hope now we are since you wed my sister."

Tarr acknowledged by offering Raynor his hand. "Our clans join, though there is the matter of the Isle of Non to settle."

"I am sure we can agree on something," Raynor said, and shook his hand.

"I am glad you two have laid the past to rest," Fiona said. "But there is one thing that has not been mentioned."

The two men waited for her to explain.

"If Giann thought Aliss and me in harm's way, enough to remove us from our home—"

Raynor finished for her. "Then the threat comes from within the clan Blackshaw."

Chapter 33

Aliss was enjoying hot mulled cider with Kirk's wife Erin when the cottage door burst open and Fiona marched in.

"What are you doing here?" Fiona went on questioning before Aliss could answer. "Are you not supposed to be resting? Have you miraculously recovered? Why is your wound no longer bandaged? And where is mother? I go to your room and you were not there, and mother was not there—"

"Fiona," Aliss interrupted abruptly, though calmly, "join us, the cider is fresh and hot."

Fiona slipped the green cloak off her shoulders, dropped it over the back of the chair she sat in, and quietly said, "I was worried when I could not find you."

"My fault," Erin said.

Aliss was quick to amend. "No one's fault, the babe was not feeling well and Erin requested my help. I thought I would return before the keep stirred."

"What of mother? And who brought you the message? It could have been a ruse. It could have been—"

"It was not. Kirk came for me and escorted me to his cottage. And as for mother, I sent her to her own bedchamber to sleep. She is exhausted from tending me and needs rest herself. I am well enough now and need no pampering or fussing, and my wound needs fresh air. And what brings you after me so early?"

"I could not sleep another wink," Fiona admitted. "The sun hit my face and that was that, so I went to your room—"

"Found me gone and panicked."

"What did you expect me to think, the sun barely risen and you are not in your bed?"

"What made you come here?" Erin asked.

"After panicking, I thought I better find out if perhaps Aliss had been summoned to help someone. The village was stirring and the few who bid me good morning had not seen you. Then I caught sight of Kirk, and he pointed to his cottage." Fiona shook her head. "I almost fell to my knees in prayer."

Aliss patted her sister's hand. "I am not foolish. You need not worry so much."

"Someone tried to kill you. I need to worry."

"I do not blame your sister for worrying," Erin said, and looked down at the babe sleeping in the cradle beside her. "I do not know what I would do if my son went missing."

"I am sorry. I was so concerned with Aliss I forgot to inquiry about your son. How is he?" Fiona asked.

"No more than a tummy ache," Erin said with relief. "I feel terrible about disturbing your sister when she still recovers from her wound."

"I am fine and I am glad to be out of that room. I could not bear another day's confinement. Tarr promised me a cottage, and today I intend to find one that will suit me."

"You cannot leave the keep yet," Fiona ordered.

Aliss understood her concern for she worried for Fiona as well. They both still were at risk, but soon, two days to be exact, Fiona would wed and begin a new life, and Aliss wished to begin her own.

"I know, Fiona, but I would like to prepare so that when this culprit is found and dealt with, I can move to my cottage."

"Are there any empty cottages close to the keep?" Fiona asked Erin.

"I think there is one, though it is small. There is a good-size cottage that borders the woods and has plenty of land for a garden."

"It sounds like it is a distance from other cottages," Fiona said.

"It does sit off on its own, but it is not completely removed from the village."

"We will look at the one closer to the keep, and if it is too small I will have Tarr build you a bigger one," Fiona said.

Aliss realized her sister wanted her close, and she did want to be close. But she was also eager to have a cottage all to herself so that she could work with her herbs and tend the ill.

"I would like to see if the one nearer the woods suits me."

Fiona shrugged. "If you want to we will look at it."

Aliss smiled at her sister's reluctant surrender, though she had far from capitulated. Fiona would find reasons why the cottage would not suit Aliss, when it was Fiona who it did not suit. She would be patient with her sister as usual, and if the abode were to her liking she would have Fiona agreeing in no time.

Fiona smiled and perked up when she said, "You know there is much to do for the wedding celebration, perhaps the cottage should wait until afterward."

"I heard your mother has everything well in hand," Erin said, to Fiona's dismay.

Aliss kept her smile steady, though she wished to chuckle at her sister's obvious attempt to delay her move. It would have been an excellent excuse to keep her busy at the keep. But Erin was right. Anya did have everything well in hand, which was why she was so exhausted and needed rest, though it would not surprise her to find Anya right now in the kitchen seeing to the food preparation or with the women who volunteered to stitch the wedding dress or with the women who gathered the garlands and berries for the decorations.

"Mother is tenacious like you," Aliss said teasingly.

"And you are not, wanting to find a cottage now when there are other important matters to consider?"

"I but take a look, Fiona," Aliss said and stood. "Let us go now."

Fiona hurried out of her seat and wrapped herself in the cloak. "Good then we can be done with it."

"It sits at the end of the village, on the side that borders the woods," Erin explained. "It has been empty some time and needs repairs."

That bit of news seemed to make Fiona happy. "It may be beyond repair."

"We shall see," Aliss said, and out the door they went, Fiona bumping into Tarr as they turned the corner.

Tarr grabbed her arm anxiously. "Never go off without telling me where you go."

"You were sleeping."

"And I woke to an empty bed with no one in the keep able to tell me where you had gone. And imagine my shock when I could not find your sister, or your mother." He sent Aliss a look that warned he had yet to deal with her.

Aliss ignored it. She was more concerned with her mother's whereabouts. "Have you found mother?"

"She is in the kitchen ordering everyone about," Tarr confirmed.

"Kirk knew—"

"And should have informed me immediately where you both had gone," Tarr finished. He glanced from one twin to the other. "While I want to believe you both safe here on Hellewyk land, I would be a fool to assume that. We now believe the person who poses a threat to you both could be here right now. I do not intend to take any chances. While there are numerous guards posted, you must be diligent in keeping me informed as to your whereabouts at all times."

"He is right," Aliss agreed. "I trusted Kirk and I still do, but Tarr should have been told that I left the keep."

"I also agree it is wise, for the moment," Fiona was quick to add.

Tarr grinned and shook his head. "I can see that your tenacious manner is going to challenge me."

"What is life without a challenge?" Fiona asked, and gave him a quick kiss.

"Peaceful," Tarr answered as she stepped away from him.

"Boring," Fiona countered. "Aliss and I were just about to go look at the cottage near the end of the village to see if it would suit her needs."

"That is a good-size one. I think you may like it," Tarr said.

Fiona quickly mentioned it needed repairs.

"None that cannot be done easily," Tarr said, and hooked Fiona's arm over his. "I will go with you and show you where it is."

Raynor waved to them and hurried over, joining with them as soon as he learned of their destination.

Aliss saw the cottage before any of them, and when she did her eyes rounded. It was much larger than she had thought with two windows and remnants of a garden that wrapped around from the front of the cottage to the back. The front door hung open, the hinges broken, shards of broken pottery lay strewn about, and a bench tilted precariously on one leg. She stared for a moment imagining how it would look once repaired, the garden renewed and bursting in the spring with herbs and flowers. She hurried forward eager to see what other repairs would be necessary to her new home.

"Great," Fiona mumbled. "She likes it."

"What is wrong with that?" Tarr asked.

"It is far from the keep."

Tarr glanced over his shoulder. "The keep is directly behind us."

"It is not next to it," Fiona snapped, and walked off to join her sister.

"Fiona is so accustomed to protecting Aliss," Raynor said. "It is not easy to relinquish that responsibility after all these years."

"I can take care of them both. She need not worry, though I do understand it," Tarr admitted hesitantly. "I wonder what Fiona will do when the day comes that Aliss weds."

"Aliss claims she will never wed."

"Not likely," Tarr said, "but the choice will be hers to make. I will see to it."

"Good, I am pleased to hear that. Now, let us go help Aliss convince her sister that this cottage is perfect for her."

Raynor remained with an ecstatic Aliss who was busy making mental notes of the repair work needed before she could move in while Tarr and Fiona returned to the keep.

"You are upset with your sister's intended move," Tarr said, their pace unrushed.

"She is so happy." Fiona looked off, avoiding Tarr's eyes.

He slipped his arm around her to snuggle her close to his side as they kept walking. "Of course she is, she has a home here with her sister. She is relieved and finally feels settled, and makes plans to be a permanent part of the clan Hellewyk."

Fiona turned a sudden smile on him. "You are right. I had not thought of it that way. She is happy here because we are together and shall remain so."

"Then you approve of the cottage?"

Fiona stopped and turned her head to glance over her shoulder. "She will be safe there?"

"Once this matter is settled, she will be safe anywhere on Hellewyk land."

She took hold of his hand, locking her fingers tightly around his. "I once thought you selfish and demanding. I see now that you unselfishly provide for your clan. They come first to you—"

"You come first to me," he whispered, almost as if it were a prayer on his lips. "I no longer think of you as the woman I will wed but of the woman I love." His smile came slowly as he pushed the fiery strands of her red hair out of her face. "You stole my heart and glad I am that you did."

She brought his hand up to her mouth and kissed it. "I may have stolen your heart, but I gave you mine."

"I would have stolen it if you had let me."

"You were taking much too long; it was easier to just give it to you."

Tarr wrinkled his brow. "Easier? When was that?"

She poked his chest with their joined hands. "I was not that difficult."

Tarr laughed, drawing several glances their way.

"Make fun of me it matters not. I love you and you are stuck with me."

"I like being stuck with you," he whispered, laughter rippling along with his words. "Besides who else would have you?"

They continued walking, Fiona remaining silent. They entered the keep and she released his hand to walk away but he held firm.

"What is wrong?"

"Nothing," she answered, forcing a weak smile. "I will see you later." She freed her hand and backed away from him. "There are things I need to tend to." She turned and rushed off.

She made it the bedchamber she shared with Aliss and shut the door. She leaning against it, wanting to cut off everyone for the moment and have a bit of solitude.

She was upset and wanted no one to know why. She walked over to the bed and sat wondering over this weakness she felt. She prided herself in her strength and boldness, and did not understand why she should allow this to upset her now.

Who else would have you?

Fiona knew Tarr only teased her, but his words had struck her like a slap in the face, for he spoke the truth. No one else had ever wanted her. No men had sought her affection or spoke kind words to her or had even attempted to kiss her.

Was she that unlovable?

What had Tarr seen in her that no other man had?

"I will not feel sorry for myself," she mumbled. "I have a good man who loves me and that is all that matters."

The opposing ache in her stomach refused to abate, and she shook her head. It made no sense to feel this way. She loved Tarr and was not interested in any other man, so why should this disturb her?

"I am foolish," she declared out loud.

"Why?"

She jumped off the bed at the sound of Tarr's voice. "I did not hear you enter."

"You were lost in thought." He walked over to her.

She nodded not wanting to share those thoughts with him, for he would think her more foolish than she thought herself.

"Tell me what is wrong?"

"Nothing is wrong." She attempted a smile that faltered much too easily.

He ran his hand up her arm slowly. "We will wed soon and I hope to *share* a life with you. I had hoped we would *share* everything, even our troubled thoughts. Had we not agreed upon *sharing*?"

She rolled her eyes, groaned, and plopped down on the edge of the bed. "I thought myself knowledgeable about love, but I was wrong. Just because you want to love does not mean you know how to love, and I have recently come to realize that I know nothing of love."

Tarr sat beside her. "Neither do I."

"You sound as if you do."

"I try because I love you."

"See." She waved her hands in the air.

"See what?"

"How good you are."

He grabbed her chin. "Stop and tell me what is wrong. It does not matter who is good at love and who is not, we both love each other and that is what matters."

"I told myself that."

"Then what could be wrong?"

She really felt foolish and wondered how she could avoid telling him the truth, then thought better of it. She would expect honesty from him; she could give him no less.

"You asked who else would love me."

"I but teased you."

"I know but the truth is that there is no other man who would love me. No man ever showed interest in me. No man ever attempted to kiss me."

"I can understand that."

"Really?" Fiona asked, affronted.

"Aye, you are too much of a woman for just any man. You required a man of strength and fine character. One who was not intimidated by your power but admired it and understood it. A man who would not attempt to bend you to his will but who would accept your passionate spirit and honor it."

An eager smile surfaced easily on Fiona.

"As for never being kissed?" He ran his thumb over her lips. "These belong to me and honored I am that you saved them for me. I am glad no other has kissed you but me; it makes our kisses that more intimate and special."

She threw her arms around his neck. "I love you so very much."

Her hugged her. "That is good for I am the *only* man—"

"I ever want in my life," she finished.

The door burst open and Anya stood for a moment

startled, then she shook away her shock and grew apologetic. "How rude of me not to have knocked. I thought Aliss might have returned—"

"It is all right, Anya," Tarr said. "We have set things right here."

"There was something wrong? Fiona, you are all right?"

"What is wrong with Fiona?"

Fiona heard her sister's worried voice before she saw her push past her mother at the open door to enter the room. Raynor followed, though remained just outside the door near his mother.

"Fiona?" Aliss asked with concern. "I came to join you for the morning meal and did not find you downstairs. I worried since you never miss a meal."

Fiona smiled at her sister and gave a quick glance around the room at everyone present. They loved her, each and every one of them in their own special way; she truly was lucky.

She jumped up tugging Tarr along with her. "I am starving."

Aliss laughed. "I suggest we get to the table before her or else there will be nothing left for us."

Fiona zipped past her sister, leaving Tarr in her wake. "I will beat you there."

Aliss yelped and hurried after her while a laughing Anya attempted to catch them.

Tarr walked over to Raynor. "The buttery is stocked, we are safe and will not starve."

Raynor grinned and, as they walked, said quietly, "We have received word from the Wolf."

Chapter 34

"What does the Wolf say?" Tarr asked, entering his solar, Raynor shutting the door behind him.

"That Giann will meet with us in five days time."

"Five days? Why the delay?" He was anxious to have this done with. He wanted Fiona and Aliss safe once and for all.

"He gave no reason."

"What does he want in return?"

"Nothing," Raynor said skeptically. "Though I question that."

"As do I, except . . ." Tarr shook his head. "He could know something that we do not. He does have Giann to advise him."

A knock sounded before Fiona entered without permission. "What goes on here?"

Tarr had grown accustomed to her interference, though he no longer thought of it that way. She was part of his life and as he had told her, he wished to share everything with her.

"Word from Wolf," Tarr said, and Fiona quickly shut the door behind her.

Raynor reiterated what they had already discussed.

"So then it was Giann who has decided this delay," Fiona said.

Tarr watched her nibble at her lower lip, a habit of hers when she gave serious thought to a matter. Her rosy lip would plump from her chewing and look delectable enough to kiss, which he had done on occasion and thoroughly enjoyed.

He doubted she was fully aware of how often he wanted to make love to her. She responded to his every touch and kiss. There was not a time she would deny his passion and there were many times she had seduced him. There was no way he intended on losing this precious woman.

He was stuck with her as she had told him, and nothing or no one would ever separate them. He would kill anyone who tried.

"Giann obviously knows something we do not, and waits," Fiona said.

"Why does she wait?" Raynor asked.

"I do not know, but I know we are missing something here," Fiona said, pacing between where Tarr and Raynor stood. "A connection, something that connects all the parts of the past that brings us to this point in time."

"Are you saying Giann knew this time would come?" Raynor asked.

Fiona stopped pacing. "I would say she prepared for this time."

Another knock interrupted them and Tarr bid the person to enter. Anya popped in, bubbling with excitement. "Your father has arrived."

Fiona and Aliss found themselves exhausted after all the introductions. It seemed as if the whole Blackshaw clan had arrived for the wedding celebration, which appeared to take place as they spoke. Food and drink flowed all day while arrangements were made to house the many visitors.

Aliss was approached by Glenor, a woman well into her years and gentle in tone and manner. She was the Blackshaw healer and was eager to talk with Aliss. They fast became friends and were soon deep in conversation.

Anya was busy helping the servants arrange the various rooms to accommodate the overflowing crowd, and Raynor was not wasting a minute in introducing Tarr to boyhood friends.

That left Fiona on her own, though she did not lack for conversation. She just did not feel like playing hostess to strangers. She had too much on her mind to celebrate. Aliss and she were in more danger than ever before. She feared whatever was brewing within the next five days, for she had no doubt it had to do with her and Aliss.

She meandered her way toward the door and was just

about to slip out unnoticed when her father stepped out of the shadows.

She jumped, her hand going to her chest. "You frightened me."

"You would not be frightened if you were not sneaking."

"I need a breath of fresh air," she protested.

He leaned close to whisper. "I think you were making an escape, and shame on you for not taking your father with you."

Fiona grinned, and with a finger to her lips warning him to be silent as they snuck out of the keep together.

A cold wind greeted them. Oleg took his fur cloak off and draped it around Fiona's shoulders.

"What of you?" she asked, though favoring the warmth of the fur.

"I am well protected with the many wool garments I wear."

He was donned in layers of wool from leggings to tunic, and all the garments in between, leaving Fiona feeling less guilty and more grateful for accepting his generosity. "Thank you."

"It is good to offer my daughter warmth while I share a walk with her."

They strolled the village, though after several interruptions from those needing introductions to either Fiona or Oleg, they changed course and walked to sit in a favorite spot of Aliss and Fiona's near the meadow that afforded them more privacy.

"Blessed quiet, how wonderful," Oleg said

"I had not expected so many of the Blackshaw clan. Are there any left defending your land?"

"You have a bold humor like your mother."

"I notice I am much like Mother. Does that mean Aliss inherited your nature?" Fiona asked.

"If Aliss possesses a quiet strength, then she has my nature."

Fiona looked into his gentle brown eyes and knew there was much more to this man than of what he spoke. And she decided there was much she could learn from him.

"I would like to hear of your younger days," Oleg said. "If you would share those memories with me?"

Fiona obliged him as she had Anya, and soon she had him laughing with tales of her stubborn spirit and endless curiosity.

Fiona jumped at what she thought was a crack of thunder. She scampered to her feet when she realized the booming shout had come from Tarr.

"Damn it, Fiona," he said walking up to her and not stopping until they were chest to chest. "You promised to let me know your whereabouts."

She winced realizing her error. "I am sorry; I completely forgot."

"You cannot forget," he scolded.

"I am sure the excitement of our arrival caused her to forget," Oleg defended.

Tarr vehemently disagreed. "No excuse is acceptable."

"It was a simple mistake—"

"That could have cost her her life," Tarr informed her father.

"Tarr is right, father. I gave him my word. It was inexcusable of me not to have informed him I was leaving the keep."

Tarr turned silent, then smiled. "Did I just hear you correctly? You are admitting you were wrong?"

She smiled too, for she knew he meant to tease and to lighten the situation. "Just this one time."

"It is a promising start." He took her in his arms and rested his forehead to hers. "I grew worried."

She heard his concern and felt, in the way he held her, his fear. "I am truly sorry. I will be diligent about informing you of my whereabouts."

"Perhaps I should just keep you by my side at all times."

"You would grow tired of me."

"Never," Tarr said, then wrinkled his eyes as if giving it second thought. "Though maybe—"

"You could live without me," Fiona finished with a defiant tilt of her chin.

"Believe me, he would not want to do that," Oleg said seriously. "He would miss you terribly and think about you every day, and wait impatiently for your return."

"Fiona is not going anywhere," Tarr said adamantly. "Tomorrow we take our vows and she will be mine, and I will be hers. We will be forever bound to each other and that is just fine with me."

"This is good to hear," Oleg said, and slapped Tarr on the back. "Now, let us go and drink to it."

Chapter 35

Tarr whistled as he walked to his bedchamber. He was happy, very happy, enthusiastically happy. He laughed out loud then quickly looked around to see if anyone saw him drunk with happiness. But then what did he care? Everyone was pleased with the wedding plans. He had left his future father-in-law and brother-in-law in the great hall debating about the merger of the clans that the wedding would bring. He had seen Fiona leave the hall and head up the stairs, and he had decided to follow. Tonight belonged to Fiona and him.

"And tomorrow night, the night after, and the night after that." He laughed to himself and placed his hand on the handle to his bedchamber door. He hoped Fiona waited inside. He had taken his time talking with the men so that Fiona would have time with her sister. He had hoped he had given her enough time and that she was now waiting eagerly in his bed.

He opened the door with a smile.

Fiona sat on his bed crying.

His heart pained him. He felt his stomach wrench and quickly rushed to her side. "What is it? Are you all right? Is Aliss all right?"

She repeatedly nodded in answer to his rapid-fire questions.

"I am—" She sniffled.

He waited anxiously for her answer.

"I am happy."

Relief flooded him, a rushing wave that returned with joy. He threw his arms around her and they fell back on the bed together.

He laughed deep from within his soul, though it sounded gentle. He kissed away her tears.

She sighed, wrapped contentedly in his arms. "Promise me it will always be like this."

"You want me to promise that you shall cry often?"

She smiled and hugged him, and when he went to kiss her she yawned.

It was contagious and soon yawn followed yawn.

"I thought to make love to you tonight, but—"

"We are both tired," she said, attempting to stifle another yawn.

"Tomorrow night—"

"Will be ours."

Her eyes drifted closed and he was grateful she was in her nightdress. He lifted her so her head would rest comfortably on the pillow and covered her. Then he undressed and slipped in beside her, hugging her close. In seconds they fell asleep.

Fiona rose with the sun, kissed a waking Tarr on the cheek, and announced, "I am starving. I go to fetch my sister and then to eat."

"I will meet you in the great hall," he said, stretching, the blanket slipping down to below his waist.

"Mmm," Fiona said with a delectable sigh. "You look tempting."

"Keep the thought, for I promise you will not sleep a wink tonight, *wife*."

She grinned with joy. "Wife. I love it and I love you."

With a quick wave she rushed off, Tarr yelling after her, "It is food you love more."

He laughed, swinging his legs out of bed and stretching as he stood. He winced, a recurring pain stabbing his arm. He rubbed at the scar that was left from Wolf's arrow. He was a formidable opponent and one of unequal strength. He knew of no man who could pierce the flesh straight through with a single blow of a handheld arrow.

Wolf would make a better friend than foe.

He hoped to make such beneficial arrangements when he visited with Giann.

He dressed quickly, hungry and eager to join Fiona for the morning meal and more than eager to wed her and be done with it. He would feel safer when she was officially his wife.

He was about to leave when a knock sounded and the door opened, Anya entering with several servants.

"A new shirt has been stitched for your wedding day,

and I will have a bath made ready for you after the meal."

Tarr listened as she went on to detail what was expected of him, and then she patted his arm and smiled.

"You will make my daughter a fine husband." She was gone along with the servants who assisted her as fast as she had appeared.

He shook his head, mumbling to himself as he left the room.

Tarr entered the great hall to a flurry of activity. A feast had been spread on the tables, clan members mingled, and tankards were raised when he was spotted, and shouts of congratulations rang out for him and his bride, who he had not yet spotted.

She and her sister were probably lost in talk and would arrive soon. He accepted the tankard spilling over with ale that was shoved at him, and with a smile he joined in the merriment.

Aliss had expected to see Fiona early. She usually woke with the rising sun, as did her stomach, which by now would be rumbling with hunger. Fiona would be expecting her to join her for breakfast as always, particularly since she probably continued to feel guilty about not spending the night with her.

She smiled; perhaps she and Tarr were preoccupied.

She dressed in her brown skirt and white blouse so that she could help with whatever needed doing, then she intended to change into the beautiful sapphire wool dress mother had had stitched for her. She could not wait. She had never seen a garment as beautiful as that dress, and she was eager to feel the soft wool against her skin.

She pulled her hair back to tie with a strip of leather when there was a knock at the door.

She smiled, expecting to see Fiona enter, though curious as to why she would knock first when she had always entered unannounced.

Anya entered and peeked about as she offered Aliss a smile and a good morning. She sighed, obviously disappointed. "I thought to find Fiona here."

"She is with Tarr."

"No she is not."

"In the hall stuffing her face," Aliss said, a sudden chill prickling her skin.

"She is not there either." Anya's eyes widened.

Aliss dropped the leather tie and sped past Anya, the startled woman followed fast on her heels.

Tarr kept a keen eye out for Fiona. He had expected her to arrive by now, but since Aliss also was not there, he was certain they had to be together. He stood by the hearth with Raynor and Oleg trying to remain attentive.

He grew alarmed when he saw Aliss rush into the hall and survey the room with a worried glance.

He dropped his tankard to the table and cut a swift path to her side. "What is wrong?"

"Fiona, is she with you?"

"She left me earlier to go to you."

"She never came to my room," Aliss said, panic straining her voice.

Anya heard as she came up behind Aliss. "No, God, not again."

Oleg and Raynor had joined them, Oleg going to his wife's side to wrap his arm around her shoulder.

"Fiona could be anywhere in the keep lost in what she is doing and forgetting time," Raynor suggested.

Aliss and Tarr shook their heads.

"She made that mistake twice already and made certain to tell me it would not happen again. She is a woman of her word," Tarr insisted. "She would have told me before she went elsewhere."

"Besides, she would not miss the morning meal. She has always woken hungry and eager to eat."

"Aliss is right," Tarr confirmed. "She told me she was starving."

"Something has happened to her," Anya said.

"If it has, then it would have been when she left Tarr's room on her way to Aliss," Oleg said. "Did anyone hear a commotion?"

Tarr shook his head. "Anything unusual would have been reported to me."

"Someone had to have seen something," Aliss said, and pushed past the men to climb on a table and shout. "We need your help."

All sound ceased.

"Has anyone seen Fiona this morning?"

Eyes rounded, hushed whispers rushed around the room, and then a man spoke up.

"I saw her leave the hall."

"Alone and willingly?" Aliss asked.

"With Odo, and she did not look like she objected."

"Kirk," Tarr shouted. "Take men and see if you can find Odo."

Talk resumed in the hall, though it was now solemn not joyous.

"What would Odo want with her?" Anya asked, and grabbed her chest. "He could not mean my daughter harm? He tirelessly searched for her all these years."

"But for what reason?" Tarr asked. "To save her or condemn her?"

"But why? What reason would he have?" Oleg asked upset. "He is my brother. He taught Raynor to fight, to hunt, to track and he was more worried than anyone when the twins were abducted. The first to go in search of them. I agree with Anya, he could not mean her harm."

"The clan means everything to Odo," Raynor said. "He would not do anything to bring disgrace to its name."

Aliss had climbed off the table and stood beside Tarr. "Which is probably the reason Giann had us sent away."

They all stared at her not understanding.

"It is probable that she knew no one would believe she had a vision of Odo harming the babes, so to protect us she had Shona take us to people who would protect us."

"That is nonsense," Oleg said. "Odo never meant you or your sister harm."

"You prove my theory true," Aliss said sadly. "Giann could never have convinced you of Odo's deceit."

Kirk rushed into the hall and yelled to Tarr. "Odo, several of his men, and Fiona's horse are all gone."

"Prepare to ride," Tarr shouted to his men.

"Blackshaw joins the search," Raynor cried out.

The men from both clans hurried out of the hall to ready for the search.

"I am going this time," Anya insisted. "I will see my daughter safe."

Aliss went to her mother's side. "This is for me to do. I will find my sister and bring her home safely. I promise."

Anya's eyes teared. "I have been promised before by those who I thought I could trust. Now I know not what to think or who to trust."

"This is your daughter who makes the promise. Fiona knows I will rescue her, as I knew she would rescue me. You can trust I *will* bring her home safely."

Tarr stepped up behind Aliss, placing a hand on her shoulder. "*We* will bring her home."

Raynor stepped forward. "You can count on *us*, Mother. I will either defend Odo or deal him the punishment he deserves if it should prove necessary."

Anya held her chin up. "Do not keep me waiting long."

"Do whatever must be done, my son," Oleg said.

"If he does not, I will," Tarr warned, and grabbed Aliss's hand. "A moment alone." He tugged her along after him to the corner of the hall where they had a bit of privacy.

Aliss spoke before he could. "You worry that I do not possess Fiona's warrior skills and that I will be more of a hindrance than a help."

"You read the situation well, and I know you will do what is best for your sister."

"And that would be for me to go with you."

Tarr stared at her. "Speaking with you is like . . ." He turned his head away.

Aliss placed her hand on his arm, drawing his attention back. "Our identical features may be just what we need to rescue Fiona."

"I would not put you in harm's way—"

"If it meant a chance to free my sister, you most certainly would. Now, we waste precious time. Let us ride and find Fiona."

They were on the trail in no time, tension as sharp between the two clans as the cold air that stung their faces and chilled their bones.

"This will not do," Aliss said, looking to Raynor and Tarr who rode on either side of her, stiff in posture and form. She glanced around her at the men who duplicated their leaders, sitting straight and alert in their saddles. "They are on edge, not sure of their enemy. Is it the clan who rides beside them, the man they chase? This is dangerous and must be settled before we go any farther, or it is certain to produce disastrous results."

"You think like father," Raynor said.

"Sensibly," she confirmed. "Now, do something, both of you."

Tarr nodded his agreement as did Raynor, and they called a halt.

Tarr spoke first. "We find Fiona this day so that we can all celebrate tonight."

Smiles from both clans greeted his message.

"Celebrate the joining of two strong and proud clans.

We ride together in purpose and strength and to discover the truth behind the mystery that has plagued the Blackshaw clan all these years. We ride united and fight united against common foe."

Cheers rang out and Aliss hoped that Fiona heard it, for then she knew they were not far behind.

Raynor brought his horse beside Tarr's. "We have a mission to save my sister and return her so that she can wed the chieftain of the clan Hellewyk. This blessed union strengthens our clans throughout the Highlands. We become an unstoppable force, and I alone will see to dealing out justice to those who have betrayed the Blackshaw name."

Cheers sounded yet again, and when the journey continued the cold, stinging air remained but the sharp tension was gone and the two clans rode as one.

"We lost the trail again," Tarr said, frustrated after returning from talking with his trackers.

Aliss shook her head. "We must hurry and find it for it feels as if the first snow may fall this day."

Tarr agreed. The temperature had dipped sharply since they first left.

"My uncle is excellent in covering his tracks," Raynor said.

"He taught you his ways?"

Raynor nodded. "Though, I am not nearly the tracker he is."

"We shall test that theory right now," Tarr challenged. "Snow seems likely, and if we do not find his trail before the flakes fall we will not find it at all."

"I will do my best," Raynor said.

"Your best is not good enough," Aliss snapped. "He

taught you. Think like him, breath like him, distrust like him, and you will track like him."

"You are much stronger and much wiser than anyone realizes," Raynor said, and rode off shaking his head.

Tarr rode silently alongside Aliss, lost in thoughts he dared to hope did not come true. He feared he would lose Fiona, and he did not know what he would do without her. He was a warrior skilled in battle, but this was a far different battle than he was accustomed. This battle, if not victorious, would bring an unbearable pain to his heart and soul.

He could not allow that; his only choice then was to be the victor.

"He has not harmed Fiona yet."

Tarr turned with a jerk to stare at Aliss. "You know this for sure?"

"Think about it," Aliss advised. "If he wanted her dead, he would have killed her by now, disposed of her body, so she would not be found and he would not be implicated."

"Then he takes her somewhere on purpose."

"Perhaps to make certain what he does is for the greater good."

"What greater good?" Tarr asked with a snort. "His own?"

"The missing piece we search for. When we find it; all will make sense."

"We hope," Tarr said skeptically.

"You are aware of Fiona's skills. She can well defend herself."

"She is outnumbered."

Aliss laughed. "They are outwitted."

Tarr could not help but laugh along with her. "True enough. Should I then feel sorry for those who abducted her?"

"I do."

"You have faith in your sister."

"As she does in us," Aliss said.

"I envy the bond between you two," he admitted.

"Which is the reason why you did not want me around," Aliss said with no animosity. "Yet you and she have an even stronger bond."

"It took me time to realize it and—"

"That I pose no threat to you," she finished with a smile. "I forgive you for you are a man and know no better."

"You are as fast with your wit as is your sister." He gave his head a quick shake. "No, you are faster and none realize it."

"An advantage I have."

Raynor's rapid approach silenced them suddenly.

"I know where he goes," Raynor said out of breath.

Tarr and Aliss waited.

"He travels to the land of the Wolf."

Chapter 36

Fiona wanted to kick herself ten times over for being a fool. Odo had grabbed her with an urgency that had her immediately worrying about her sister. When she had insisted on telling Tarr, he quickly dispatched one of his men to get him.

Aliss had suffered a horrible accident and she begged for her sister, that is what Odo had told her. Fear had ripped through her stomach like a dull blade, burning and paining her with each pounding hoove of her mare as she rode, until she realized too late that it had been a ruse to trick her, right into the arms of her enemy.

She had had no reason to distrust Odo. He was the uncle who had searched so unselfishly and endlessly for her and her sister, but for what end?

In a few hours time she was to wed. She should rightfully be preparing for her wedding at this very moment.

Instead she rode through woods, the trees barren in their winter sleep, the ground hard and the cold air biting her cheeks.

She had no idea where they went or Odo's intention, and she wondered what the next few hours would bring?

Her answer came suddenly.

Freedom.

She may have fallen prey to her enemy but she would not remain so. She would free herself, starting with the ties that bound her wrists, and then once free she would go after Odo. He was fit and strong for a man well into his late years, but all men were vulnerable somewhere. She would wait and watch and discover his weakness, then she would strike. Without their leader's guidance, the men would be easy to deal with, and besides Tarr and Aliss could not be far behind.

"You think to plot your escape," Odo said with a chuckle. "There is no getting away from me this time. I have searched too long and hard for you."

"Not for my sister and me?"

"You will do, or so the prophecy says."

"I am getting tired of this Giann and her foolish prophecies—"

"They are not foolish," Odo snapped. "They are wise and they have alerted me to the possible destruction of my clan."

"Did the prophecy have to do with why you wanted us gone?" Fiona asked, fishing for answers.

"Actually, the opposite."

"You wanted us around?"

"Aye, so that I could make certain the prophecy never

saw fruition," Odo admitted. "Shona abducted you, why I still cannot understand, and ruined everything. I had no choice but to search and pray that you had not survived."

"Then you did plan on killing us."

"I thought only one would need to die, but I was not certain whom," he said.

"Yet you made an attempt on both our lives. Tell me, did you fire the arrow that hit Aliss?"

"My men are faithful and do what I ask of them."

She shook her head. "No wonder we found no tracks after Aliss was hit. You covered your own when you volunteered to search for the offender."

"I do what is necessary to protect my clan."

"Tell me of this prophecy that predicts doom and gloom for the clan."

"No one heard it but me," Odo whispered, his eyes darting in all directions to see that his men did not ride too close and hear the dire words. "Giann whispered them over your mother as she slept. I was in the shadows. She did not see me, but I heard her."

"What did you hear?" Fiona asked impatiently.

Odo gave another anxious glance around before reciting the prophecy. "On a full moon two babes are born; and with their birth sounds the horn; eyes of green; hair of red; destruction comes when the first one weds."

A chill ran up her spine, though she refused to shiver, she simply shrugged. "My marriage unites two fine and powerful clans. It does not cause destruction."

"According to the prophecy it does."

"And you believe such nonsense?"

"I believe the truth," he said harshly. "You and your sister were born on a full moon, the horn sounded from a distant village, you had green eyes and a thatch of red hair. The rest was sure to prove true. It was yours or your sister's life or the clan's demise. There was no other choice left to me."

"And what choice do you have now? You have betrayed one of your own. You will be hunted and punished."

He laughed. "I am no fool. You were seen freely leaving Hellewyk land with me. You did not protest or scream that I was abducting you. We rode off together in a common cause. And if you should die in pursuit of that cause?"—he shrugged—"heroes are born from less."

Her green eyes glistened with a tangible fury and she raised her tied wrists, shook her fisted hands at him. "*You* will bring destruction."

"Blackshaw clan will gladly unite with the clan Hellewyk and seek revenge against the Wolf clan," Odo said with pride. "Of course, if Tarr should die in battle the Hellewyk clan would have no leader; my nephew being a strong chieftain and following my wise opinions, would take leadership and unite the two clans."

"It will never happen. Tarr is no fool, he will not believe you."

"My brother, his wife, and my nephew Raynor would never doubt me. They know I serve the clan with honor."

"Your own deceit will be your defeat. Tarr knows I would not ride off without first—"

"What makes you think Tarr will live to hear an explanation of your sudden disappearance?"

She glared at him, gritting her teeth to prevent spewing oaths at him.

"I know he follows; I counted on it." He pounded his chest. "It does my heart good to see that young men remain foolish when it comes to love."

"Raynor will know you are traitor to your people when you murder Tarr."

"I will raise no weapon against him."

His intentions dawned on her and fueled her already boiling anger. "You plan to make the Wolf clan look responsible for his death—"

"Do not forget yours," he chuckled. "Between both your deaths, there will be no man, woman, or child of the Hellewyk clan who would refuse to battle the Wolf clan. Add the Blackshaw warriors to the mix and victory is guaranteed."

Fiona wanted to shout, scream, cry out her rage but that would only please him, instead she chose words that would strike doubt in him.

"You forget one thing."

"I forget nothing; it will all come to pass."

She snickered to herself, pleased that she was about to land a solid blow to his confidence. "Will it? *You* forget the prophecy."

"Why would Odo take Fiona to the land of the Wolf?" Aliss asked, pulling the hood of her wool cloak up on her head, the wind having whipped it off for the third time.

"Perhaps he learned something that would help us to—"

"You refuse to believe your uncle a traitor," Tarr accused.

"He could be protecting Fiona."

"Why not tell us his intentions?" Tarr asked, appearing as unsettled as his stallion that snorted and pawed the ground. "Why did he not seek our help? Why sneak off without a word?"

Raynor remained firm in defense of his uncle. "I am sure he will have a good answer when we confront him."

"Can you tell how far they are from us?" Aliss asked.

"If we keep a swift pace, we may be able to meet up with them by midday."

"They will be expecting us," Tarr said.

"There you have answered Odo's intentions yourself," Raynor claimed. "He does not hide from us; his trail was easy to follow."

"For you his nephew."

Raynor reared up in his saddle. "You accuse me?"

"*I* take no chances with Fiona's life."

"You think I do?"

"By refusing to admit that your uncle may be culpable for your sisters' abduction then, yes, you take a dangerous chance. You risk your sister's life."

"Tarr is right, Raynor," Aliss said. "We must assume and prepare for the worst, and if we are wrong we hurt no one, but if we are right—"

"We rescue Fiona and finally bring an end to this madness," Raynor finished.

"You stand with us or against. I need to know," Tarr demanded.

"I would die to keep my sister safe."

"You may get that chance," Tarr said. "I have a feeling Odo has planned well and I think he involves the Wolf clan."

"We should hurry," Aliss urged. "The weather does not bode well for us. We must attempt to beat the approaching storm."

Tarr's dark eyes narrowed. "I will unleash a storm far more destructive than you have ever seen if Odo hurts Fiona in any way. Let us go. I grow tired of the hunt; it is time to attack."

Fiona had worked the leather ties loose that bound her wrists without anyone being the wiser. She would be able to slip her hands free when she was ready. She took stock of her situation. Only two men rode with Odo, a third always out scouting the area.

She slipped her cloak over her hands when she saw that Odo approached on his horse.

"You watch, wait, and plan. I admire your warrior skills, so unusual in a woman. I think it is time to put them to a test. Give me your hands."

She obliged him and he laughed when he saw the loosened ties.

"Finish ridding yourself of them, your attempt to free yourself has set for a better scene."

She worked her way out of the ties and tossed them to the ground.

"Dismount."

She slipped off her mare giving her rump a pat, letting her know she was to stay close by. She watched with curiosity for Odo's next move.

"Tarr cannot be far behind, so we have little time—and I do want your body found on his land. He will be livid when he thinks the Wolf clan invaded his property and killed his bride-to-be on their wedding day."

"Your plan is flawed. Even if you manage to kill Tarr and me, there is still my sister to deal with. She will demand answers—"

He snickered. "I have plans for Aliss."

That did it, now she was going to have to kill him. There was no doubt about it.

"You do know I am going to take great pleasure in gutting you."

"You will be too busy fighting the Wolf clan." He gave a wave and out of the woods stepped several men garbed in wolf skin, the head and face of the wolf forming a helmet of sorts and concealing their faces.

She counted six as they formed a half-circle in front of her.

"Do I get a weapon to defend myself?"

"You expect me to make it easy for the warrior twin? Be grateful I give you a chance to run before the wolves descend on you. Worry not about Tarr, he will follow you into death." He laughed. "Now run. Run for your life."

Fiona sprinted into the woods, her first thought to put distance between her and her enemy, time later to fashion a weapon. She heard the crack of a branch a distance behind her. The wolves had been let lose; she had no time to spare for thought. She put all her effort into running.

Raynor had dismounted a few feet ahead of the column of men and examined the ground when suddenly he jerked his head up.

Tarr caught his abrupt reaction and rode over to him; Aliss close behind him.

"What is it?" He asked dismounting.

"Someone is close by."

Tarr signaled his men for attack when suddenly one of Odo's men ran out of the woods, blood dripping from his head, and dropped on the ground in front of Raynor.

Aliss dismounted, prepared to go to his aid but Tarr stopped her, shoving her behind him. Another wave of his hand had his men off their horses and spreading in a protective circle around them.

"Odo needs help." The man took deep breaths, grasping for air. "The Wolf clan attacked."

"Fiona?" Tarr demanded.

"Odo saw her safely to the woods and ordered her to run," he gulped for another breath.

"What brought Odo here?" Raynor asked.

"I follow orders, I know not his plans."

"Take us to where he fights," Raynor instructed.

"The woods," the man said with a wave of his hand. "The wolves give chase through the woods."

A scream pierced the cold air.

"Fiona!" Aliss yelled and took off, bursting through the circle of warriors before she could be stopped.

Tarr followed in quick pursuit along with several of his men.

Aliss was far lighter on her feet and was soon out of sight, fearing not that they would lose her trail. Besides, if she could reach her sister sooner it might make all the difference.

She sprinted over fallen trees, ducked beneath branches, and avoided holes that could tear at the ankles until in the distance she spotted her sister's green wool cloak on the ground. She was traveling in the right direction. She picked up speed.

Fiona knew the man was almost on top of her. He would catch her soon; she had only one choice. She dropped like a felled branch to the ground. Her pursuer could not halt soon enough; he tripped over her hitting the ground hard. Fiona picked up a thick rock with both hands and, with a shrilling screech, brought it down with a heavy thud on his head, knocking him out cold.

She hoped her painful scream would convince at least one or two of her pursuers that she had met her demise and they would wait for the victor's return. By then, she would have put farther distance between them.

She got up to run and caught a movement out of the corner of her eye. She turned, and there in front of a boulder stood a man draped in wolf fur. His large size warned her he would not go down easily.

Her only chance against him was to keep her distance and flee if she could, though she had the dreadful feeling this man would not be easy to outrun.

Another sudden flash of movement caught her attention that for a moment Fiona thought was a giant bat descending on the man. Until she realized it was her sister, her dark green cloak spreading out like wings as she jumped off the top of the boulder, landing directly on the wolf below.

She hit her mark, sending his head flying back against the boulder; he hit the ground with a solid thud.

Fiona helped a dazed Aliss up and as soon as she saw the unconscious man, her eyes turned wide.

"Yes, you did that to him and, no, you are not going to see if he is all right," Fiona said. "There are more of them and we need to get out of here."

Aliss nodded, her breath short.

"Are you all right? Is Tarr close by?"

Aliss nodded and pointed in the direction she had left them.

"He could not keep up with you, could he?"

Aliss shook her head.

"I should have warned him that you are light and fast on your feet. I do not suppose you thought to bring a weapon?"

Aliss's eyes rounded.

"I did not think so."

Aliss looked around her and pointed to large stones.

"Their weight will slow us down and we need to reach Tarr as fast as we can. Odo plans to kill him."

Aliss made ready to sprint but Fiona grabbed her arm.

"Do not outrun me; we need to remain together and keep alert. There are more wolves around."

Aliss nodded and they took off.

They had barely set a pace when suddenly Odo

stepped from behind two trees that had entwined and grown into one large one.

"How lucky, I now have both twins."

Fiona pushed her sister behind her. "You will never get us both."

"How touching, you give your life for your sister, but you only delay her death. You cannot prevent it."

Fiona bared her teeth and let out a blood-curdling scream as she charged at Odo full force, lowering her head at the last moment to ram him in the stomach.

Her speed was her ally; he had no time to react and she took him down fast. Her fists pummeled him in rapid succession, and Aliss wasted no time in joining in.

When he regained his breath and wits, he made short work of Aliss, tossing her off him.

"Run, Aliss, run," Fiona screamed, and took a blow to her chin that sent her flying.

Aliss was about to charge him again when out of nowhere Tarr sprung and charged at Odo like a raging bull, nostrils flaring and teeth gritted.

They locked in battle and Aliss hurried to get Fiona out of the way before the fighting men trampled her.

The two men tore at each other like wild beasts claiming their territory. Fists smashed again and again against flesh and bone, and blood spewed forth, raining down on both of them.

Several of Tarr's men emerged from the woods and cheered their leader on.

Fiona got to her feet, refusing to let her sister tend her jaw that was deepening in color. She would watch the man she loved fight, for he fought for her.

Cheers sounded every time Tarr landed a blow and there was no doubt who would emerge the victor.

Raynor finally arrived in time to see Tarr deliver the final blow that ended the melee.

Tarr turned, blood pouring from the corner of his mouth, his cheek and eye swelling, blood covering his shirt, and he spread his arms out to Fiona.

She ran into them and hugged him tight.

Chapter 37

Snow fell softly outside as Tarr and Fiona exchanged wedding vows before the roaring fire in the great hall. The room was overflowing with Hellewyk and Blackshaw clan members alike. They came to celebrate, to rejoice, to praise the joining of the two people who would lead their clans.

Fiona made a beautiful bride in her deep purple wool dress, her bruised jaw matching perfectly in color.

Tarr's bruised eye, swollen lip and jaw did not detract from his handsome features, and he looked every bit the powerful chieftain in his newly stitched shirt and his green and black plaid.

After their return to the keep, Odo was quickly dispatched to the dungeons until a fitting punishment could be determined for him.

Tarr refused to be denied his wedding day and demanded that the ceremony take place as planned. So they were wed, just a little later than expected, and the celebration followed.

Tarr and Fiona managed to slip away from the festivities early on in the evening. They climbed the stairs slowly, pains and aches grabbing hold of them here and there, reminding them of the recent battle for their lives.

Fiona sighed, relieved when Tarr closed and latched the door behind them. They would not be disturbed tonight. Tonight was theirs and theirs alone and she was grateful.

"How I have longed for this moment, just you and me," she said, and stretched her hand out to him.

He grabbed hold with a strength that let Fiona know he never intended to let go, and that was fine with her for she had no intentions of ever letting him out of her sight. She squeezed his hand tightly as they drifted up against each other.

"I meant to kiss every inch of your body tonight." He laughed and it was followed by a wince. "This swollen lip will not let me do that, but I will see you pleased on this special night."

She smiled, lucky to have wed a man with such a loving heart.

Tarr tenderly stroked the bruise on her chin. "I have felt rage before, but nothing like I felt when I saw Odo strike you. I wanted to rip him apart piece by piece."

"You almost did."

"He deserved it. It pains me to know that you were not safe in your own home."

"It pains me to have been so foolish. Odo was so convincing, telling me how my sister begged for me. His words wrenched at my heart and all I could think about was Aliss, though I did want to tell you and have you go with us. Odo ordered one of his men to inform you of our absence, convincing me there was not a minute to spare. He also claimed that you would catch up with us in no time, and knowing you I had no doubt you would, that was if you were aware of our departure."

"When did you grow suspicious?"

"When we entered the woods and I attempted to turn my mare around, it finally dawned on me that I had erred terribly. His men attacked and had my wrists tied in no time."

"And here I had expected to see your abductors tied in knots when we arrived to rescue you." He tried not to laugh but could not help it and suffered the consequences.

She winced, sharing in his pain. "I did take care of three of Odo's men for you."

"Two, not three," he corrected and joined her by the side of the bed.

She held up three fingers suddenly switching to two. "Three, no actually two, the third man Aliss knocked out when she jumped off the boulder."

"We found two in the woods, not three." Tarr shook his head. "Aliss jumped off a boulder?"

"Landed right on the large wolf, saving my life."

"Remind me to kiss her when my lips heal."

"Me first," she sighed, already missing his kisses.

He leaned over and rubbed his cheek against hers. "I may not be able to kiss you but I can touch you."

His fingers glided slowly over her neck, his faint touch tickling her.

She giggled soft and sexy, stepped away from him with reluctance, and slipped off her dress and slippers to stand naked in front of him.

He smiled, ignoring the pain, rid himself of his clothes, and walked over to her. He lifted her up into his arms and gently laid her on the bed stretching out on his side next to her.

"I am going to touch you all over."

"Promise," she murmured.

"You have my word."

He kept his word, and his caresses wore on with the night until they both lay beside each other content and smiling.

"I thank the heavens for bringing us together," Tarr said.

"Do not forget to thank our stubbornness; it held us fast."

He took her hand and brought it to his chest to rest over his heart. "Love. We cannot forget to thank love for finding us."

She rolled on her side. "Time for a prediction, I shall make one greater than Giann."

"A greater prediction than Giann," he teased. "How will you know it to come true?"

"It is an easy one; you know it as well."

"Now I am a prophet?"

She nodded, wrapping her arm around his. "You will agree when you hear it."

"I do not need to hear it; I know the prediction."

"You do?" she asked surprised.

He turned and pressed his forehead to hers. "Aye, every word."

She faintly brushed her lips over his. "Tell me."

"The prediction that will surely come true is that we will love each other forever and ever and ever and . . ."

Fiona fell asleep with whispers of love echoing in her ear.